The Mystery of Druid Forest

NANCY POTTS

WESTIE
PUBLISHING

Nancy Potts

Published in 2020 by Westie Publishing
Enon, OH 45323, U.S.A.

Potts, Nancy
The Mystery of Druid Forest
by Nancy Potts

ISBN 978-1-7340061-6-2 (paperback)

Cover Art by Daniel Kinney

In Memory Of

William Patrick Flanagan, Jr.

Nancy Potts

Acknowledgments

A special thank you to my team of copy-editors, Dan, Cindi, Bob, Amy, and Riley. I am extremely grateful for all the time, thought and diligence you gave to this project.

A very special thank you to Daniel Kinney for his wonderful cover artwork. You are such a talented artist and always come up with the perfect covers.

Books by Nancy Potts

YA Books

The Mystery Tunnel
The Jericho Head
The Mysterious Abyss
The Mystery of Druid Forest

Children's Books

The Buzzard Tree
Raccoons in the Attic
The Adventures of Chuck the Groundhog
The Misadventures of a Christmas Elf

Chapter One

Andy Parker slowly opened his eyes and listened. The house was silent, not one sound coming from anywhere. He turned over in his bed and pulled the covers over his head to block the early morning sunshine peeking through his bedroom window. It was a wonderful feeling. They were all gone. He shifted the blankets enough to glance at his clock. It was only 7:30 but he knew his mom, dad, and sister were all in Ireland by now. He was free! For an entire week he was free! It was Spring Break. No school, no parents to tell him what to do, no little sister to cause him trouble. It was going to be great!

He still couldn't believe his folks agreed to let him stay home while they went to Ireland to help with an archaeology dig. It had been fairly easy convincing his father but getting his mother to agree had been more difficult. Eventually his dad persuaded her by pointing out that as of March first he was eighteen, therefore he was technically an adult and they should let him stay home. *"Yes,"* thought Andy, *"this was going to be a great week."*

Emily adjusted her backpack as she followed her parents out the doors of the Shannon Airport. She had thought they would never get through customs, not because they were slow but because her father decided to carry on a long conversation with the agent. It seemed the guy recognized her father's name and just had to bend his ear about all the archaeology sites in Ireland. She was relieved when they finally were able to pick up their luggage and leave.

The sunshine was warming the entrance's large glass windows and the pavement. Emily stood there in the sunlight absorbing the warmth. It felt great. When they had left Ohio yesterday morning it had been cold, cloudy, and
windy. This was a very welcome change. She slipped past her mother and over to her father. "Dad, is Mr. Flanagan supposed to

be picking us up or do we need to rent a car and meet him?" she asked with concern.

Martin glanced at his daughter, smiled, and slightly shook his head. "Don't worry, Pat will be here to pick us up." He set the suitcases down and scanned the nearby parking lot. In the distance he noticed a man making his way in their direction. He was about as tall as Martin with brown wavy hair and a bit of a middle-age spread. As the man got closer Martin's eyes began to crinkle with amusement. It was Pat all right but it appeared he'd put on a few pounds since the last time he saw him. The man jogged the final few yards before stopping in front of the Parkers.

"Sorry I'm a bit late," apologized Pat. He grabbed Martin's arm and gave him a hug. "You haven't changed a bit in the past ten years, except for maybe that touch of silver along the temples." He cast his eyes on Anne and gave her a hug as well. "It's good to see you Anne. If anything, you've gotten lovelier over the years." Finally he stepped back and looked with surprise at Emily.

"Now, don't tell me," he said with a broad smile. "This must be little Emily." He wrapped his arms around her and lifted her off the ground. "The last time I saw you, you weren't much taller than the daffodils growing in the garden. Just look at you now. What a fine young lady you've become and just as lovely as your mother."

He picked up the two suitcases. "Come along. I'm parked over there," he said as he nodded his head in the direction of the nearby parking lot. "Mary Jo and Rowena are anxious to see you all. They've been cleaning the house and getting the guest room ready for the last two weeks." He turned his head to glance at Emily. "I hope you won't mind sharing a room with Rowena for the week that you're here."

Emily looked a bit puzzled. She had no idea who Rowena was. "I'm sure it'll be fine Mr. Flanagan," she told him kindly.

"Ah, sure an' you wouldn't be remembering who Rowena is," he said when he noticed the confused look on her face. "You were only three the last time we saw you. Rowena is my daughter. She's about three years older than you, so let me see. You're about thirteen and Rowena is sixteen. She'll be seventeen in October."

Emily smiled slightly and nodded. "It'll be fine, sir."

Pat stopped at the trunk of a light blue Toyota and put the suitcases on the ground. He opened the trunk then turned to look at Emily. "My dear, please don't be so formal. Call me Pat just like all my friends. Okay?"

Emily looked at her father for his approval. He nodded his head and smiled.

She took a deep breath and sighed. "Okay … Pat."

"Good girl," he said sliding the suitcases inside. "We're gonna get along fine." He walked toward the side of the car and opened the back door for Anne and Emily. "Hop in and we'll get going. I don't know about the rest of you but I'm ready for lunch."

"Sounds good to me," said Martin as he climbed into the front left passenger seat. "Afterwards maybe you can
take us out to the excavation site."

"Be glad to," said Pat as he slipped into the right front driver's seat. "I think you might find some of what we've discovered to be interesting. At least I hope so." He drove out of the parking lot and headed toward Limerick. "It's almost an hour and a half to the house so I thought maybe we'd stop in Limerick for a bite if that's all right with everyone."

Martin glanced in the rearview mirror at Anne and Emily before turning toward his friend. "I think that will be fine. They did offer breakfast on the plane but it wasn't much so I know we'd all welcome a good meal. Right?"

"Oh, absolutely," answered Anne happily. She looked at Emily and could tell from the expression on her face that she was more than a little anxious and worried but she didn't know why. She reached over and took her hand, hoping it would provide some comfort. "Are you all right?"

Emily blinked and wiggled in her seat. "Yeah, sure Mom," she answered. "Why wouldn't I be?"

"I don't know. You just look a bit nervous, that's all."

8

Emily glanced out her window at a passing truck and moved closer to the center of the car.

Anne observed her daughter and smiled to herself. "It's traveling on the opposite side of the road that's got you worried. That's it, isn't it?"

Emily took a deep breath and tried to calm herself. "I guess," she replied apprehensively. "It's just kinda weird."

Anne patted Emily's hand. "I understand. It takes a little getting used to. Guess I should have had you sit on this side. After lunch we'll change seats. Okay?"

"Okay," answered Emily solemnly.

"In the meantime just lean back, close your eyes and try to relax."

Emily's eyes gave her mother a 'you've got to be kidding' look but tried her best to settle back and calm down. She closed her eyes and soon the gentle hum of the car lulled her to sleep.

It wasn't long before they reached a nice little bistro in Limerick and Pat pulled into the parking lot. He surveyed the half full parking area as he switched the engine off. "They don't look too crowded yet so there shouldn't be a wait," he told them and got out of the car.

Anne looked at Emily sleeping so soundly beside her it was almost a shame to wake her. "Emily, hey honey, wake up. It's time for lunch."

Emily jerked and quickly opened her eyes in surprise. She appeared a little bewildered and looked at her mother. "Guess I must have fallen asleep."

Anne just smiled. "Well, it has been a long trip and I'm sure you needed that extra slumber time. Now, let's have something to eat." Martin opened her door while Pat helped Emily out of the car and they headed inside.

They found a nice quiet corner table and settled in just as their waiter arrived with the menus. "I don't think we'll be needin' those young man. Just bring us four orders of Irish stew and some soda bread. Bring the young lady some milk and a pot of tea for the rest of us." The waiter left and Pat looked at the Parkers and raised his eyebrows. "I hope that's all right. I guess maybe I should have asked before ordering."

Martin just laughed and slowly shook his head. "That's fine. It's been awhile since we've had real Irish stew or soda bread."

"I've been meanin' to ask you why you didn't bring your son Andy along."

"He didn't want to come," answered Martin bluntly. "I'm afraid he's just not interested in archaeology, which is fine. He's eighteen and a senior in high school. It's time for him to decide what he wants to do with his life."

"And has he?" asked Pat.

"Don't know. Right now he's into flying drones."

A small smile crossed Pat's lips. "Is that so. It's kind of funny that you mentioned drones."

"Why's that?"

"Well, because it was a video taken by a drone pilot that led us to our current dig."

Martin gave his friend a puzzled stare. "I don't think I understand."

"It's quite simple really," said Pat matter-of-factly. "The guy was out flying his drone around some fields and videotaping the flight. When he looked at things afterwards he noticed some unusual looking circles in one of the fields. At first he thought maybe they were made when the crops were harvested but on closer examination he realized that wasn't the case because the only thing growing in that field was grass for the sheep and horses." Pat laughed and fidgeted with his silverware. "Anyway, a friend told me about it and I asked if we could explore these unusual circles. The farmer gave his okay and so that's what we've been doing for the past few months."

"So, what have you discovered so far?" asked Emily excitedly.

Pat leaned back slightly in his seat and gazed with interest at this inquisitive teenager. "Well, so far, we've found what appears to be an ancient cemetery and a possible settlement from the same time. It's very interesting. Of course our discoveries aren't nearly as unusual as your dad's find in that cave in January."

Emily's eyes flashed at her father with a trace of annoyance. Martin loudly cleared his throat to get his friend's attention. "I'm afraid you have that wrong, Pat. It was Emily who made that discovery, not me. My class and I just helped with the investigation."

"Oh, I see," said Pat humbly and looked toward Emily. "I didn't know. Well, I'm grateful that you are here, Emily. I'm sure you will be a major asset to our excavation."

"I'm looking forward to helping you," she answered with a grin.

Just then the waiter arrived with their food. "It certainly looks good," said Anne as she placed her napkin on her lap. While the others buttered their bread and dug into their stew she poured the tea for Pat and Martin as well as herself then settled down to enjoy her lunch.

It was nearly 3 o'clock by the time the little group reached the town of Blarney in County Cork and Pat pulled into his home's driveway. His wife and daughter were waiting patiently by the front door as everyone emerged from the car. Martin grabbed their luggage and handed Emily her backpack.

Mary Jo quickly walked over to greet everyone. "It's so good to see all of you," she said and bent down to give Anne a hug. At 5 foot 7 she was a good three inches taller than Anne and half a foot taller than Emily. "I can't believe it's been ten years."

"I know," said Anne. "It doesn't seem that long ago that we were exploring the bogs up north."

"Oh those were grand times," stated Mary Jo releasing her arms from around her friend. She stepped back, smiled, and took a quick look at Emily. "And this is little Emily. My how you've grown." She gave her a hug also and guided her toward her daughter.

"Emily, this is our daughter Rowena. I'm sure you don't remember each other. You were only three and Rowena was six but now you have a chance to really get to know each other."

"Hello," said Emily. "It's nice to meet you Rowena."

Rowena looked down at Emily, smiled and brushed her dark red bangs out of her warm brown eyes. "It's nice to meet you too Emily. Hope you don't mind sharing a room with me."

"It'll be fine," Emily assured her. She noticed that both Rowena and her mother had lovely red hair but Mrs. Flanagan's was more reddish blonde and Rowena had inherited her father's dark brown eyes and not her mother's emerald green.

"Come along then and I'll help you get settled," said Rowena leading her into the house and to her bedroom.

As they entered the room Emily noticed a golden brown pile of fluffy fur on one of the beds. Rowena turned on a light and quietly approached the object. She sat on the bed and began to stroke the fur. "Hey there sleepy head, wake up. We've got company." She picked up the furry object and placed it on her lap. Slowly it opened its sapphire eyes and looked up at Rowena. "Shea, meet our house guest Emily Parker, Emily this is Shea, our cat. He's a good little guy most of the time. He usually sleeps at the foot of my bed and sometimes he gets to go to the dig sites. He's a great explorer and every once in a while he's been known to uncover an interesting artifact or two."

Emily walked over and sat down next to Rowena and Shea. "May I pet him?"

"Sure. He's really pretty friendly unless you're a mouse or one of the neighborhood dogs. He's not very fond of dogs, especially the ones who bark a lot."

"Can't say that I blame him. I don't like noisy dogs myself." She reached over and ran her hand down the cat's head and back. He closed his eyes and began to purr.

"He likes you," Rowena assured her.

Emily smiled. "I'm glad. I like him too." She was enjoying

this quiet time and decided she was going to like getting to know Rowena.

Just then her father appeared in the doorway. "Hey, kiddo, you want to come along and see the dig site or do you want to stay here and entertain the cat?"

Emily glanced up at him and quietly laughed. "Of course I want to go to the dig site."

"Well, come along then. What about you Rowena? Are you coming?"

Rowena stroked Shea and shook her head. "No, I will stay here for right now. I've been there lots of times. Perhaps I'll go tomorrow afternoon. You go and enjoy yourselves."

"Okay, we shouldn't be long," stated Martin as he guided Emily out of the room and down the hallway.

"Is the site here in Blarney?" asked Emily enthusiastically.

Martin shook his head. "No, it's in a little village called Donoughmore, about eighteen minutes east of here."

"I guess that makes sense since Pat said they found the circles in a sheep field. There aren't many farms in the city."

Martin grinned. "How about there aren't *any* farms in the city, darling.'"

Emily laughed as they headed out the door toward the car. "Is Mom coming?"

"Not today," he told her. "She'll go tomorrow. Right now she just wants to rest. It's been a long couple of days."

"Hop in everyone," said Pat as he started the engine. "They should be shutting things down in another hour and a half, so we should have just enough time for a quick tour."

On a quiet country road just on the fringe of Donoughmore, Pat parked his car at the edge of the excavation site and led Martin and Emily to the field. A small team was busy working on the west side of the barrow. Pat and the Parkers made their way to the group and stopped at the edge of one of the shallow pits. "Hey there

Vince!" shouted Pat getting the man's attention. "I want you to meet some people!"

Vince laid his shovel on the nearby short stone wall and walked over to the group. "Hello, Boss, glad to see you made it back all right."

"Me too," said Pat. "I want you to meet my friend and fellow archaeologist, Martin Parker and his daughter, Emily."

"Hello," said Vince. "Nice to meet you." He removed his hat revealing his short blondish brown hair and wiped some dirt from his forehead with the back of his gloved hand. He removed the glove and extended his hand.

Martin cordially bent over to shake it. "Nice to meet you, Vince."

"Marty and I go back a good twelve years or so when we were working together on a few excavations up in Meath. He finished up a major dig in Israel last year and decided to try his hand at teaching college students. A couple of months ago they made an interesting discovery in the States, isn't that right?"

Martin smiled and nodded his head.

"Have they ever found any more about that unusual skeleton or that strange sphere?"

"Afraid not," answered Martin. "It's all still an enigma. Eventually I'm sure someone will find the answers."

"Anyway," continued Pat, "the college is on holiday this week so I invited him to join us."

Vince thoughtfully rubbed the stubble on his jaw. "Well, we certainly welcome all the help you can give us."

"I'm just going to give them a quick tour of the site and we'll be here tomorrow after church."

"That'll be fine, sir," Vince replied putting his hat and glove back on. He turned and walked back to continue his work.

Pat led Martin and Emily on a tour of the circle then over to a tent. Inside were a few tables and a couple of buckets of water. On one of the tables were a few pottery shards and some bones. There were also several boxes of objects from the site that still needed to be cleaned, photographed, and recorded. Pat picked up a thigh bone and gave it to Martin so he could inspect it. Emily watched as her father turned the bone around and rubbed his hands carefully over it from the top to the bottom.

"It's interesting," Martin stated and ran his fingers to an indentation near the middle of the bone. "It appears to have a mark here, possibly from an axe or sword."

Emily stood close to her father to get a better look at the mark. "Does that mean he was hurt in a battle or maybe was killed?"

Martin shook his head. "This looks like it healed completely. That doesn't mean he didn't die in battle; it just means that he didn't die from this blow."

"A number of the skeletons and bones we've uncovered so far show signs of injury. My best guess is there were several battles fought here over the years," said Pat as he took the bone from Martin and placed it back on the table.

Emily stood at the table observing all the objects. She noticed a bracelet that appeared to be made from copper and silver. "This is interesting," she said picking it up. "Does Ireland have copper and silver mines?"

"Oh my yes," Pat told her. "We even have a few gold mines."

"Well, do you think anyone would have been able to own this bracelet or just someone who was wealthy?" she asked placing the bracelet back on the table.

"That's difficult to say, dear. Our idea of wealth and what wealth was thought to be when these people lived are quite different ideas indeed." Pat started to head out of the tent just as a loud boom exploded, shattering the afternoon silence.

Emily yelped, jumped backward, and collided into her father. Martin reached out and snugly wrapped his arms around her. "What was that?" she whispered to her dad as she tried not to shake.

Martin smiled and leaned his mouth to her ear. "It's just thunder," he told her soothingly. "You've heard it before."

She turned around and looked up at him. "But it was nice and sunny when we came in here."

Pat had walked to the tent entrance and was gazing out the opening at the sudden downpour of rain. "To be sure, that's Ireland. One minute it's calm and sunny and the next it's pourin' rain. Give it a few minutes and it'll turn into a drizzle."

There was a crack of lightening in the distance and a rumble of thunder just as far away. The curtain of rain began to turn into a drizzle just as Pat had predicted. "There, now, what'd I tell ya? Shall we be leavin' now?"

Martin took Emily's hand and led her out of the tent.

"I think you're right, it's time we are getting back." They followed Pat to his car where he opened the door to the backseat.

Emily hesitated getting inside. "Do you have some-thing to put over the seat? I don't want to get it all wet."

Pat opened the trunk and pulled out a couple of towels. He spread one on the backseat for Emily and gave Martin the other. "You don't really need to be concerned. The seats have been treated with a special spray that'll keep them dry but the towel should make you feel a bit better."

"Thank you," said Emily as she climbed inside and fastened her seatbelt.

Martin and Pat slid into the front seats and Pat started the engine. "Thank you for the tour," said Martin as Pat eased the car out of the excavation site and onto the road toward Blarney. "I think this should be an interesting week."

"I'm hoping it will be," stated Pat. "And while you're here I'm wantin' to get your thoughts about some rocks we found."

Martin gave his friend a sideways glance and Emily noticed a look of curiosity fleetingly cross his face. "I'd be more than happy to," Martin replied. "I think tomorrow is going to be an interesting day."

"I know it will," said Pat with a grin.

Chapter Two

Andy stood in his backyard giving his drone a preflight check. The weather was perfect. The sun was shining, the wind was calm and the air was a mild 58 degrees. Life was great! He turned the drone's controls on and began to fly it around the yard. He had set up a small obstacle course so he could practice. Some of the obstacles at the past few competitions had been a bit tricky and he wanted to be prepared for the next race after Spring Break. He was enjoying himself immensely. He could do what he wanted, when he wanted, however he wanted and there was no one around to tell him otherwise.

He flew his drone through a couple of hoops and around a tower of boxes before bringing it in for a landing on the backyard picnic table. He turned the controls off and was on his way into the yard to pick up his drone when he heard some loud clapping.

"Hey, that was great!" shouted Gracie Taylor as she continued to clap. "You are really good at this, you know that?"

Andy quickly turned around, startled. He blinked his eyes and shook his head. "How long have you been standing there?" he asked apprehensively.

Gracie smiled. "Oh, long enough to watch you fly through your obstacle course. I'm sure you will give that team from Dayton real competition. I'll be surprised if you don't come in first place."

Andy blushed a bit, slowly shook his head and grinned. "Yeah, right. We both know I'm not that good. So far I've only managed to place third. It'll take a lot more practice for me to even come close to first place."

"I don't think you give yourself enough credit. You're better than anyone else in our club. Even Major Reese thinks so."

Andy retrieved his drone from the table, walked back to the porch, and sat down on the top step. "You're pretty good yourself, you know."

"I'm not as good as you. You're a natural," said Gracie as she joined him on the step. "So, how're things going?"

"Everything is fine. Why?"

"Just curious, that's all." She leaned against the porch railing and shoved her hands into her jacket pockets. "I mean it's gotta be a little weird being alone in a house."

He looked at her and frowned. "They only left yesterday. It's not like they've been gone for months. And frankly, it's been nice. I'm enjoying the peace and quiet."

"I see. Then I suppose you wouldn't want to join us for supper this evening."

Andy jerked back stunned. "Is that why you came over, to invite me to supper?"

"Yes," answered Gracie quietly. "But if you'd rather not, well I understand if you want to be alone. I'll just tell my dad and Gwen you made other plans." She stood up to leave and Andy reached for her arm.

"Wait, I'm sorry, " he apologized and stood up beside her. "I'll be glad to come to supper. Thank you for asking. What time and do you want me to bring anything?"

"We'll be eating at six so you can come a little before then and the only thing you need to bring is your appetite." She walked down the steps and headed across the street for her home.

"Wait," begged Andy as he followed her. "Would you like to go to the movies afterward?"

Gracie smiled to herself before turning around to face him. "Sure, I'd be happy to. See you in a few hours."

Andy watched her cross the street and go into her house. "You can be really stupid sometimes," he muttered to himself. He quietly gathered his drone and controls and headed inside. As he deposited his stuff on the kitchen countertop he noticed the light flashing on the answering machine.

He pushed the play button. "Hi Andy, it's just Mom. Thought I'd check in to see how you were doing. Your dad and Emily are at the dig site and I'm here with Mrs. Flanagan and her daughter.

I know it's early afternoon there but it'll be dinner time here in just a little while. Please give me a call when you get this. Oh, before I forget. Remember to take the trash out Sunday night. Sometimes they like to pick it up early. Love you."

Andy hit the erase button and grabbed his cell phone off the table. He noticed there was a new message and saw it was from his mother's cell phone. "The woman just doesn't give up," he groused. "Wonder what she'll do in the fall when I leave for college."

Reluctantly he called his mother. "Hi Mom. Sorry I missed your call but I was outside flying my drone." He listened impatiently while she gave him a detailed account of everything that had happened since they landed in Ireland. "Yes, everything is fine. Yes, I got the mail, it was mainly junk and the electric bill. I've been invited to the Taylors for supper so you don't need to worry about me eating. Besides, you left enough frozen meals to last a month. Stop worrying, okay? Just enjoy yourselves. And yes, I'll remember to take the trash out tomorrow night. All right. Tell everyone I said hi. 'Bye." He ended the call, slipped his phone into his jeans pocket, grabbed a Coke, and went into the family room. He turned on the television, opened the soda can and stretched out to watch a movie.

When Andy reached the Taylors at ten till six he was greeted by Jim Taylor, Gracie and Gwen's father. "Good evening, Andy, come in," said Jim welcoming him into the house. "I'm glad you could make it." He took Andy's jacket and hung it in the coat closet near the front door. "Hope you like lasagna and apple pie. The girls have been baking all afternoon."

Andy smiled. "Yes, sir, I like lasagna and apple pie just fine. I'm sure whatever Gracie and Gwen have made will be great." He followed Mr. Taylor into the dining room. "Is there anything I can do to help?"

"I think the girls have everything under control," stated Mr.

Taylor. "What would you like to drink? We've got milk, water, coffee, tea, soda."

"Whatever everyone else is having is fine," said Andy as he observed the table layout. He could tell they had gone to a lot of fuss with a linen tablecloth and fancy dishes. Gwen rolled her wheelchair into the dining room bringing the salad and placed it on the table while Gracie filled the glasses with water. Italian bread, salad dressing and butter were already there. Andy was trying to figure out where he was to sit when Mr. Taylor brought the lasagna in and set it on the table.

"You can sit over here," said Mr. Taylor pointing to the chair to his right. He looked at Gracie. "Have we forgotten anything?"

"No, that's everything," she told him and took her seat at the foot of the table while her father sat at the head and Gwen sat across from Andy. Mr. Taylor offered a prayer and began dishing out the lasagna while Gwen began to pass around the salad and bread.

"This is really good," Andy declared looking at Gracie and Gwen. "You two are really good cooks."

"Glad you like it," said Gracie with a smile.

"Emily said this was one of your favorite meals," Gwen added and took a bite of her salad.

Andy looked at her a bit suspiciously. "You talked to my sister about what I like to eat?"

Gwen eyed him with amusement. "Not really. It just came up one day when we were talking about our favorite foods. She said she liked chocolate milkshakes and chicken cacciatore."

"I see," Andy said good humoredly. "And what is your favorite food?"

Gwen crinkled her wide gray-blue eyes and laughed.
"I don't have a favorite. I like just about everything except fish. I can't stand anchovies or sardines. Yuck!"

Everyone laughed.

"So, tell me Andy, have you given any thought as to what you want to do after graduation?" asked Mr. Taylor casually. "Gracie tells me you're very good at flying drones. Is that something you might want to pursue?"

These questions caught Andy completely off guard. Not even his parents had posed those questions. Andy put down his fork and took a swallow of water before he replied. "To tell you the truth, sir, I really haven't given it much thought. I've been so focused on what I don't want to do that I just haven't thought about what I'd like to do."

"Well, I know the military is looking for drone pilots. Of course those drones are much larger than what you kids are flying in the drone club. But I think drones may be the future of aerospace. It's something to think about, anyway."

"Yes, you may be correct," admitted Andy giving Gracie a questioning stare before looking back at her father.

"I never thought my daughter would be interested in engineering as a career, much less aerospace engineering," said Mr. Taylor with a small smile. "But she seems to really like it which is the important thing."

Andy glanced at Gracie. "Yes, you're right and Gracie is very good at math and the sciences. I think she'll make an excellent aeronautical engineer. Have you decided on what college you want to attend?"

Gracie shrugged her shoulders. "I've applied to Ohio State and Purdue but haven't heard from either yet."

"I think you'd do fine at either school," said Andy calmly.

Mr. Taylor noticed everyone's plates were empty and excused himself to retrieve the pie from the kitchen. "Does anyone want ice cream with their pie?" he asked as he left.

Andy shook his head no, as did Gwen. "No Dad," shouted Gracie. "We just want the pie."

"Okay," he said entering the dining room with the pie and dessert plates. He sliced it up and soon everyone was busy devouring their dessert. As they finished Andy glanced at his watch. It was after seven o'clock. He began to gather up his dirty dishes to take them to the kitchen.

"You don't need to do that," Mr. Taylor told him. "Gwen and I can take care of them. I know you and Gracie want to go to the movies."

Andy shook his head and continued to head for the kitchen. "It wouldn't be right for me to leave you with the dishes," stated Andy. "The least I can do is help clear the table."

Mr. Taylor followed Andy toward the kitchen. "No, really young man. Take Gracie to the movies and leave the cleaning up to Gwen and me." He took Andy's dishes from him and placed them on the counter. "She needs to get out of the house for a while. Go on, it'll do you both good."

Reluctantly Andy surrendered and did as Mr. Taylor requested even though he didn't think it was the right thing to do.

"It looks like our services are not required," he told Gracie as he re-entered the dining room. "You get your coat, the temperature has dropped quite a bit since this afternoon, and I'll bring the car over."

"All right," replied Gracie seeing him out the front door. She watched him enter the garage before she told her father and sister good bye and grabbed her coat.

It was nearly midnight when Andy dropped Gracie off at her front door. "Thank you for a wonderful evening. It was fun and I really enjoyed the movie."

"I'm glad you could come." Andy bent his head and gave her a kiss. "See you tomorrow. If the weather's like it was today maybe we can go drone flying in the afternoon."

"Sounds good to me. Goodnight."

Gracie went into her house while Andy climbed back into his car and drove across the street to his garage. He put the car away and slowly headed for the back porch. His brain was occupied with at least a half dozen thoughts but mainly he was thinking of Gracie and his future. The conversation with Mr. Taylor at supper got him thinking about his life. What was he going to do with it? He didn't know. He was so preoccupied with his thoughts he didn't see the strange pile of fur curled up asleep in a dark corner of the porch.

Andy got up late Sunday morning. He'd missed church which he knew would make his mother upset when she found out. *"Oh well, there's nothing I can do about it now,"* he thought as he scrambled himself some eggs and buttered his toast. When he finished eating he took the eggshells out to the compost pile. It was there he noticed some animal had been foraging among the dirt and rotten vegetables. "Probably a raccoon or skunk," he muttered. When he turned to head back toward the house he noticed a set of light brown eyes peeking out at him from the nearby woodpile. The animal began to whimper. Andy stopped. He crouched down to get on the animal's level. It stopped making any sound and it's eyes fixed themselves on Andy. He wasn't sure what kind of animal it was but he was hoping whatever it was it wasn't vicious. He got on his hands and knees and quietly began to talk to the animal as he slowly crawled toward the woodpile.

"It's all right little buddy. I won't hurt you. Don't be afraid, now. Everything's going to be okay." As he got closer he held out his hand toward those sad brown eyes and hoped the animal understood what he was saying. A few feet from the woodpile Andy leaned back on his legs and sat still. He watched the animal stick it's little brown nose through a gap of the sticks in the pile of wood. Soon it drew it's head away from the sticks and slowly made its way around the end of the pile of logs. Andy continued to stay very still as he tried to determine what the animal was. Finally he saw its head. It looked like it might be a dog. It just didn't resemble any type of dog he'd ever seen. Its face reminded him of a kid's teddy bear with some crooked lower teeth but the top of its head and back were blondish brown and curly. "Come here little buddy," urged Andy as he held out his hand toward the dog. "Are you lost? I'll bet that's it and you're hungry. If you come here I'll help you get back home and I'll even find you something to eat." The dog cautiously made its way toward Andy, stopping now and then to sniff the ground. Eventually the dog walked to Andy's knees and sat there, staring. Carefully Andy reached his hand out to stroke the dog's fur. The dog didn't move. Andy got closer and ran his hand down the dog's back hoping to find a collar under all the fur but there was none. The dog bent its head toward Andy's other hand and began to lick it. Andy laughed. "Would you like something to eat?" The dog continued to lick Andy's hand. Gradually Andy stood up but kept his hand close to the dog.

"Come along little guy. Let's go up to the house and I'll get you something to eat." Little by little Andy led the dog to the back porch. The dog ran up the steps and into the far corner where he had spent the night. Now Andy faced a dilemma. Should he bring the dog into the house while he found something for it to eat or should he leave it outside where it might run away. He looked at the dog then at the door trying to decide. Carefully he opened the door and called to the dog. It looked at Andy, then out to the backyard. Slowly it got up and walked over to Andy and through the door into the kitchen.

"Good dog," Andy told him as he closed the door. The dog snapped it's head around looking at the door. He appeared to be a little frightened so Andy gently stroked the dog's ears and back. "It's all right. I promise. Calm down. I'm going to get you something to eat."

Andy rummaged through the refrigerator and the freezer finally finding some frozen hamburger patties. He put one on a plate into the microwave and set the cook time for about five minutes. While the burger cooked he dug an old bowl out of the cupboard and filled it with cold water. He placed the water bowl near the dog who wasted no time at all slurping until his thirst was satisfied. As soon as the hamburger was done Andy cut it up and cooled it off before placing it on the floor near the water dish. In less than a minute the plate was empty and the dog was stretched out on the kitchen rug in the sunshine.

While the dog enjoyed its quiet rest Andy sat at the kitchen table and tried to decide what to do with the mut. He thought maybe he should make up some lost and found posters and put them up around town. In the meantime he needed to get the dog some food and probably a collar and leash. The problem was what to do with the dog. He didn't want to leave the animal alone in the house.

Just then Gracie arrived at the backdoor and Andy raced to let her in before she could knock. "My weren't you quick? You'd think you were expecting me." She walked into the kitchen and the dog raised its sleepy head. When Gracie saw the dog she stumbled backwards into the cupboards. "Where did that come from?" she whispered.

"Don't know. I found it down by the woodpile this morning." Andy motioned for Gracie to join him on the kitchen stools at the counter away from the dog. "I figure it's lost. Anyway I brought it into the house, gave it some food and water and now it's zonked out there."

"So what are you going to do with it?"

Andy shrugged his shoulders. "Well, I thought maybe I should put up some signs to let its owners know where it is. I also figured I should get it some food and maybe a collar and leash but I didn't want to leave it here alone." Andy looked at Gracie and smiled. "You wouldn't want to stay here with the dog while I run to the store for those things would you?"

Gracie looked at the dog then at Andy and took a very deep breath. "You've got to be kidding!"

"Oh come on. It shouldn't take me long to pick those things up at the grocery store in town." He looked at her with his best soulful face. "Please?"

Gracie laughed and playfully punched his upper arm. "Oh you! All right, I'll stay with the dog but don't be long. We still need to go fly our drones."

"Thanks," said Andy and he kissed her cheek. "I promise to be quick." He grabbed his jacket, wallet and car keys as he headed for the door. The dog watched him leave and started to get up. "It's all right little buddy. I'll be right back. You be good and Gracie will stay with you." He pointed his finger at Gracie and the dog looked at her before laying back down. He quickly slipped out the door and was gone.

Gracie watched the dog for a few minutes trying to decide if she should go over and make friends with it. But before she could make a move the dog got up and walked over to her. Gracie slid off the stool and kneeled on the floor. She scratched the dogs head and ran her hand down its back. The dog turned over on its back and looked up at Gracie. "Oh, you want a belly rub don't you boy?" She spent the next several minutes rubbing the dogs belly before getting off the floor and walking into the living room. She sat on the couch and the dog quickly joined her laying his head in her lap and falling asleep.

When Andy returned twenty minutes later that's exactly where he found them. "I think the dog is feeling at home."

Gracie looked at Andy and smiled. "I believe you're right. He's definitely feeling right at home." She scratched the dogs ears and he opened his eyes to look at her.

"So the dog's a male?" asked Andy sitting on the other side of the dog.

"Yep. And I've been thinking, why not just run an ad in the town newspaper that you found the dog. It'd be easier then printing posters and hanging them up everywhere."

"I hadn't thought of that."

"I figured you might not have. So, call Mr. Morgan and give him the information. Then we can take this little rascal and go to the park to fly our drones."

"Sounds like a good idea to me." Andy took the new dog collar from the grocery bag and fastened it to the dog's neck before making the phone call. "There you go little rascal." He looked at Gracie and grinned. "You know, that might be a good name for him. We'll call him Rascal, at least until his owner shows up and we know his real name."

"Sounds fine to me, agreed Gracie smiling and gently petting little Rascal.

Chapter Three

Emily and Rowena wandered around the Donoughmore dig site while their parents explored one of the trenches and reminisced about their last excavation in County Meath ten years ago. Rowena had brought Shea along as well and he was out investigating any small thing he found scampering in the area.

The girls strolled to a section of a rock wall and sat down. Emily leaned back and looked up at the bright blue sky. "This place is amazing. I can't get over how green it is. The grass, the trees and the flowers are so beautiful. It must be wonderful living here."

Rowena observed her companion thoughtfully. "You're right. Ireland is an amazing country and I've seen most of it. The people, for the most part, are friendly and I can't imagine living anywhere else. But from what my dad has told me, you and your family have lived lots of places."

Emily sat up and smiled. "Yes, that's right. It's been fun living in different countries. My dad has mostly explored Neolithic sites but he's done other things as well. He's done at least one Iron Age excavation and a few Medieval ones as well. I've found them all interesting."

"What about that cave you found in January? I understand that was very unusual."

Emily nodded her head. "Yeah, it was. They still aren't positive about some of it and no matter how much my father tells me I'm wrong, I still think the skeleton is an alien from another planet."

Rowena rubbed her forehead and smiled. "I suppose it's possible." She stood up. "Come on I want to show you something." She helped Emily to her feet and took her to an area where there were several large boulders near a forest.

Emily stood in disbelief staring at the rocks. She dropped to her knees and ran her hands over the rock's surface. "This is remarkable." She gazed at Rowena in awe. "Some of these petroglyphs are identical to the ones we found in the cave back in the States."

"That's what my da said when he saw them." Rowena kneeled down beside Emily. "Some of them are quite unusual. I mean look at this figure. It looks like a guy with some kind of hood on his head and this thing that he's carryin' with the lines comin' out of it. It almost reminds me of old Mr. Dodd's portable oxygen tank."

Emily nodded her head. "I see what you mean. There was a similar drawing on the cave wall we found. And these spirals are the same too."

Rowena traced one of the spirals with her finger. "They kinda remind me of the ones at Newgrange."

"Yes, but do you see these circles on some of the spirals? They sort of remind me of maybe planets. You know like if you drew our solar system you'd put in each planet and the route it traveled around the sun. They seem similar to me only this is a different solar system."

Rowena studied the drawing more closely. "I see what you mean. Wouldn't that be weird if these turned out to be just that? Where do you suppose that system could be?"

Emily shrugged her shoulders and wrinkled her forehead. "I have no idea."

While the girls studied the drawings Shea came running across the top of the rocks and into the forest. Rowena jumped up and ran after him. "Come back here Shea! Shea! Come here!"

Emily got off the ground and followed them. "Here kitty, kitty!" She had no idea which direction the cat took and she had lost sight of Rowena as well. She couldn't find anything that even resembled a foot path so she just wandered aimlessly hoping she would find either Rowena or the cat.

As she ambled deeper into the forest through the rustling dead carpet foliage she heard something scampering ahead of her. She began sprinting in the direction of the sound hoping it was either Rowena or the cat and not some wild animal. The trees new spring leaves allowed splotches of sunlight to filter through to the ground below but there were also unanticipated deep shadows hiding the unexpected tree limb or animal hole. It was such a hole that surprised Emily as she raced through the inches of dead leaves and she fell hitting her head on a large tree root nearby.

Emily opened her eyes and reached up to touch the side of her head. "There, there, dear, just lay still. Everything's going to be all right," the soft soothing voice told her as someone took a cloth to the cut on her head. Emily tried to see who it was but everything was so dark she was frightened that she may have lost her sight.

"Who are you and where am I?" she asked in a hushed voice.

"I am Epona. You're in my home. I found you in the forest." Epona finished cleaning the cut on Emily's head and helped her sit up. "There that's better," she said as she rinsed the cloth in a basin of water.

Emily tried moving her head and when she did she saw a candle sitting on a nearby shelf. "I remember running in the forest. I was trying to find my friend Rowena and her cat Shea. I think I must have stepped in a hole or something because I remember falling but nothing else." She tried to get up but couldn't. "I don't know how long I've been here but I need to get back. My parents will wonder where I am." She tried to see her watch but it was too dark. Slowly she looked around at her surroundings. Her vision was getting better but she felt a bit dizzy. She seemed to be sitting on a cot of some kind but the room reminded her of the inside of a large tree. The floor was dirt and the walls were wood.

"Here, dear, drink this. It'll make you feel better." The woman gave Emily a porcelain cup with some kind of warm liquid inside.

"What is it?" Emily asked nervously. "It's not some kind of poison or something. My mother told me never to take any sort of food from strangers."

The woman just smiled kindly and shook her head. "It's not anything that will harm you. I promise." She took a spoonful of the liquid from the cup and put it in her own mouth. "See? It will get rid of your headache and you won't feel so lightheaded."

Emily looked at the liquid, smelled it and took a deep breath. She took a small sip then looked at the woman. "It tastes good." She drained the cup and gave it back to the woman. "Thank you."

"You're very welcome." Epona took the cup to the sink where she washed and dried it. She walked back to Emily and sat down. "Are you feeling better now?"

"Yes, much better, thank you."

"Good. Now, shall I take you back to the rocks?"

Emily's eyes grew wide with wonder. "How did you know I came into the woods near the rocks?"

"Because that's usually where people enter the forest. Come along. We don't want your folks to worry, now do we?"

Once outside Emily got a better look at the woman named Epona. She was on the thin side, with long strawberry-blonde hair and bright green eyes. She walked almost like a dancer through the woods and her dress was the color of the forest. As they got closer to the clearing with the rocks Epona allowed Emily to travel ahead of her and by the time Emily reached the rocks Epona was nowhere in sight.

Rowena was standing next to the rock cuddling Shea when Emily finally emerged from the woods. "Where have you been? I was getting worried." Rowena told her.

Emily blinked her eyes. Compared to the forest the sunshine in the clearing was very bright. "I was in the woods looking for you and Shea," she answered shading her eyes.

"I've been looking for you for over an hour. Didn't you hear me calling?"

Emily gave Rowena a very puzzled stare and shook her head. "No, I never heard you. I fell and hit my head on a tree root or something. When I came to I was in some lady's house and she was cleaning my head." Emily brushed her light brown curls away from the cut to show Rowena.

"It doesn't look too bad to me."

Emily gingerly touched the spot. "It was bleeding and it hurt so much I had a headache. But this lady cleaned it up and gave me something to drink. She said it would take care of the pain and she was right. My headache is nearly gone."

Rowena stared at Emily in disbelief. As far as she knew no one lived in the forest. "Did this woman tell you her name?"

"She said she was Epona. I had never heard that name before but there are plenty of names I've never heard of. Her house was strange. It was almost like she lived in a tree or something. The floor was dirt and the walls were like the inside of a large tree."

Rowena sighed heavily and put her arm around Emily. "I think we need to be gettin' back to our parents. I think you may have hurt your head more than you know."

Emily frowned and allowed Rowena to lead her back to the area where they had left their folks. They were sitting on one of the stone walls examining some bones and a piece of copper.

"There you two are. Come see what ..." Pat stopped in mid-sentence when he noticed the girls slowly walking toward them. "What happened?"

"Emily fell in the woods and hurt her head," stated Rowena walking Emily over to her parents. "Shea went running and we ran after him. During the chase Emily fell and hit her head on a log or something. I wasn't with her when it happened so I'm not sure what it was."

Both Anne and Martin got up from the wall to check Emily's injury. By now the cut had nearly disappeared and all that remained was a small lump near the hairline on her forehead. However, there was some blood on her shirt and plenty of dirt on her jeans.

"How are you feeling, sweetheart?" asked her father with concern as he inspected her injury.

"I'm feeling fine. I don't know what all the fuss is about."

Rowena quickly glanced at her parents and shook her head indicating that things were not fine at all. "I think maybe Dr. MacDonagh should have a look at her. She may have a concussion."

Mary Jo looked at her daughter a bit bewildered. "What makes you think that?"

Rowena moved her parents out of hearing from the Parkers and told them the story Emily told her about the woman Epona and how she helped her.

"Maybe you're right," her father agreed. "It certainly couldn't hurt to have him check her out. Let me talk with her folks." He looked at his daughter. "Why don't you take Emily and Shea back to the van and we'll be along directly."

"Come on Emily," said Rowena taking her arm. "Let's go sit in the van while the old folks finish up."

As the girls slowly made their way to the other side of the dig Pat filled the Parkers in on everything Rowena had told him and Mary Jo.

"I don't understand what is so odd about this woman finding Emily in the woods and helping her," Anne said rather confused.

Mary Jo nodded her head. "Well, it's like this. No one lives in those woods. At least we've never found any evidence of someone living there."

"Well, maybe this woman is just camping there or something," suggested Anne hopefully.

"It would be nice to think so," stated Pat kindly, "but your daughter described the woman as livin' in some type of house with a dirt floor and walls that looked like the inside of a tree. That doesn't sound like someone who's just out there camping."

"No, I suppose not," agreed Anne. "Do you think she really might have a concussion?"

"I'm not a physician," said Pat. "But it couldn't hurt to have Dr. MacDonagh check her out just to be sure."

Martin glanced at his watch. "It's getting late. Where do we need to take her to get this Dr. MacDonagh to see her?"

"He'll come to the house. I'll just give him a call and he can be there when we get home." Pat noticed the confused look on his friend's face. "Mike's a friend of ours and he lives in Blarney just a few streets from us. If he thinks she needs to go to hospital he'll make arrangements after he does his evaluation. And don't worry about the cost. Like I said, he's a friend."

Martin looked at Anne and shrugged his shoulders. "All right. Let's do this." He was still holding one of the bones they had found in the nearby trench. "What should I do with this?"

"Just leave it," said Pat as he made the call to MacDonagh. "I'll have one of the staff come and get this stuff." He saw Vince Walker in one of the trenches a few yards away and motioned for him to take care of the items.

Soon they were all back at the van and on their way to the Flanagans.

Dr. MacDonagh finished examining Emily and then deposited his stethoscope and pen flashlight in his medical bag. He took one last look at her head, winked and patted her hand. "I think you're going to be just fine darlin'." He turned around to look at all the adults gathered in the living room. "Outside of the small bump on her head I can't find one other thing wrong with this young lady. It doesn't appear that she'd had any type of concussion. So, I don't see any reason to limit her activities while she's here. I would suggest that maybe she should take things a little easy for the next day or so." The doctor gathered his bag and stood up to leave. He took a careful look at the Parkers. "Do you have any questions for me?"

Martin looked at his wife. "No, I don't believe so. Thank you for coming, we really appreciate it. I'd like to pay you," and he reached in his pocket for his wallet.

MacDonagh held up his hand. "Please, don't embarrass me by offering me money. I won't take it. Just enjoy the rest of your stay with us. It's been a pleasure meeting all of you." And he headed out the door.

Anne sat on the couch next to her daughter and gave her a hug. "I'm glad you're all right."

Emily looked at her mother and smiled. "I did tell you I was fine. I don't know why no one believed me."

Martin stood in front of her and stared down at both his wife and daughter. "You know how we parents are. We just worry too much about everything."

"Oh Dad!"

Martin just smiled and sat down in a chair next to Pat while Mary Jo and Rowena retreated to the kitchen to check on supper.

"Now, I was thinking tomorrow we could either continue digging in the trench we were in this afternoon," stated Pat, "or there's a spot on the other side that I've been wantin' to explore."

"And just what do you think might be in this other spot?" inquired Martin.

"I have no idea. Given' what we've found so far this afternoon anything's possible. Why we might even find a fairy fort or leprechaun village," laughed his friend.

Both Martin and Pat broke out in laughter.

"Then I say let's find out what's hiding there!" Martin exclaimed holding his sides. "Ooh it's been a long time since I've laughed this hard!"

Pat was laughing so hard he couldn't speak.

While the men were trying to control their laughter Mary Jo came into the room. "I don't know what's so funny but if anyone is interested supper is on the table."

Anne just watched the men and shook her head. She stood up and grabbed Emily's hand. "Come on, Em. Supper smells delicious."

That evening when Emily was ready to crawl into bed she was watching Rowena with some interest. She sensed something wasn't quite right but she had no idea what it was. Finally she couldn't contain her curiosity. "You want to tell me what's going on? Ever since this afternoon there seems to be some kind of mystery that everyone knows about but me and I'd like to know what it is."

Rowena, who had been vigorously brushing her long dark red hair stopped, and turned around to face Emily. Her brown eyes softened and she sat down next to her and fluffed the covers over her. "How much Irish history do you know?"

"Not a lot. I know about their fight for independence, St. Patrick, the potato famine, and leprechauns but that's about it."

Rowena rubbed her finger across her freckled nose and smiled. "So, you wouldn't be knowin' anything about the Druids."

Emily crinkled her forehead. "Never heard of them. Why?"

"Well, it's quite possible the person you encountered this afternoon is one."

"I don't understand. She was a little different than most people I know but there's all kinds of people in the world."

"Let me explain to you about Druids. There isn't much information about them before the second century B.C. because they didn't usually write things down. They had to memorize the information. But they have been a part of our culture for a very long time. They were sort of like priests before there was Christianity. But some of them were also teachers, scientists, judges, philosophers, doctors, musicians and even poets. They had a lot of power and respect. And Druid women were equal to men. They observed nature and worshiped times like lunar, solar and seasonal cycles. Some were said to have magical powers but no one can prove this. It's mostly just legends and such. These people knew about astronomy and mathematics and they were pretty good engineers because they built huge mounds like Newgrange

"When the Romans arrived here in the first century A.D. Druidism was banned and by the second century they sort of disappeared. No one knows why. They could have been wiped out by war, disease, famine, it's anyone's guess. Or they could have been converted to Christianity. It's a fact that many things about the Druids were written down by the Christian clerics. Even St. Patrick wrote down all the old Irish Druid laws.

"Then in the seventeen hundreds there was sort of a Druid revival in England and Wales. There are still groups around who are studying the Druids and their language and traditions."

"Boy, you sure know a lot about Druids."

"Yeah, Druids, and mythology are sort of a hobby of mine."

"Well, I still don't understand what Druids have to do with what happened this afternoon."

Rowena took a deep breath. "The woman you said helped you today said her name was Epona. Well, there was a Druid goddess by that name and one of the things she was noted for was healing."

Emily's dark blue eyes widened to the size of nearly half dollars. "Are you trying to say this woman is a Druid goddess?"

"I don't know. I don't believe in gods and goddesses. I only believe in one God. I do think this woman knows something about medicine. I also think she's a bit strange to be living in a tree in the woods. That's all."

"Well, I agree living in a tree in the forest is odd. I don't know of anyone who has ever done that. But she did help my head so I don't think that's a bad thing."

"I agree. I think it's a good thing too." Rowena turned off the bedroom light and climbed into bed. "Goodnight, tomorrow is going to be a busy day."

"Yeah, Goodnight."

Chapter Four

Gracie was sitting in the Parker's kitchen watching Andy put the new leash on Rascal. He was certainly the funniest looking dog she had ever seen with his little teddy bear looking face and his blondish brown curly hair going from the top of his head down his back. It almost looked like he'd had a perm and it was starting to grow out, and those soulful light brown eyes. The rest of him looked like he could be part fox. "So, what are you going to do with old Rascal here if you can't find his owner?"

Andy softly stroked the dog's head and kneeled down on the floor beside him. "I don't know. Hadn't really thought about it." He gave the dog a hug. "This village isn't that big. Someone will see the notice and this little guy will be back with his owners by tomorrow. You'll see."

"But what if he isn't? Will you keep him?"

"Well, I'm not going to give him to the dog pound or something. I couldn't do that to the little guy."

"Will your folks let you keep him?"

Andy's gray-green eyes flashed in Gracie's direction. He ran his fingers thoughtfully through his short curly dark brown hair. "I don't know. We've never had a pet before. With all the traveling we did it just didn't seem practical. You know?"

Gracie watched the two. They seemed very comfortable together, like they belonged with each other. "Well, now that you've settled down here and won't be doing all that traveling maybe they'll let you have a pet."

Andy looked at the dog then at Gracie and smiled a little. "That'd be nice but I probably wouldn't get to spend much time with any pet. Afterall, I'll be going to college this fall. Don't know where but it won't be close."

"You could stay here and go to Leinster University. You're dad works there so you could get a discount and you could live at home. You might even be able to get a job at the university or nearby."

Andy stood up and frowned at her. "You don't understand. I want to get away. Away from my parents, my sister and archaeology." He walked to the kitchen table and sat down across from Gracie. "I want to do something on my own, something that isn't connected to my parents. I don't want any special favors because of someone they know. I need to see what I can do for myself."

Gracie quietly studied the floral placemat on the table for a few minutes before she responded. Slowly she lifted her head and gazed at Andy. "You know, you're right. I guess I don't understand. I never felt like I needed to run away from my family. I've always been allowed to think for myself and do my own thing. But I also know they need me and that I need them. That really became evident several years ago when my mother died and Gwen was injured in that awful car accident. I miss my mom and so does Gwen and my dad. We've become more dependent on each other. I worry about my sister and how she's going to get along without me when I go to college in the fall. I know she has learned to do quite a lot for herself over the last twenty months but there are still things she needs help with. Dad does what he can but he's not always available. And she can be stubborn because she doesn't like to ask for help. So, I guess I don't understand your need for independence from your family. I've always been able to be myself and I want to be there for my sister and father."

She silently brushed a tear from her cheek. "And from watching your father I'd say he wants you to think for yourself and to be whatever you want to be. I don't think he expects you to be an archaeologist. I think he's happy you enjoy flying drones. I've watched him at some of the competitions cheering you on and he's really excited and supportive of your accomplishments. It doesn't matter to him if you win or lose. He's just excited seeing you enjoy yourself."

Andy reached for the tissues at the side of the table and gave her one. "Hey, I'm sorry. I didn't mean to get you upset. Our lives are different, I know that. I also know that my father supports my drone flying. But I didn't know until recently that he wanted me to do anything besides archaeology. I had always just assumed that's what he expected me to do. But like I said last night, I've been so focused on what I didn't want to do that I haven't thought about what I'd like to do with my life."

Gracie wiped her face and put the tissue in her pocket. "Well, I guess it's time you gave it some serious thought." She stood up and Rascal walked to the back door dragging his leash with him. "I think Rascal wants to go out." She gathered her drone and looked at Andy. "Are we still going drone flying?"

"Absolutely." He put on his jacket, grabbed his drone and the dog's leash. He checked his pants pocket to be sure he had the house key and they left.

"I was thinking maybe we could go someplace different," said Gracie as they walked down the driveway. "You know, someplace more challenging than the park on Harper Avenue."

Andy was trying to hold on to his drone and the dog's leash and doing neither one successfully. Gracie grabbed the drone from his left hand to he could get control of the lead with both hands. "Thanks," he said. "Do you have any place particular in mind?"

"I was thinking maybe the other end of town. It's only a few miles and I'm sure Rascal would welcome the walk. There's some empty space down by the old MacAllister house and the wetlands. Then there's the other cemetery down there too."

A little shiver ran down Andy's spine at the very thought of a cemetery after what had been found next to St. Michael's Cemetery in January. He took a deep breath and exhaled. He looked at Gracie and shrugged his shoulders. "I suppose we can go down to that old abandoned house near the wetlands. I've been by it and there does seem to be a nice open area."

They were at the abandoned MacAllister house and flying their drones about forty-five minutes later. Rascal was enjoying himself running around the weed infested field and chasing the chipmunks hiding in some nearby logs. Andy was hesitant at first to let the dog go free but eventually Gracie convinced him that it would be all right. From his observation he could tell the dog was having a good time.

"See if you can fly your drone around that old well," suggested Andy to Gracie.

She looked skeptically at Andy. "Okay, but this isn't going to be easy. I sure hope I don't crash."

"You can do it," he told her. "Just tell yourself you can and give it your best. Think positive."

"Okay, here goes." The drone took off, straight up and then she moved the controls to send it on its journey toward the well. She was glad the covering was still over the opening because she sure didn't want her drone to end up in the water. She noticed the boards that held the well roof and spindle were looking as sturdy as ever given the fact they were over 200 years old. She managed to fly around the well twice before bringing the drone in for a landing on the house porch steps. She turned the drones controls off and wiped the nervous perspiration from her forehead.

"That was great!" shouted Andy racing over toward her. "I told you, you could do it. You just have to believe in yourself."

Gracie stared at him. "Right." In the distance she heard a dog barking. "Do you hear that?"

Andy quickly looked around for Rascal. He didn't see the dog anywhere. "Do you think that's the dog?"

Gracie picked up her drone and listened at the barking. "It sounds like it's coming from over there." She pointed to her right in the direction of the town cemetery. "Come on!"

"Oh great," muttered Andy. "Just where I want to go, NOT!" He ran after Gracie through the field and finally into the cemetery.

"Here doggie, here Rascal!!" Gracie kept shouting and running through the tombstones in the direction of the barking. She stopped just before reaching the mausoleum. Andy soon came up right behind her and stopped also. Before them sat the dog staring at a man laying in front of a tombstone.

"Oh no! I knew I didn't want to come over here." Andy stepped around Gracie and over to the dog. He grabbed the dog, put on his leash and handed it to her. Carefully he approached the man. He was fairly certain the man was dead but he thought he should check for a pulse just to be sure. Gently he put his fingers on the man's wrist then tried the artery in his neck. There was none either place. He turned to look at Gracie and shook his head. "I'm afraid he's dead." He looked at the headstone beside the man and noticed a bouquet of flowers in his outstretched hand. The name on the headstone read Brigid Murphy, wife of Fanin Murphy and her birth and death date. "We should call the police."

Gracie was dialing the number before he finished the sentence. "Hello, this is Gracie Taylor. I need to speak with Captain Scott. It's very urgent. Yes, I'll hold." She gave Andy an 'I'm doing the best I can' look as she waited for the captain. "Hello, Captain Scott. Yes. I need you to send a police officer to the cemetery on the south side of town. That's right. Down near the old MacAllister house. There's a dead man near one of the tombstones. No, I don't know who he is or how long he's been there. We just found him. Yes, there's someone with me. Andy Parker. Thank you. We'll wait." She put her phone in her jacket pocket. "Captain Scott said he will come here and we need to wait for him."

Andy rubbed the back of his neck and looked up at the cloudless crystal blue sky. "Why, lord? Why couldn't you have let someone else find the body?" He noticed a little bench between this row of graves and the mausoleum. He took the dog's leash and Gracie's hand leading them to it. "We might as well be comfortable while we wait."

The dog began to whimper and stare at the body. "Do you suppose the dog knows who this person is? Maybe he's the dog's owner," Gracie speculated as she watched the dog. "He looks so sad."

Andy stroked the dog's ears, head and back trying to comfort him and keep him calm. He was at a loss for words. Something like this never happened to him. Oh, sure, he helped dig up old skeletons, lots of old skeletons but he never came across a real dead body before. When Andy noticed the dog was shaking he picked him up and held him in his lap. Andy gave the dog a hug and continued to stroke him and whisper in his ear.

At last Captain Scott arrived with the coroner and another police officer. Gracie walked to the police car while Andy picked Rascal up and followed her. "Thank you for coming so quickly," said Gracie gravely as she looked at the three men.

"I don't believe we had any other option," replied Scott seriously. "Where's the body?"

"This way." Gracie led the men to the Murphy grave and the man's body.

The coroner, Dr. Henry Duncan and officer Robert Brady knelt down to check the body and turn it over on its back. The dead man was quite old, perhaps in his 80s or 90s with snow-white hair, thin eyebrows and very rosy cheeks. He was all dressed up like he was going someplace important. His dark blue sportscoat was buttoned just so neatly, and his white dress shirt appeared freshly ironed. He wore a navy flowered tie and gray dress slacks. The slacks had a few patches of grass and dirt on the knees where he had fallen and his shiny black shoes looked like he had just polished them.

Dr. Duncan removed the flowers from the dead man's hand and laid them on Brigid's grave. Although it was very apparent the man was dead the doctor gave the body a thorough check before turning to talk with Captain Scott. "I'd guess he's been dead at least twenty-four hours, maybe longer."

"Does he have any identification," inquired Scott gravely.

"Haven't checked," stated Duncan. "But I know who he is. He's Fanin Murphy. Looks like he came to visit his wife's grave for her birthday. Probably had a heart attack but I'll know for sure once I've completed the autopsy."

"Does he have any family?" asked Scott. "Children, grandchildren, siblings, nieces, nephews that sort of thing."

The doctor nodded his head. "His granddaughter teaches at the grade school and I'm not sure about his son. He was in the Air Force but I believe he's retired. I just don't know where he's living. I'm sure his granddaughter can give us the contact information. I think he may have a daughter also."

The dog jerked his leash from Andy's hand and ran to Murphy's body. He began to lick the dead man's face and whimper.

Andy swiftly strode over to the dog and grabbed the leash. Carefully he gathered the dog in his arms and began to walk away but the dog kept trying to turn its head to look at Murphy.

"Did you find the dog here with Mr. Murphy?" asked Duncan with interest.

Andy finally put the dog on the ground but held tightly to the leash so it wouldn't get away again. He looked somberly at the doctor. "No sir, I found the dog in my backyard this morning. Why?"

Duncan scratched the top of his head. "I think he might belong to Murphy. I could be wrong. It's been a while since I've seen him but this little guy looks like a dog Murphy might have adopted. We can check with Doc Schafer in the morning. Schafer is the vet Murphy used and his office is just over on Main Street."

"All right," agreed Andy. "I can do that." He looked at Dr. Duncan with a puzzled expression. "It is all right if I keep him isn't it?" He glanced apprehensively at Duncan and Captain Scott. "You aren't going to take him and put him in the dog pound or something are you?"

Scott shot Duncan a hesitant glance then looked back at Andy. "Normally we give a pet to a relative or take it to the animal shelter."

"I think, until we're positive about the dog's ownership it would be all right for Andy to take care of it," suggested Duncan calmly. "The dog seems to be responding well to him and it does seem like he found Andy on its own. Did it have any tags or collar?"

"No sir. He didn't have anything like that. I went to the store this morning and bought the collar and leash and some dog food."

Duncan glanced at Scott and smiled then turned his attention back to Andy and the dog. "I think the dog will be just fine with you for the time being. I believe the vet's office opens about eight thirty and I'm sure I have one of his cards." Duncan pulled out his wallet and found the card he was looking for. "There's his office hours and phone number. Just give him a call and tell him I want him to see the dog. Once you get there you can give him the rest of the story if this dog is in fact Murphy's."

"Thank you," said Andy taking the card and stuffing it in his pocket.

Gracie gazed at Mr. Murphy's body and at Duncan, Scott and Brady. She was anxious to be finished here so they could leave. She strolled over to Captain Scott and touched his arm. "Do you need us for anything else?"

Scott patiently looked at her and slowly shook his head. "I think we have everything under control. If I need any more information I will give you a call. Thank you for your help and I'm very sorry you were the ones who had to discover the body." He suddenly noticed the drones resting on the bench. "Guess this sort of messed up your drone practice didn't it?"

Gracie smiled at him. "Yeah, just a bit but we've got the rest of the week to practice." She walked to the bench and picked up the drones then joined Andy and little Rascal. "Shall we go home?"

Andy nodded. "I think that might be a good idea. I've had all the excitement I want for one day. In fact I have had all I want for the rest of the week or maybe the rest of my life."

As they made their way home Gracie couldn't help but remember how Andy reacted to the unusual things that happened to his sister. He liked to say trouble was drawn to her like a magnet. After today she was inclined to believe Emily wasn't the only one in his family with this trait.

Chapter Five

Monday began early at the Donoughmore excavation site. There were a number of college students and volunteers working in various trenches on the inside of the circle. Flanagan assigned his man, Vince Walker, to oversee this group while he took the Parkers to an area outside the circle.

"You see these boulders?" stated Pat when they reached the rocks Rowena had shown Emily the day before. "These petroglyphs have some similarities to the ones you found in that cave in January. See these circles and the people figures? The circles remind me a bit of the ones at Newgrange but a couple of them are different." He pointed to the circles Emily had told Rowena looked like solar systems.

"I see what you mean," commented Martin. "They do look similar to the ones we found. The people also resemble one of the drawings in the cave also but not the other drawings of people we found. Those people were in some type of object. It sort of looked like a spaceship."

Pat nodded his head and smiled. "Exactly. But so far we haven't found any petroglyphs like that here. That's why I thought if we dug here, near the rocks, maybe we could find something that would give us more clues about these drawings."

"Well, that does make sense," agreed Anne as she walked around the boulders and took pictures.

"The question is, where to begin," said Mary Jo glancing around the ground.

"That's why I asked Morgan to bring the laser scanner and bulldozer over," explained Pat with a wink. He turned toward where the cars were parked about a quarter of a mile to the east of the dig. "And speak of the devil, here he comes, right on time."

Pat left the group and headed for the tall man trudging across the field carrying the scanner. Behind him was Ben Nolan driving a small bulldozer and Paul O'Malley one of the college students from Trinity College helping at the site.

"Hey there, Morgan, my man, so glad you could make it."

"Hi Flanagan, I wouldn't want to miss out on this. I can't wait to see what we'll discover."

"Well, I'm hopin' it'll be something important. Come along I want you to meet some friends from the States. You come along too Paul and Ben."

Pat guided the group over to the boulders. "Now this is Martin Parker, a famous Neolithic archaeologist who is now a professor at a college in the States. We've been friends for over twelve years. Isn't that so?"

"Now there you go exaggerating Patrick. I am not famous. I'm just an archaeologist and right now I am teaching at Leinster University in Ohio." He held out his hand to the three men and shook each as Pat introduced them.

"This is Riley Morgan, his buddy Ben Nolan and this is Paul O'Malley one of the college kids who's been helping us out."

"It's very nice to meet all of you," said Martin warmly. "I'm looking forward to seeing what we might discover while we're here this week."

Pat directed the men to the small group of women standing nearby. "And over here we have Marty's lovely wife, Anne and his adorable daughter Emily. The other two you know."

"It's a pleasure to meet all of you," said Anne greeting each with a nod and a handshake. Emily stood beside her mother smiling politely.

"All right, let's get started," Pat said. "Morgan, how about starting here by these rocks with the scanner. O'Malley, fly the drone over this acre outside the stone circle. Then, if we find anything we can bring in the bulldozer and start digging."

Emily and Rowena sat on one of the rocks and watched the guys at work. "This has to be the most boring part of the dig," grumbled Emily as she dropped her backpack to the ground. "I know it's important so they have a good idea where to find stuff and if you're the one doing the detecting it would be fun. It just isn't any fun watching someone else do it. I'd bet even my brother would enjoy flying his drone out there."

Rowena was watching O'Malley maneuver the drone methodically over the field. "You're brother flies drones?" she asked switching her vision from the field to Emily. "I sort of remember him. It's been a long time and I was only six. So Andy likes to fly drones. That's interesting. He's about seventeen or eighteen isn't he?"

"He turned eighteen on March the first. He'll graduate from high school in May."

"What's he goin' to be doin' after graduation?"

"He has no idea. He won't be going into archaeology that's for sure. He hates it." Emily stretched her back and stood up.

"Well, I can understand that. It's not a profession for everyone. I like finding the history behind the different things we find but usually I'm not that interested in digging the stuff up." Rowena stood up and began to wander around the clearing. She glanced into the woods then back at Emily. "You know, while they are out there detecting maybe we could go into the woods and you could show me where you fell and maybe we could find this place where Epona lives."

Emily stared at Rowena as though she'd lost her mind. "Are you nuts? After everything that happened yesterday you want me to go back in there! I don't think so."

Rowena's face took on a mischievous look. "It's up to you of course, but I'd like to find this unusual woman. Maybe she knows something about the history of this place."

Emily fixed her eyes on Rowena trying to decide if she was sincere or if she was joking. "She may know something about this area but that doesn't mean she will share it. She seemed more of a recluse to me."

"Well, suit yourself, stay here and be bored," said Rowena. "I'm going hunting."

Emily watched her run into the woods and disappear. "And people think I'm crazy," she muttered sitting back down on the rock. "Compared to her I'm perfectly sane."

Emily's parents were across the field with the Flanagans talking with Mr. Morgan so they had no idea Rowena was off playing detective in the forest. She was debating with herself about whether she should try to go after Rowena or if she should tell her parents or if she should do nothing at all and just wait for her to return. "I really should do something," she mumbled putting her elbows on her knees and resting her chin in her hands.

"You should do something about what?" asked O'Malley coming over to the rock with his drone.

Emily jerked her head up and nearly slipped off the rock. "Oh my goodness! You scared me half to death. You really shouldn't sneak up on people like that."

"Sorry," said Paul O'Malley. "I didn't mean to frighten you. I just saw you sitting here alone and thought you might like some company. So, what is it you should do something about?"

Emily looked into his light blue eyes and sighed. "Rowena went into the woods and didn't tell anyone so I was trying to decide if I should let her folks know."

O'Malley carefully held his drone in his hands and tried to understand her concern. "These woods aren't that big so I don't think you need to be worried she will get lost." He sat down next to Emily.

Emily slowly shook her head. "That isn't it. You see, yesterday her cat went in there and while we were running around looking for him I fell and hurt my head. We weren't together when it happened. Anyway, I must have knocked myself out because when I came to I was in some woman's house in the forest and she was cleaning up my head. She gave me something to drink to make me feel better then helped me back here. But the woman wasn't with me when I came into the clearing so no one but me saw her. When I told Rowena the lady's name she acted as though she thought I made it up or that I had really hurt my head worse than it looked. So now Rowena has gone into the woods to try and find this woman."

"I see," said O'Malley rubbing his chin thoughtfully. "And what exactly was this woman's name?"

"Epona."

He abruptly stopped rubbing his chin, sat up straighter and stared at Emily. "Epona?"

"Exactly. You think it's weird too don't you?"

"Let's just say it's been a very long time since I heard that name."

"I never heard the name until yesterday. After Rowena told me about the Druids and this Epona goddess I'm in no hurry to go back in the woods to find her."

O'Malley chuckled. "I don't think you need to be concerned that the lady who helped you is a Druid goddess."

Emily sadly shook her head and stared at the ground. Reluctantly she raised her head and looked at him. "You're probably right. It's all just part of Gaelic mythology. The woman is just someone living in the woods. That's all." She wished she could believe what she said but she knew if it wasn't there was going to be trouble. There always was.

She looked at the drone and decided to change the subject. "So, did you discover anything interesting?"

"As a matter of fact I did," O'Malley stated with a grin. "About fifty meters from here there appears to be some metal artifacts. There were some bones as well. And over in that corner, near the tree line, there's more bones and something else but I couldn't get a good reading."

Emily's face brightened up. "Oh that's wonderful. How soon can we start digging?"

"Don't know. Still waiting for Morgan to finish his scan of the area."

"Well, I hope he hurries up. Half the morning is gone already." She slumped backwards on the boulder and pouted.

O'Malley laughed slightly. "I'm sure he'll be done before dinner."

"Dinner?!"

"Oh, I'm sorry, you Americans call it lunch," said O'Malley with a smile. "Some call it lunch here also."

"I see. I'll have to remember that."

Emily glanced across the field and noticed her mom and Mrs. Flanagan headed in their direction. "Uh, oh."

"We've got good news," said Anne smiling broadly. "Mr. Morgan has found some objects in the field in addition to the things you've found Paul. Pat is going to have Mr. Nolan bring in the bulldozer and begin digging."

"It looks like we'll be able to have several areas to explore," stated Mary Jo. She looked around the area and suddenly realized her daughter wasn't there. "Where's Rowena? I'm sure she'll be happy to know we've found some promising areas to excavate."

Emily stared at the ground not wanting to look at anyone. She especially didn't want to look at Mrs. Flanagan.

"What's happened?" asked Mary Jo apprehensively.

Paul cleared his throat, placed his drone on the boulder and eased over to her. "It's nothing to be concerned about," he assured her. "It just seems she has gone into the woods to do some exploring."

Mary Jo's eyes flashed wide with surprise. "What kind of exploring and why didn't she let us know or take someone with her?"

Emily couldn't decide if she should be worried or guilty. She should have told them Rowena went into the woods alone but then maybe she should have gone with her. "I'm sorry Mrs. Flanagan I should have told you but you were all so busy I didn't want to interrupt. Besides, I didn't think she'd be gone very long."

"Just how long has she been gone?" Anne inquired firmly.

Emily looked at her watch and answered meekly. "About an hour."

"What on earth could she be doing in there so long? The forest isn't that big," Mary Jo stated uneasily.

Emily nervously played with the zipper on her jacket before answering. "This is probably going to sound silly but she wanted to find the lady who helped me yesterday after I fell."

Mary Jo look toward the forest fearfully. "I have to go find her." She anxiously headed into the woods and began calling Rowena's name.

Anne glanced tensely at her daughter and Paul. "We should probably go with her just in case there's some trouble."

Paul turned on his drone controls. "I can maybe use my drone to help find her. It might be faster than trudging through the entire forest."

"All right," agreed Anne. "Now, Emily, did you happen to notice which direction Rowena went?"

Emily quickly but carefully scanned the entrance area. "Over that way, to the left." She led the way through some of the trees. "Do you think we should let Dad and Pat know where we are and what we're doing?"

"I can try," said Anne, "but I don't know how good the reception is in here." She pulled out her phone to check and slipped it back in her pocket. "There's no reception. They'll just have to wait. Besides, they're going to be so busy digging they won't even notice we're gone. Come on."

Emily began to inspect the area making mental notes of disturbed dead leaves on the ground, as well as any bent or broken limbs on various plants. "Over this way," she called motioning to her mother and Paul. "I think she may have come this way. There's some bent branches and the ground leaves are all messed up."

Paul scratched his head. "Mrs. Flanagan could have done that when she came in."

Emily shook her head. "No, because she went in the opposite direction."

"All right, let's see what we can find." He launched his drone in the general direction Emily had indicated and the three of them followed it.

Emily kept a cautious eye on the vegetation as they went. "Over this way." She pointed to a small tree limb with several strands of dark red hair. "She came this way. See some of her hair got caught on this."

Paul blinked his eyes in amazement. "Are you sure you're not part American Indian? You're pretty good at this tracking business."

Both Emily and her mother laughed. "As far as I know there's no American Indian in our ancestry," volunteered Anne.

"It's just something I learned from books I've read."

"You'll have to let me know what books they were. I think that skill could come in handy."

Emily smiled. "Sure, I'll be glad to."

The drone was making its way deeper into the woods and they still hadn't found Rowena. They hadn't found the house or the woman who had helped Emily either. They started to head toward the right when they heard a pony whinny in the opposite direction. Paul turned his drone in the direction of the noise.

"Is there a horse farm around here?" asked Anne hesitantly as they continued to follow the drone.

"There could be but I don't know," replied Paul keeping a careful watch on his machine. "I'm new to this area. There are farms here so maybe someone owns a horse and we just don't know it."

"Sure, that could be," agreed Anne tentatively.

Emily began to walk faster keeping up with the drone until she reached a small clearing. There, sitting near a tree stump was Rowena talking to a beautiful white pony. Emily abruptly stopped, mesmerized by what she saw. She was soon joined by her mother and Paul. The drone was floating in midair going nowhere and Paul brought it back landing it on the ground at his feet.

Rowena hadn't noticed them and neither had the pony or if they had they decided to ignore them.

"Well, at least we found her," said Emily encouragingly. "Now we just need to get her and find our way back."

"Okay, you two stay here. I think it would be best if just one of us went to her," Anne explained quietly. "We don't want to startle the pony or Rowena by everyone descending on them."

Anne carefully followed the tree line toward Rowena and the pony. The closer she got the more she noticed that Rowena seemed to be just staring into space, almost as though she were in a trance. She made a bit of noise but Rowena didn't react. It was as if she hadn't heard anything. She certainly didn't want to startle the girl. Anne walked around to face Rowena, but there was still no response from her. Finally Anne knelt down in front of her and reached out for her hand. "Rowena, it's Anne Parker, we need to go. Your mother needs you."

Rowena slowly turned her face away from the pony and stared at Anne rather dreamy eyed. "My mother?"

"Yes, Rowena, your mother needs you. Come along."
Anne helped Rowena to her feet but before she left Rowena stroked the pony's nose. "Good-bye Niamh (Nee-av)." Slowly Anne led the girl to where Emily and Paul were waiting.

As they entered the forest Rowena stopped, shook her head and rubbed her eyes. She looked at Emily in surprise. "I didn't think you wanted to come with me." She looked around a little more and noticed Paul and Anne and was even more startled. "Where'd you come from? I thought you were all exploring the field."

"They're done exploring the field," Emily told her kindly. "They've found several interesting places to explore."

"Oh. Well, I'm glad for that," said Rowena dimly.

Cautiously the small group retraced their steps through the forest to the boulders near the clearing. As they exited the trees Emily led Rowena to one of the rocks and had her sit down. The girl still seemed to be in a daze. The men were in a far corner of the field digging up dirt with the bulldozer. It was quite noisy there and they were so focused on their work they never noticed the group's return.

"Mary Jo hasn't returned," noticed Anne with a frown. "Do you think she may have gotten lost?"

"I hope not," said Emily taking a seat beside Rowena. "If one of you will stay with Rowena I'll go see if I can find her."

Anne stood with her hands on her hips, commandingly in front of her daughter. "You are not going into those woods. Understand? Paul and I will go look for her. You will stay here with Rowena until we return. You have that?"

Emily looked soulfully up at her mother with her big dark blue eyes. "Yes, Ma'am."

"Good. Now you said she went in the opposite direction from the one we took."

"Yes."

"Fine. Now if your father or Pat should happen to come over here you can tell them what happened but don't go over there on your own. There's no reason to tear them away from their work and get them worried over nothing." Anne glanced at Paul and motioned for him to come with her. "Hopefully, she hasn't gone too far into these woods."

"Yes, Ma'am, I hope so too," agreed Paul promptly following after Anne.

Emily watched them disappear into the trees silently hoping they would be able to quickly find Rowena's mom. She picked up her backpack and rummaged around inside until she found a couple of water bottles. She took them out and gave one to Rowena.

"Thank you," said Rowena opening the bottle and taking a nice long drink. "I never thought watching guys digging up a field could make a person so thirsty."

Emily gave Rowena a puzzled glance before turning her attention to the men digging up the field. She looked back at Rowena. "I think the long walk you took in the woods is what's made you thirsty more than watching all that digging."

Rowena took another gulp of water. "I don't know what you mean. I didn't take a long walk in the woods."

Emily blinked her eyes and rubbed her knees. Rowena's remark made absolutely no sense. "Do you know what time it is?"

Rowena shrugged her shoulders. "I didn't wear my watch but it's probably about eleven."

Emily shook her head. "No, it's almost a quarter to one." She stared at Rowena trying to understand why the girl didn't remember what had happened.

"That's ridiculous," insisted Rowena blandly. "I would certainly remember taking a walk in the woods."

"I'm afraid you don't remember," stated Emily emphatically. "About ten thirty you decided to go into the forest to look for Epona, the woman who helped me yesterday. You asked me to go along but I didn't. You went alone. An hour later Paul O'Malley came along and not too long after that your mom and mine came here to let us know they found some places to dig. When they saw you weren't here and where you had gone your mother got concerned and went into the woods looking for you. Then my mom, Paul and I went looking for you too. We found you in a small field with a white pony and brought you back here. Right now my mom and Paul are in the woods trying to find your mother."

Rowena leapt to her feet glaring angrily at Emily. "That's a lie. You're crazy." She began stomping around in front of the huge rocks. "I've been right here the whole time!" She began to swiftly move toward the group with the bulldozer.

"We can't go over there right now. We have to stay here until our mothers and Paul return," Emily said grabbing Rowena's arm.

"Let go of me!" shouted Rowena. "I'm not going to listen to any more of your insane stories."

Just as she began to sprint away again her mother came racing out of the woods. "Rowena! Rowena!" yelled Mary Jo running to stop her. Rowena hesitated just long enough for her mother to reach her and lead her back to the boulder. "I'm so glad they found you!" Mary Jo gave her daughter a tight hug and had her sit back on the rock.

Soon Anne and Paul joined the little group. Paul sat on the ground and rested his back against the boulder while Anne sat down beside Emily.

Mary Jo knelt on the ground in front of Rowena and took her daughter's hands in hers. "You had us so worried. Are you all right?"

Rowena stared at her mother and frowned. "Look, I don't know what's going on. Of course I'm all right. Why wouldn't I be?"

Mary Jo looked questioningly at Anne, Paul and Emily. "She doesn't remember going into the woods or anything," explained Emily sadly. "She thinks she's been here the entire time watching them dig in the field."

"Oh, no," lamented Mary Jo. "I can't believe this has happened. I've got to call Dr. MacDonagh and take her home."

Anne nodded her head in agreement. "That would probably be a good idea. It could be wandering around in those woods was a little confusing and stressful. Take her home and let her rest. I'll tell the guys if you like."

"This is more than being confused or stressed from being in those woods," stated Mary Jo. "This has to do with Epona and the forest."

Anne looked very bewildered. "I guess I don't understand what Irish myths has to do with this."

Mary Jo stared at Anne. "Perhaps you will one day." She got her daughter onto her feet and led her to the parked cars.

"Do you think they need a ride home?" inquired Emily. "Maybe we should tell Pat."

"That's all right. I'll tell him," offered Paul. "She usually has her own set of keys for the car. Of course, all of you may need a ride back to the Flanagans if you all came in the same car."

Nancy Potts

"Luckily for us we rented a car yesterday so we came in separate cars this morning. We can give Pat a ride home," stated Anne plainly. "Come on, let's all go see how things are going and fill them in on the latest developments."

When they reached the group Ben Nolan and his bulldozer had made a significant trench in the area. Emily wasted no time rushing to the hole to investigate. In fact, she nearly fell in.

"Hey there darlin' you better watch where you're going. Don't want you gettin' hurt, now do we," said Pat as he grabbed her by the waist to keep her out of the trench.

Emily looked up at him in surprise. "Thank you," she whispered as she tried to catch her breath. "Guess I got a little excited and didn't watch where I was going."

Pat smiled. "That's all right dear. You're safe now."

"You're making good progress," observed Anne standing at the edge of the trench. "Have you found anything yet?"

"Not yet. We're almost deep enough to go in. Ben just needs to remove one more little layer of dirt," Martin explained happily.

"So, where's Mary Jo and Rowena?" asked Pat, all of a sudden realizing they weren't there.

Anne chewed nervously on her bottom lip as her blue-violet eyes darted first to her husband then to Flanagan. "Mary Jo took Rowena home," she said at last.

"Home?" asked Pat looking worried. "Is Rowena sick or something?"

"I'm not sure," answered Anne uneasily. "You see, Rowena went into the woods looking for the woman who helped Emily yesterday. Anyway, when the three of us found her she was sitting in a little pasture with a pony. After we brought her back here she said she'd never been there and didn't even remember going into the woods. So, Mary Jo thought it best to take her home and call the doctor."

"I see," he replied hesitantly and stared at the ground before raising his head to look at Anne.

"Would you like me to take you home?" inquired Martin with concern. "I could take care of things here for you."

"I can't ask you to do that. Besides, if it's anything important Mary Jo will call."

Martin watched his friend with concern. "Well, if you change your mind let me know."

"Of course I will. Now, let's see what Ben has unearthed."

Emily had been watching Ben as he scraped off the recent layer of dirt. They were down several feet now and they should be able to begin to find a few things. Paul was standing beside her making a mental note of where they were and where his drone had noticed one of the burial sites. Part of that area was right here.

"They're making good progress don't you think?" she asked Paul excitedly. "We should be able to get in there and start finding things. Are they near any of the places you picked up with your drone?"

Paul smiled and nodded his head. "As a matter of fact they are." He walked down beside the trench a few feet and she followed. He paused and stared inside. "I believe we should find a skeleton and a few objects right about here."

Ben parked his bulldozer to one side of the trench and hopped down to the ground. "I hope I've cleared enough area to at least get started," he said as he stood beside Paul and Emily observing his handiwork.

"I believe you've hit the right spot," stated Paul with a grin. "At least it's one of the areas I found with my drone."

Emily picked up a trowel and small brush then slid into the trench. She looked at the guys still standing near the edge. "Are you guys going to spend all afternoon yakking or are you going to get down here and get to work? It's not getting any earlier, ya know."

Both Paul and Ben looked down at her standing in the ditch and laughed. "We'll be right with you, darlin'" chuckled Paul as he grabbed a trowel and brush and joined her.

"I'll join you right after I have a bite to eat. Driving that dozer has made me hungry," said Ben with amusement as he left to get his lunch.

Paul looked at Emily and shrugged his shoulders. He glanced at his watch. "It *is* after one thirty. Would you like something to eat before we get started?"

"Yeah, I guess. I am sort of hungry. Sometimes I get so carried away that I forget about eating."

"All right then. Let's eat and then we can get back to discovering all the mysteries hidden beneath the soil," Paul said and helped Emily out of the trench. "Afterall they've been here several thousand years; I don't think they're going to be going anywhere in the next few minutes."

"Right," giggled Emily. "Let's eat."

It was nearly 4 o'clock. Emily, Paul, and Ben along with Emily's father, as well as Pat and Riley Morgan had been digging in the trench for several hours. Anne had remained on the ground nearby with her camera and notebook so she could photograph whatever they might find. Emily's trowel suddenly struck medal making a sound that got everyone's attention.

"What did you find?" Martin asked as he moved to her side.

"I'll know in a minute," she answered taking her brush to sweep away the dirt. "It looks like it might be a shield or something." She quickly kept digging and sweeping revealing more of the metal shaped disk. There were carvings of horses and some type of plants on the disk. The carvings looked like they were made of bronze. Carefully Emily brushed more dirt away until the entire object was visible. Anne quickly snapped a few photos of everything. "I was right. It is a shield," she said lifting it out of the ground and showing it to everyone. "Isn't that beautiful?"

Her father smiled and helped her lift it higher. "It is lovely," he agreed and slid it out of the trench and onto the ground above.

Once the shield was gone a skeleton was discovered that had been lying beneath it. "Interesting," said Riley. "I think we found us an important warrior."

Being stuck in the ground for several thousand centuries hadn't done a great deal for the bones. True, they seemed to be laying on a metal sheet of some kind which did help but it wasn't as good as if they had been in a stone coffin or something.

Emily gently brushed more dirt and debris from the bones. "Oh, look!" she exclaimed. "There's an armband on this upper arm." She was very careful not to touch or remove it until her mother had taken pictures to record the find. Very delicately Emily removed the metal band and handed it to her father. "This looks like it's made of gold," she told him. "But would they have done that back then?"

"It does look like it's made of gold and there's some silver on it also," Martin remarked. "But since we haven't determined what time frame we're dealing with yet it's difficult to say if they would have made jewelry from gold and silver. One thing is fairly certain, however, whoever this was, he was wealthy. He may even have been the chief of this area."

Emily gave him a cynical stare. "What makes you so sure this skeleton is a male. Maybe it's a female. Ireland did have female warriors you know."

"You're absolutely right, dear, Ireland and other Celtic countries had women warriors. They were a feisty little group for sure," he responded enthusiastically.

"Aye, that they were," remarked Riley with a broad grin, "and there's still plenty of their kind around. You won't be finding a fcisticr woman than an Irish one and a redhead is really dangerous!"

All of the men laughed vigorously at that comment. Emily and her mother eyed the men rather belligerently.

"Just remember this Pat Flanagan," stated Anne energetically, "both your wife and daughter are redheads. And Martin, a female doesn't need to be either Irish or a redhead to be feisty and fight for what she believes in."

The laughter abruptly ceased and the men all looked at each other in surprise trying to understand what exactly had happened. Pat quickly picked up his trowel and brush.

"Come on, let's get back to work. It'll be getting dark soon."

By 5:30 they had found a metal helmet, and a sword in a fancy scabbard. Emily was working on another end of the trench when she discovered partial remains of several strips of leather. It was difficult to tell just how long they were or where they would end. She wanted to continue digging but she saw everyone was getting ready to leave. Whatever was there would just have to wait until tomorrow.

Chapter Six

Andy and Rascal sat in the examining room at the local animal hospital. Rascal was shivering, and refused to leave Andy's lap. "There, there, boy, calm down. Everything's going to be all right," said Andy quietly as he stroked the dog's head to comfort him.

Last night had been interesting, Andy remembered. The dog had followed him everywhere when they returned home from flying the drone. When he went to bed the dog was right there, curled up beside him all night. When the first rays of sunlight made it into the bedroom the dog was energetically licking Andy's face and nuzzling his nose into Andy's armpit. Andy nearly fell out of his bed. The dog tried to follow him into the shower but raced out of the room when Andy turned on the water. The dog didn't go far though. He was laying in front of the bathroom door when Andy opened it.

Andy leaned down and gave Rascal a hug. "Good boy. Maybe we can go for a walk in the park when we're done."

The examining room door opened and the veterinary technician came in. "Hi, I'm Heather, Doc Schafer's assistant," she said as she walked over to the exam table. Andy guessed she was maybe in her late twenties. Her long dark brown hair was pulled back into a pony tail and her hazel eyes were looking lovingly at the dog. "Can you get him up here?" She placed her well-manicured hand on the table.

Cautiously Andy stood up and put the shivering dog on the table as she had asked. Rascal didn't want to stay and tried to jump down but Andy held on to his collar and continued to whisper in his ear. Eventually the dog sat down and Heather wrote down his weight.

She pulled out a thermometer from a nearby drawer. "If you could hold his front I'll take his temperature." Rascal was in no mood to be cooperative and refused to stand up. Eventually, with Andy's help they did get him to stand long enough to get his temperature.

"Thank you," said Heather as she petted Rascal's head. "Doc should be with you in a minute." She left and closed the door leaving Andy and Rascal alone again.

Andy continued to do his best to calm the dog talking to him as he glanced around the room. This was a new experience for him and like Rascal he was a bit nervous.

Soon the door opened again and Dr. Schafer along with Heather entered the room. The dog began to bark and shake again.

Doc came closer and held his hand toward the dog's nose. "There, there, Taliesin, everything's all right," said Dr. Schafer soothingly. He smiled warmly at Andy. "It was nice of you to bring in Mr. Murphy's dog for him. I hope he's doing well."

Andy took a very deep worried breath. "Well, sir, it's like this. I don't know who's dog this is. I found him in my backyard yesterday morning. He didn't have any collar or tags. But Dr. Duncan said he thought the dog might be Mr. Murphy's and suggested I bring him to you to find out."

Doc looked at Andy then at the dog. "I see. But if Dr. Duncan thought this was Mr. Murphy's dog why didn't you just take him there and ask?"

Andy glanced nervously at the vet. "Ah, well, you see, I couldn't do that because Mr. Murphy's dead."

Doc nearly dropped his stethoscope at this information. He blinked his small brown eyes and stared at Andy. "Murphy's dead? How? When?"

"I'm not real sure," said Andy trying to compose himself. "My friend Gracie Taylor and I found him yesterday afternoon beside his wife's grave. Apparently he must have gone to put flowers on her grave and he had a heart attack. At least that's what Dr. Duncan thinks. They'll know better once they do an autopsy. Anyway, Dr. Duncan said you might know who this dog belongs to."

"I see," said Doc running his hand down the dog's back. "We can check to see if he has a microchip. If he does then we can track

64

down his owners. But this dog does look a lot like Murphy's dog." Dr. Schafer turned to Heather. "Would you please bring me the microchip scanner?"

"Yes," answered Heather and she left to retrieve the device.

"I am very sorry to hear about Mr. Murphy. He was a nice old guy. But he was up there in age. I think the last time he was here he told me he was going to be ninety-six in May. I know he missed his wife a lot. They had been married about sixty-eight years when she passed," Doc told Andy.

Heather returned with the scanner and gave it to Dr. Schafer. He promptly scanned for the microchip and found the results. He checked the ID number with that of Mr. Murphy's dog. "We have a match," said Doc. "This is Mr. Murphy's dog all right."

"Well, I'm glad we know who he belongs to," said Andy somberly. "I imagine Mr. Murphy's relatives will be wanting him."

Doc viewed Andy rather seriously. "I doubt that. Neither of his kids are fond of animals and they don't exactly live close by. His son lives in California and his daughter is in Hawaii."

Andy's face perked up a bit. "Are you sure?"

"Yes, I'm sure. My parents went to school with the Murphy kids. Mr. Murphy and his wife loved animals, all kinds. They had cats, dogs, birds, fish, turtles and one time they even had a pet skunk. Eric and Wanda couldn't stand any of them. At least that's what my folks told me."

"So, you think I might be able to keep this dog then?"

"I don't see why not."

Andy scratched the dogs ears and gave him a hug. "You hear that boy? You can stay with me." Andy looked at Dr. Schafer a little puzzled. "What was the name you called him again?"

Doc smiled. "Taliesin. But you can call him whatever you like. I don't think he'll mind if you give him a different name. What did you want to call him?"

Andy grinned. "Gracie and I called him Rascal."

"That seems like a good name to me."

Nancy Potts

"I imagine I'm going to need to get him a dog license aren't I? I mean since he didn't have any tags or collar when I found him and we have no idea where they might be it just makes sense to get him a new license doesn't it?"

Doc nodded his head. "Yes, yes it does. We can give you one here. The lady at the front desk can take care of that for you."

"So when do I need to bring him back and is there anything I need to do for him?"

Doc looked over Taliesin's medical record. "He just had his annual physical in February so he's good until next year. He is on heartworm medicine as well as flea and tick medicine and I would imagine you can find that at Mr. Murphy's house but just in case we'll give you the medicine here when you check out."

"Thank you. Is there anything else I need to know?"

"Nope. You're all set." Dr. Schafer opened the exam room door that led to the lobby and reception desk. "So long there little Rascal. You be a good boy." Rascal didn't even look at Doc. He just raced out the door and tried to run out of the building.

Andy picked the dog up and went to the checkout counter where the receptionist handed him a bag containing the dog's medicine and new license. She also handed him the bill. He looked twice at the amount before pulling out his wallet with a credit card. He could only imagine what his parents reaction would be when he showed them this when they got home. He might need to get a job to pay for little Rascal's upkeep.

It was 10:30 by the time Andy pulled into his home's driveway. Rascal was so excited to be home that as soon as Andy opened his car door he jumped across Andy's lap and onto the ground. Andy barely had time to grab the dog's leash and even then the dog pulled so vigorously on it Andy had a difficult time holding on.

"Whoa there Rascal. Where are you going in such a big hurry?" The dog had stopped at the bottom of a maple tree in the backyard and was barking up a storm. It was then that Andy noticed a squirrel sitting on a high branch staring down at them. It was chattering right back at Rascal.

Andy knelt down next to the dog and tried to calm him. He looked up at the squirrel and laughed. "It's all right. I won't let him get you," he told the squirrel. "Come along Rascal. You sure are living up to your name."

On his way back to the house his phone began to chirp. It was his mother calling. He had given all his family members a special ring and birds chirping was his mom. "Great!" he growled as he pulled the phone from his pocket. "Hi Mom. How are you?" He hoped he sounded pleasant and cheerful. "Yes, I remembered to set out the trash. No, they haven't been here yet. What? No, the mail hasn't arrived yet either. It's only a little after ten thirty here Mom. I thought the mail didn't arrive until after one o'clock. Everything is fine here. Hope all of you are enjoying yourselves." Just then Rascal spotted a couple taking a walk down the street and he began to bark quite loudly. Andy stared at the dog and whispered for him to be quiet. "What Mom? It's just a dog barking somewhere. I'm outside in the backyard. No, no, it's nothing to worry about. All right. Look, I gotta go. I promised Gracie we'd go drone flying before lunch. You take care too and I'll see you when you get home on Saturday. 'Bye."

Andy looked down at Rascal who had stopped barking and was sitting quietly at his feet. Andy slowly shook his head and smiled. "You are something, you know that?"

Once inside the house Andy deposited the dog's medicine on the counter and put his new license on his collar. "There you go boy. Now you're official." He knelt down and scratched Rascal behind his ears then gave him a hug. "Well, shall we go for that walk now?"

Rascal stared at Andy then began giving him wet slobbery kisses all over his face. Andy smiled and laughed. "All right. Let's go!"

In no time at all they were out the door and jogging down the sidewalk toward the park on Harper Avenue. "Well, you sure don't waste any time do you boy?" Andy raced Rascal around the soccer fields and finally led him to a nearby bench so he could sit down. "Man, I'm definitely out of shape," he told Rascal breathing hard. The dog decided to take a break and laid down next to Andy's feet.

Andy leaned back on the park bench and closed his eyes. Even though it was only early April and still a little chilly he was enjoying the sunshine. He listened to the birds calling to each other as they perched in the park trees. *This is perfect,* he thought. *Life can't get much better than this.*

His blissful solitude was soon interrupted. Rascal jumped up and began barking. Andy opened his eyes and saw Ted Morgan enter the park with his brown Labrador Retriever, Jasper. "Well, it was great while it lasted," he muttered stoically.

"Hello Ted," said Andy sitting up straighter and petting Rascal to calm him down.

Jasper raced to the bench playfully greeting Rascal. He was definitely looking for a playmate. Rascal on the other hand wasn't so sure he wanted to play with this big dog.

Ted stood hesitantly in front of Andy and the dogs like he was trying to decide what to do. Finally he tightened his grip on Jasper's leash and stroked the dog's head.

"Quiet down Jasper," he told the dog. "Come, sit."

Jasper neither quieted down nor sat, much to Ted's dismay.

Andy chuckled to himself. "What do you say we take them over to the fenced in part of the park and turn them lose?" he suggested amicably. "That way they can run around and enjoy themselves. There's even some benches for us to sit on."

"Sure, why not," said Ted trying to make himself heard above all the noisy barking.

The guys made their way over to the dog park, closed the gate and turned the dogs lose. The dogs didn't waste any time enjoying their freedom and began to race around the grounds. Andy and Ted sat on a bench watching them.

"So, when did you get a dog?" asked Ted, his brown eyes sparkling with curiosity. "Emily never mentioned it."

Andy leaned back and stretched. "She doesn't know about it."

"Oh, I get it," said Ted confidently. "It's a surprise for when she gets back."

Andy glanced at Ted rather conspiratorially. "It's going to be a surprise for all of them."

Ted furrowed his brow in confusion. "I don't understand. You got a dog and your parents don't even know about it?"

"Actually, the dog is the one who got me," explained Andy as he filled Ted in on the whole story about finding the dog, and about finding Mr. Murphy. The more he explained the more interested Ted became.

"This is great!" exclaimed Ted. "It would make a terrific story for the newspaper."

Andy stared at Ted and scowled. "I don't think so. Do you really want everyone to know Mr. Murphy died in the cemetery when he visited his wife's grave and no one knew about it for at least a day and a half? How do you think that would make his kids feel? How would you feel if it were your dad this happened to? Which reminds me, I need to cancel that lost and found ad in the newspaper."

"I guess you're right about a story," Ted said gravely. He ran his fingers thoughtfully through his dark brown hair. "I never thought of it like that. So have his kids been notified?"

Andy shrugged his shoulders. "Don't know. I haven't talked with Captain Scott or the coroner, Dr. Duncan, since yesterday. According to Doc Schafer the man's son lives in California and the daughter's in Hawaii. But I imagine the police would have called them."

"Man, you and your family sure do lead exciting and interesting lives. I never realized just how dull and boring this place was until you got here."

Andy sat staring at Ted. The people in this town were peculiar for sure. He sure didn't find anything that happened here in the past few months exciting or very interesting. "I don't have a problem with dull and boring. And I really don't think you could say my family's life is all that exciting and interesting but you're entitled to your opinions," said Andy seriously.

The dogs had stopped running and were resting in the shade of a couple of pine trees.

"It looks like the dogs have exhausted their energy," Andy observed as he walked over to Rascal and attached his lead. "I need to be getting home. I'm going drone flying this afternoon. You take care and enjoy your week off from school."

He led Rascal out the gate and headed for home.

After lunch Andy was getting ready to call Gracie when she showed up at his backdoor. "Are you sure you aren't a mind reader?" he asked as he opened the door to let her into the kitchen. "I was just going to call you."

Gracie smiled and flipped her long blonde hair over her shoulder. "Well, now you can save yourself the phone call," she joked moving toward the kitchen table and sitting down. "I was wondering how things went with Doc Schafer."

"Everything went fine. He scanned Rascal and found his microchip. The dog did belong to Mr. Murphy."

"So, now what?"

Andy looked at her a bit perplexed. "Now, nothing. I bought the dog a new license and brought him home."

"Have you told your parents yet?"

Andy's gray-green eyes sparkled mischievously. "Nope. Figured I'd surprise them when they got home."

Gracie giggled. "Oh, you are so bad."

"I know," he laughed. "Come on let's go fly our drones. I thought maybe we could go over to the football field."

"Sure," she agreed. "Are you going to take Rascal along or leave him here?"

The dog was calmly sitting in the middle of the kitchen floor watching Andy's every move.

"He's been to the park and got plenty of exercise. I think he can stay here for a while." Andy retrieved his drone from the dining room and headed for the back door with Gracie. Rascal was right on their heels. Andy stopped and looked at the dog. "You need to stay here boy; we'll be back in a little while."

Rascal began to utter a mournful whimper and stared at Andy with his pitiful brown eyes.

"Oh, he looks so pathetic and sad," said Gracie gravely. "You can't just leave him here all alone."

"I really don't want to take him to the football field," said Andy.

Gracie's face brightened up. "I know. We can take him to my house and he can keep Gwen company until we get back."

Andy looked at Gracie, then Rascal hesitantly. "Are you sure?"

"Absolutely," answered Gracie confidently. "Gwen loves dogs. Besides, she could use the company."

Andy sighed in resignation. "Okay." He clasped the leash onto Rascal's collar, took him outside and locked the door.

They crossed the street and entered the Taylor's house where they found Gwen watching a movie on the TV in the living room.

"Hi Sis, how would you like some company this afternoon?"

Andy brought Rascal over to Gwen. She turned her wheelchair around and the dog jumped into her lap.

"Whoa! I didn't see that coming," exclaimed Andy reaching down to pick up the dog.

Gwen put her hand out to stop him. "It's all right. He can stay here if he wants." She gave her sister a questioning glance. "I thought you were going drone flying?"

"We were; are," stated Gracie. "The thing is we didn't want to take Rascal along but he didn't want to stay at home alone so we thought maybe you could spend the time together."

Gwen patted the dog's head and smiled at her sister. "No problem, he can spend the afternoon with me. You two go have fun. We'll be fine."

Nancy Potts

Gracie and Andy spent a half an hour at the football field taking turns practicing various moves and honing their flying skills. When Gracie's drone's battery quit Andy let her fly his.

"You know you're getting really good," he told her earnestly. "Keep it up and you'll be able to win the next competition."

"Thanks for the confidence but I'll need to be much better than you to even think about winning any competition." She landed his drone and gave it back to him. "Tell me, have you ever thought about flying an airplane?"

"Not really. Why?"

"Oh, I was just wondering. I was thinking about learning to fly. They're having an open house at the local county airport tomorrow and I thought it might be interesting to check it out. Maybe see about going to ground school and taking some flying lessons."

"Are you serious?" asked Andy totally surprised.

"Of course I'm serious. If I'm going to become an aeronautical engineer I think it would be useful to know a few things about airplanes and their engines. Don't you?"

Andy slowly shook his head. He was having trouble processing her thinking. "Yes, you're absolutely right," he concurred at last. "It would be very important to know how airplanes work and learning to fly one would be useful."

"Glad you agree. So, you want to come with me?"

Andy took a minute to catch his breath. Her request took him completely by surprise. He stared at her and blinked his eyes several times. "Ah, yeah, sure, I'd be glad to go with you. What time?"

"How about eleven thirty? They're going to have a BBQ and people will have a chance to meet some of the pilots and see the airplanes. It should be fun!"

Andy swallowed nervously. "Yeah, it should be fun." He gathered his drone and packed up his gear. "Shall we go home? I don't want to burden Gwen too long with Rascal."

Gracie smiled slyly. "Right. We should be going. And don't worry about Rascal tomorrow. He can always stay with Gwen. They're good company for each other."

Chapter Seven

It was almost 6 o'clock by the time the Parkers and Pat arrived at the Flanagans. The subject of Rowena and the forest had been ostentatiously avoided. They spoke of the dig and things they had found but not one word about Rowena.

Emily impatiently listened to the adults becoming more frustrated by the minute. She was anxious to find out how the girl was doing. She also wanted to discover what had happened to her in the woods. It was all very bizarre.

When they entered the house they found Mary Jo in the kitchen fixing supper. Emily didn't wait around to listen to any more of the grownups silly talk. She went in search of Rowena.

As she walked down the hallway toward the bedrooms she saw Shea sitting outside Rowena's bedroom. When Emily reached the doorway the cat turned and ran inside the room. He jumped onto Rowena's bed and laid down at the foot.

Rowena was curled up under the covers fast asleep. Emily wanted to wake her up but decided that probably wouldn't be a good idea. She noticed a bottle of pills on the bedside table and picked them up. Apparently they were sleeping pills, at least that's what it said on the bottle. She placed the bottle back on the table and quietly left the room.

Might as well see if I can help with supper, she thought as she made her way to the kitchen. *Maybe I can get Mrs. Flanagan to tell me what the doctor said about Rowena. I just hope she'll be all right.*

When Emily entered the kitchen she saw her mother fixing a salad and Mrs. Flanagan at the stove stirring some vegetables. "Is there anything I can do to help?" asked Emily trying to sound cheerful.

Mrs. Flanagan turned around from the stove to face her. "Would you like to set the table?"

"Absolutely," answered Emily with a smile.

"The dishes are in the cupboard to your left and the silverware is in the drawer beside the sink," stated Mary Jo. "Thank you."

"Oh, you're welcome," said Emily. "There will just be the five of us right?"

Mary Jo hesitated for just a few seconds before answering. "Yes, that's right. Just the five of us. Rowena needs her rest."

Emily quickly gathered the dishes and silverware and set the dining room table. She really hoped she could get Rowena's mother to talk but things didn't appear very promising. She reentered the kitchen. "Do you want me to put on cups and saucers or glasses?"

"Pat and I will be having tea so cups and saucers for us. What would you and Martin like to drink Anne?"

"Tea will be fine," answered Anne as she finished slicing the last tomato. "Emily will have milk if that's all right."

"Sure, not a problem." She took a roast from the oven and placed the pan on the granite countertop. "The cups and saucers are in the cupboard next to the dishes and the glasses are in the cupboard near the sink."

Emily retrieved the necessary beverage containers and finished setting the table. She was going to go back to the kitchen when her mother arrived in the dining room with the salad.

"Honey, would you go tell your dad and Pat that we're putting supper on the table? I believe they're in the front room."

"Yes, Ma'am," Emily said, leaving to carry out her mother's request.

She found the men sitting on the couch discussing today's latest finds. She paused at the living room entrance watching them. They appeared as excited as a couple of school boys who had found some pirate treasure chest buried in the backyard. She almost hated to interrupt.

"Ah, Dad, Pat, sorry to disrupt your good time here but your presence is requested at the supper table."

The men stopped, looked at her and chuckled. "All right, Em, we'll be right there," said her father as the men got off the couch and followed her to the dining room.

All during supper Emily quietly sat at the table listening to the adults talk about the dig site, the country and reminiscing about old times. Not once did anyone mention Rowena or what had happened that morning. She was really getting annoyed but she was a little afraid to try and bring up the subject. When Mrs. Flanagan brought dessert to the table Emily said she didn't want any even though cherry pie was one of her favorite desserts.

Anne gave her daughter a questioning look. "Are you sure, honey?"

"I'm sure," answered Emily glumly as she stared at the table, refusing to look at any of them.

"Emily, what's bothering you?" asked Martin with concern. "You've been silent all through supper as well as on the ride home."

Emily raised her head and stared hostilely at her father then at all the others at the table. She sprang to her feet and tossed her napkin onto the table. "You want to know what's wrong? I'll tell you. Mrs. Flanagan brought Rowena here this afternoon to see the doctor because she was behaving weird. Rowena didn't remember going into the woods, finding the pony or even us finding her. I am worried about her but apparently none of you are. If you are you have a very strange way of showing it."

Emily stomped out of the room grabbed her jacket and left the house. She stamped through the garden and began walking down the sidewalk. She had no idea where she was going and at the moment she didn't care. Eventually she found herself in a small park. She spotted a bench and sat down. This trip sure wasn't turning out the way she had expected.

She closed her eyes and listened to the silence. She had so many questions but no one could or would give her any answers. She leaned back on the bench and felt the tears begin to trickle down her cheeks. She didn't care.

"Ah there little one, what seems to be the trouble?"

Emily's eyes flew open and she brushed a tear from her face.

"Here, I think you could be usin' this," an elderly man said as he sat down beside her and gave her a tissue.

"Thank you," said Emily rather timidly.

"You're very welcome," said the man. "My name is Shamus O'Keeffe. I don't recall seein' you around here before. Did you just move here?"

Emily finished drying her eyes before looking at the man. He had a kind face with bright blue eyes and a very firm jaw. His hair, what little she could see under his cap, was as white as snow and matched his bushy eyebrows. His boney hands were wrapped casually around his black walking stick.

"No sir, I'm here with my parents. We're just visiting with the Flanagans for a while."

"The Flanagans you say. Nice family. He's into diggin' up Irish history if I remember right."

"Yes, he's an archaeologist like my father. We're working on an excavation in Donoughmore."

"You're from America aren't you? I can tell by your accent."

Emily gave him a puzzled look and laughed. "I didn't know I had an accent. I thought *you* had the accent."

The man grinned. "Nah, I just sound like anyone else from around here. So what part of the States are you from?"

Emily shrugged her shoulders. "I have no idea. You see, up until ten months ago we didn't live there. We lived all over the world, wherever my dad was asked to go. We didn't really have a permanent home. Now my dad is teaching at a university in Ohio so that's where we're living."

"I see. So where exactly are you excavating in Donoughmore?"

"I'm not exactly sure. There's a huge field and a small forest and some boulders with petroglyphs. They've found a circular wall that is a burial site but they aren't sure yet who all is buried there or when it was made. They have also found a settlement. Today we found the remains of a warrior, at least that's what it looks like. We'll know more once we do some testing on things we found."

"I see. It sounds interestin' for sure. It also sounds like you are enjoying being here. So, why were ya cryin'"

"It's complicated."

"Well, try tellin' me anyway. I've got nothing better to do at the moment and sometimes it helps to talk to someone."

Emily sighed. "It all began yesterday …" and she spent the next fifteen minutes telling Mr. O'Keeffe about her encounter with Epona and Rowena's journey into the woods today and the consequences. "So you understand why I'm worried about her. Something happened to her in the forest but we don't know what and she can't remember."

"I can certainly understand your concern. But I'm sure if anyone can help her it'll be Dr. MacDonagh. It'll be takin' some time though. These things always do."

"What do you mean?" Emily questioned him. "Has something like this happened before?"

"Oh, now, don't you be frettin' yourself none. It was a very long time ago, so it was. Long before I was ever even born. And it was probably just a story someone made up. There's no proof of it at all."

"Please tell me," begged Emily as she looked at him with her sad dark blue eyes.

"It's probably just a story someone made up. But according to what I've been told, once there was a young girl who lived on a farm in Donoughmore. Her father raised horses, Connemara horses. Anyway the girl had one particular pony that she was very fond of. It was white, so it was and it was very fond of the girl also. At night it would somehow get out of the barn and go to the girl's bedroom window. Sometimes it would even spend the night there. Then one day a man came to buy a pony for his daughter. They say she was a bit of a spoiled little brat, but I wouldn't be knowin' that for certain. As I said it was just a story told to me by my granny. Anyway the girl saw the pony and wanted it. When the farmer said it wasn't for sale the girl had a tantrum and her father offered to pay three times what the pony was worth. Now the farmer was in a spot. They needed the money because at the time most of the farms weren't doing too good. But the farmer knew if he sold the pony it would break his daughter's heart. He didn't know what to do. He told the man to come back the next day for the pony so he could explain everything to his daughter. Well, that night they found the girl in one of the pastures with the pony. They brought the girl back to the house and put her to bed. The next morning she didn't remember being in the field with the pony. In fact she didn't even remember having the pony. And when the farmer went back to the pasture that night after bringing his daughter home he couldn't find it. He and his brothers searched everywhere and never found it. Eventually the girl did remember going to the field with the pony but she didn't know what happened to it. But the strange thing was, the girl insisted she met a woman named Epona who promised to take care of the pony and to not let the mean girl or anyone else have it."

Emily shook her head and ran her fingers through her hair. "That's a strange story for sure. And I can see how what happened to Rowena is similar. So, you think she'll eventually remember what happened?"

O'Keeffe slowly nodded his head and smiled. "Oh aye, I'm sure she will. It'll just take some time is all."

O'Keeffe looked around. The sun was setting and it was beginning to get cooler. "Well, I think lass it's time you should be getting' back to Flanagans before they begin to get worried and come searchin' for ya."

"Yes, you're right. They have enough to be worried about. I don't need to add to their problems. Thank you."

"You're welcome. Have a good time for the rest of your visit here." The man walked off in the opposite direction from Emily, went around a corner and disappeared from her view.

Emily was walking down the sidewalk toward the Flanagans

when she spotted her father coming toward her. He appeared rather upset.

"Emily Marie Parker, where in the world have you been? We've been looking everywhere for you. Your mother and Mary Jo are worried sick."

"I'm sorry Dad," she said mournfully. "I didn't mean to cause trouble, honest. It's just that I'm concerned about Rowena. What happened at the dig today was really strange. In fact it was kinda spooky. I just want to know if she's going to be all right but no one will tell me anything. I found a bottle of sleeping pills on her bedside table so I guess the doctor just wants her to sleep but ..." Emily started to cry.

Martin put his arm around his daughter and gave her a tight hug. He gently slipped his hand under her chin and lifted her face up toward his. He kissed her forehead and hugged her again. "Everything's going to be okay. The doctor seems to think Rowena just got lost in the woods, and she was dehydrated which sort of made her disoriented. He gave her an IV to help get her hydrated and those sleeping pills. He said she should be fine by morning. All right?"

Emily blinked and brushed the tears from her face. "Okay, Dad." She looked up into his hazel eyes and gave him a hug. "Let's go."

Pat Flanagan was in his front garden with Shea when Martin came down the path with Emily. "Well, you found her, I see."

"Yes, all the women can now rest easy. I've brought her back safe and sound."

Pat gave Emily a concerned look. "And just where have you been, young lady? We've all been mighty worried."

Emily stared at the ground then looked at Pat feeling very regretful. "I am sorry to worry everyone. I know I behaved badly. It's just that I was concerned about Rowena and no one would tell me anything. But my dad has explained everything to me. And I really didn't go far, just down the road a piece to that little park."

"All right then," said Pat leniently. "Let's go inside. I think there's still a piece of cherry pie waitin' for you."

He opened the door ushering her and Martin inside. Shea scampered between his legs and raced for his food dish in the kitchen.

"Hey ladies, good news. Our young wanderer has returned."

Anne looked at her daughter, smiled and shook her head. "I'm glad you came back. Please have a seat," she said pulling out a chair at the dining room table.

"I hope it's all right that we saved you a piece of pie," said Mary Jo placing the pie and a fork in front of Emily.

Emily looked kindly at her and picked up the fork. "Thank you Mrs. Flanagan. I am sorry for my bad behavior earlier this evening. Please forgive me?"

"Oh sure, sweetheart. I understand completely. But you don't need to be worrin' yourself about Rowena. The doctor said she'll be fine."

"I'm very glad to hear that," said Emily humbly.

"Sure, and is there anything else you'd like?"

Emily quickly looked at everyone gathered near her and blushed. "Could I have a small glass of milk?"

"Here you go," said Anne who had anticipated her daughter's request.

"Is there anything else?" inquired Pat mildly.

Emily swallowed a piece of pie and looked at him. "Do you happen to have any books on Irish mythology or the Druids?"

Everyone stared at her apprehensively. "What? I just figure it would be nice to learn something about the Irish besides their history."

"Sure," answered Pat gently. "I know we have a few on the bookshelf in my study." He left and returned a few minutes later with a small stack of books on the subjects requested. "Anything else?"

"Nope," Emily said with a slight smile. "This is all I need. Thank you." She finished her pie and milk then took her dirty dishes to the kitchen sink and rinsed them. She returned to the table, opened one of the books and settled down for a long night of reading.

At 1:30 a.m. Mary Jo got up to check on Rowena and noticed the dining room light was on. *Guess Emily must have forgotten to turn it off*, she thought as she went to take care of it. She was astonished to see Emily still at the table pouring over the books.

"Emily, honey, it's one thirty in the morning. Why not let this go until later and go on to bed?"

Emily stretched her neck and looked at Mary Jo with sleepy blurry eyes. "Yeah, I guess I should." She closed the book she was reading and headed for the bedroom.

"Goodnight."

"Goodnight dear." Mary Jo turned off the light and followed her down the hallway to look in on her daughter before returning to bed.

Tuesday morning found the excavation crews back at work in Donoughmore. Vince Walker was still overseeing the crews inside the ancient cemetery area. So far they had found several skeletons that appeared to be warriors with helmets, shields and swords. These warrior graves were not like the one that had been found near the boulders with the petroglyphs. They were smaller and there were fewer items buried with them. There was also a couple of areas that contained skeletons that might be women and at least two children. There was still much more to explore in the circle and it would take many months or maybe years to find everything.

Emily was with her father and Pat at the site they began to explore yesterday afternoon. Paul O'Malley was with them as well as Riley Morgan. They were joined by another member of Flanagan's staff, a young woman named Bridin (bree + jean) Sullivan.

Emily guessed Bridin was probably in her late 20s, maybe early 30s and Pat said she had been with his staff since she graduated from college. Emily was happy to have another female helping out, especially since her mother was wandering around the site taking photos of everything they were finding in the other trenches.

"So, how are things going over here?" Bridin asked Emily as she jumped into the trench.

"They're going well," replied Emily gently. "I imagine my dad and Pat told you the things we found yesterday."

"Yes, they did. So, what are you working on over here?"

"Well, right before we left yesterday I came across something that looks like leather straps. I just don't know exactly what they are. They look like they could be fairly long but we need to find out where they go exactly. And I didn't have time to do that before we left."

Bridin knelt down on the ground and began to inspect the items. She and Emily managed to scoop out more of the dirt and brush it away from the straps. As they continued on they came across more bones.

"Wow, look at these!" exclaimed Bridin scooping more dirt away. "They look like they might belong to a large animal."

Emily sat back on her heels looking at the bones. "Do you think this could have been a horse? I mean, if this is a warrior then it would make sense that they might bury this horse with him or her. We still need to figure out if the skeleton is male or female."

"You know, I think you might be right," said Bridin, her light brown eyes fairly dancing with excitement. "Come on, let's see how much we can uncover before we break for lunch."

They had unearthed almost the back half of the skeleton by the time Martin came by to check on them. "Well, you young ladies are certainly making progress. It looks like you may have discovered a horse."

"It does look that way doesn't it?" said Bridin happily. "This is the first time I've ever found a horse at a burial site. I know they have found them other places. They even found a Celtic warrior grave in Yorkshire, England, with a horse and a chariot in 2019."

Nancy Potts

Martin nodded his head and smiled. "If I remember correctly there have been about twenty chariot graves found mostly in Yorkshire in the last century. The only thing missing here is the chariot."

Emily wiped the back of her hand across her forehead and frowned. "Why do you suppose there isn't one? I know the skeleton is laying on some kind of metal but it isn't a chariot."

"Maybe this warrior didn't use one. Maybe he or she just rode the horse," suggested Bridin.

"If that's the case then maybe we'll find a saddle," said Emily hopefully.

"Unless the warrior rode bareback like the American Indians," advised her father smiling slightly.

Emily screwed up her mouth and squinted at him. "You know, you can be a real spoil sport sometimes."

Martin chuckled. "Yes I can. But it is something to consider. Now, come along. It's time for lunch."

He climbed out of the trench and helped Emily and Bridin out and onto the ground. He opened an old blanket and spread it on the grass beside the cooler that contained the food and drinks. They were soon joined by Pat, Paul and Riley.

"We're making decent progress," stated Pat grabbing a sandwich and a thermos of tea before sitting down. "How about the rest of you?"

"We've discovered a horse," Emily told him excitedly. "Have you figured out yet if the warrior is male or female?"

Paul sat down with his lunch next to Emily and Bridin. "You two will be delighted to know, that after careful examination it has been determined that the skeleton is a female."

"Like I said, Irish women are fighters," Martin reminded them and took a bite of his sandwich.

"That they are," commented Bridin with a grin. "That's why the wise man knows to stay on the good side of an Irish woman. It makes his life happier."

"That's for sure," agreed Riley.

84

While the rest of the team continued with their lunch Paul leaned close to Emily and whispered, "How is Rowena doing?"

Emily looked at him solemnly. "It's difficult to say. The doctor gave her medicine to make her sleep and she was still asleep when we left this morning. Mary Jo said the doctor expects her to be all right and said her behavior was due to dehydration. I'm having a hard time believing that though."

Paul nodded gravely. "Me too."

"I understand Rowena isn't the first person something like this happened to."

"What do you mean?"

"Last night I walked to a park near the Flanagans' home and met an older gentleman. He told me about this girl who had a pony. When he described it, it sounded like the horse we saw in the field with Rowena. Anyway, it seemed the girl's father was going to sell her pony to some spoiled little girl. But the night before this was to happen the man found his daughter in a field with the pony. He brought his daughter home but she didn't remember being there or the pony for quite a while later. Also, when the father went back to the field for the pony it was missing. They never found it. But apparently this girl did finally remember going to the field with the pony and she said she met a woman named Epona who promised to take care of the pony and to not let the mean girl have it. Now, isn't that odd?"

"I'll say," agreed Paul. "It's really strange."

"I'll tell you something even stranger. Do you remember when Rowena got ready to leave the field with my mom she patted the horse and called it Niamh?"

Paul nodded, "Yes, I remember."

"Well, I was doing some reading about Druids last night and there was a goddess named Niamh. She was supposed to be the daughter of the sea god Manannan and she rode a white horse that could walk on water."

"I must admit that I really don't know that much about the Druids and mythology," admitted Paul finishing his lunch. "I had heard though that Rowena is really into that stuff so maybe there could be a logical explanation behind it all."

"You could be right, but it doesn't explain about the lady I met in the forest. I mean I knew nothing about Druids or Irish mythology before we came here. So, who is this woman Epona that I met when I fell and hurt my head?"

Paul shrugged his shoulders and gave her a perplexed look. "I have no idea." He glanced at his watch and noticed everyone was gathering up their trash.

"Guess it's time to get back to work," observed Emily as she put her empty Coke can and sandwich wrapper in the trash bag. "I can't wait to uncover the rest of this horse. Who knows, we might even find a saddle or maybe some spurs."

Chapter Eight

Andy brought Rascal to Gracie's and Gwen's house around 11 o'clock Tuesday morning. "Thanks for taking care of Rascal for me. I brought his water bowl. He just went to the potty so hopefully he'll be all right for a while." He took the dog's leash off and put it on the coffee table and filled the water bowl. "But if he needs to go out …" Andy began as he set the water dish on the kitchen floor. "Are you sure you wouldn't like to come along?"

"Yes, I'm sure. I have some programs I want to watch and a book that I am reading. Now don't worry," said Gwen. "If Rascal needs to go out we have a fenced backyard so I can just let him out the backdoor." She moved around in her chair and stretched her back. "You two go on. Rascal and I will be fine. Go, and have a good time." She rolled her wheelchair toward the front door and opened it.

"Yes, Ma'am, we're on our way," Andy said winking at her and smiling. "Come along Gracie." He ushered her out the door and into his car. As he backed out of the driveway he waved at Gwen.

"Do you know where the county airport is?" asked Gracie dubiously as they traveled down the street. "I mean it is just a small airport."

"Yes, I know," he replied stopping at the stop sign at the end of the street. He touched the map app on his phone that was in the phone holder on the dashboard. "I admit I didn't know where it was but I looked it up last night and the directions are on my phone since this car doesn't have a GPS."

"Oh, well then that's fine." Gracie leaned back in the seat and tried to relax. "The Aero Club at the airport has this open house every year. It's really neat. They even offer rides in the little planes. Of course you have to pay for the ride."

Andy gave a quick glance at Gracie. "Little planes? How small are they? And you didn't say this was going to cost anything. I didn't bring much money."

"I just mean the planes are those single engine, private planes. They only seat two or four people, including the pilot. They're really neat."

Andy took a deep breath and slowly exhaled. "I see. I take it you've been here before."

Gracie glanced at him nonchalantly and smiled thinly. "Yes, my grandfather took Gwen and me last year. It was fascinating. That's where I met Major Reese and we discussed flying drones."

"Interesting. And just how much will it cost us to take a ride in one of these single engine planes? Do we have to pay for the food too?"

Gracie laughed. "The food is free. I think the Aero Club foots the bill for that. The plane rides are twenty-five dollars per person. But don't worry, I have the money to pay for that."

Andy looked at her and frowned. "I'll pay my own way thanks. I just wish you'd told me this yesterday, that's all."

Gracie slumped into her seat and pouted. "I didn't tell you about the cost because I figured if I did you wouldn't come. I talked you into doing this so the least I can do is pay for you to go flying."

"Listen, no one pays my way for anything. I pay my own way, understand?" He gripped the stirring wheel tighter and glanced at his phone.

"Oh, Andy Parker, you are so stubborn sometimes!" She crossed her arms across her stomach and silently stared out her side window for the remainder of the trip.

When they reached the airport the parking lot was already getting full. Andy, however, did manage to find a spot not too far from the entrance. He got out of the car and walked over to open Gracie's door but she got out before he could reach it.

"I can be just as self-sufficient and independent as you," she told him huffily and began to briskly walk toward the airport office entrance.

Andy jogged to catch up with her. "Listen, there's no reason for you to get all bent out of shape over this. You can pay for your own ride. No problem. I'm just not comfortable letting someone pay for me, no matter who they are."

Gracie stopped and turned around to face him. "I just don't understand you. I'm only trying to do something nice and say thank you for taking the time to come here with me. That's all."

Andy scratched his head and sighed. "You don't need to do that. I am more than glad to bring you here."

"You don't get it, do you? I know I don't have to do it, I want to do it, it's that simple."

He studied her bright blue eyes for a second and noticed they were beginning to tear up. "I'm sorry," he said humbly. "I appreciate your offer and if it will make you feel better then I accept. I didn't know it meant so much to you." He pulled a tissue from his jacket pocket and gave it to her.

She took the tissue and wiped her eyes. "Thank you."

He kissed her forehead and gave her a hug. "All right?"

"Yes, I'm all right,' she answered with a small smile and put the tissue in her pocket. "Shall we go?"

"Absolutely." He took her hand and they made their way inside the building.

There were several people handing out flyers and packets of information while a few others were at a counter signing people up to go flying. Major Reese was one of the club members signing people to fly.

"Well, hello there Gracie and Andy," he greeted them eagerly. "It's good to see you. Are you interested in taking a ride around the countryside?"

"Of course we are," stated Gracie excitedly. "That's one of the reasons we're here. I wanted Andy to see just how much fun it is to fly in a regular prop airplane."

Major Reese surveyed Andy with curiosity. He was fairly certain the young man had flown on more than one occasion and probably on more than just huge passenger planes. "All right then, let's get you scheduled for a flight. I know you were here last year Gracie, so is there any particular airplane you're interested in flying on today?"

"No, I don't think so."

"What about you Andy?" Reese inquired cordially.

Andy looked at Major Reese and grinned. "Well, since I don't know what planes you have available it's a bit difficult for me to say. But if you have a Piper Warrior that would be great, if not then I guess a Cessna would be fine. I did notice a few of them on the tarmac when we came."

Gracie looked at Andy and her jaw dropped in astonishment. Andy looked at her and winked. "I think you might want to close your mouth before a wayward bug decides to fly inside."

She closed her mouth and shook her head quickly several times. "I ..."

"I know, you didn't think I knew anything about small airplanes, right?"

Both Andy and Major Reese watched as Gracie attempted to gather her thoughts. "It's all right," Andy told her politely. "On more than one occasion I've had to fly on a small plane to go somewhere from one of the digs to a city. I even flew on a helicopter once. It was fun."

Major Reese could see Gracie was still in a state of minor shock. He coughed to break the uncomfortable silence. "Well, you're in luck," he said looking at Andy. "We do have a Warrior available in about a half hour. Why not go have something to eat and then go over to the runway?" He gave them a slip of paper. "Give this to one of the guys over there and they'll fix you right up."

"Thank you," said Andy taking the paper and putting it in his pocket. "Do we pay for the ride here or out there."

"Pay here," said Reese amiably.

Andy turned to Gracie who was slowly recovering from her shock. "We need to pay Major Reese," he whispered in her ear.

"Oh, yes, of course," she murmured digging into her pocket for the money. "It's twenty-five dollars a person, right?" Major Reese nodded his head as she handed him $50.

"Thank you. Go and enjoy yourselves," he told them putting the money in the cash register drawer.

They made their way outside to some tables and chairs and the BBQ grills. "It sure is a nice day," commented Andy. "What would you like to eat?"

Gracie wandered to one of the grills to see what they were cooking. It was hot dogs and hamburgers. She walked back to Andy and took his arm. "How about a hot dog and a Coke?" she asked.

"Anything special you want on it; ketchup, mustard, relish?"

"Ketchup and mustard will be fine."

"Got it." Andy went to retrieve their food while Gracie found them a place at one of the tables.

When he returned he found his friend Simon Gallagher seated at the table with Gracie. "Here you go Gracie," said Andy placing the hot dog and Coke in front of her. "Hope I put on the right amount of ketchup and mustard. I brought you some chips too."

"It's perfect," she answered opening her can of soda.

He sat down across from Gracie and next to Simon. "Well, Simon, fancy meeting you here. I thought you were only interested in piloting drones, not airplanes."

"Yeah, I am but I thought since I plan on joining the Air Force after college it wouldn't hurt to see about flying airplanes. So, I signed up for ground school. It's only a couple of evenings a week for about six weeks."

"And after ground school, then what?" asked Andy.

"Well, then you take a written test and if you pass you get to take flying lessons," answered Simon confidently.

Andy chewed a mouthful of hamburger and took a large gulp of his root beer. "Just how much does this ground school cost?"

"The total for tuition and books is three hundred and thirty-five dollars," stated Simon proudly. "The classes and everything are right here."

"And how much are flying lessons."

Simon shrugged his shoulders and glanced at Gracie for a second then back at Andy. "I didn't ask. I figure take it one step at a time."

Gracie looked at the guys and just shook her head. "It's over three thousand dollars for flying lessons to get your private pilot's license. I already checked. It could be more, depending on how fast you learn and what type of plane you learn how to fly."

"Guess if I want to learn to fly I'm going to need to get a job," said Andy. "I haven't a clue what kind of job though."

"Why not just let your folks pay for them?" asked Simon. "That's what I'm doing."

Andy frowned and stared hard at Simon. "I'm not going to do that. I'll pay for them myself."

"Andy believes in paying his own way," explained Gracie with a slight smile.

"That's right," affirmed Andy staunchly.

Simon watched his two friends for a few minutes. Andy certainly seemed determined, that's for sure. He just couldn't understand his friend's thinking. His parents always paid for everything. He figured that's what they were supposed to do. He certainly never thought about paying for anything on his own.

"Does that mean you're going to pay for college yourself too?" inquired Simon seriously.

Andy stared at Simon. "I don't even know for sure if I'm going to college. I might decide to just get a job that doesn't require a college degree or any degree except a high school diploma." He got up from the table and threw his trash in a nearby trash can. He looked at Gracie. "Are you ready to go see about that ride?"

Gracie finished her Coke, got up and got rid of her trash. "Absolutely. See you later Simon." She glanced briefly at him then briskly followed Andy around the buildings and to the tarmac. For some reason today Andy seemed very irritated but she didn't know why. At first she thought it was because she didn't tell him it would cost money for the airplane ride and because she wanted to pay for both of them. But the more she thought about it the more she realized there was something more bothering him. She remembered he was a bit on edge the other night when her father had asked him about college. She was fairly certain his parents intended for him to get a college degree of some kind so maybe that was it. He had admitted before that he didn't know what he wanted to do with his life only what he *didn't* want to do. She thought he probably just needed some time to figure things out.

When they reached the gathering point beside the runway there was only one person ahead of them. It was a little boy about seven-years-old who wasn't real sure that he wanted to go up in an airplane. His mother finally convinced him that it was safe and he'd have fun so off he went.

Major Reese was standing nearby and walked over to greet them. "Well, are you two ready for that ride?" he asked pleasantly.

"Yes," answered Andy. "Just show us to the plane and our pilot."

"Come with me," instructed Reese leading them across the tarmac to a waiting Piper Warrior. "Do either of you want to sit up in the co-pilot seat?"

Andy and Gracie just stared speechless at each other.

"Why don't you go ahead and fly up front Gracie?" suggested Andy. "I'll sit in the back. So, where's the pilot?"

Major Reese grinned. "I'm the pilot. This is my plane." He turned to Andy. "You get in the back, then Gracie can get in."

"Oh, I don't mind sitting in back if Andy would like to fly up front," Gracie told them hesitantly.

Andy looked at her and shook his head. "I've ridden in the co-pilot seat plenty of times. Now it's your turn. The experience will be good for you, especially if you plan on learning to fly." He smiled deviously and climbed into the plane.

The major helped Gracie onto the plane's wing and inside then walked to the pilot's side and got in. "Put on your seatbelts," he told them as he fastened his and started the engine. He handed them both headphones and asked, "Is there any place special you'd like to go?"

Gracie shook her head no and Andy replied, "Wherever you want to fly is fine."

"Okay, then sit back and enjoy the ride." He taxied down the runway and headed east, then north, over farms and houses.

As they headed toward some fields he turned to Gracie. "Would you like to fly for a while?"

Gracie's blue eyes flashed wide with excitement. "Are you sure?"

"Of course I am. Just keep the wings level, and fly straight," and he pointed to the attitude indicator and the turn coordinator on the instrument panel.

She carefully placed her hands on the yoke then glanced at the instrument panel. Both the major and Andy noticed that her hands began to tremble slightly.

"Take a deep breath and relax," directed Major Reese.

Gracie complied as best as she could. She glanced out the side window then at the instrument panel. "Keep the wings level," she whispered to herself. "Stay calm." She took another breath and exhaled slowly.

"That's it," the major said encouragingly. He glanced back at Andy cheerfully.

"You're doing great Gracie," Andy told her reassuringly. "You're a natural for sure." He leaned back and smiled. "You could finish ground school and get your private pilot's license by the end of summer. Don't you think so Major Reese?"

"Most definitely," said Reese. "Ground school classes begin next week."

"I think you better take back the controls, Major Reese," said Gracie timidly. Once the major had control again Gracie leaned back in her seat and breathed out slowly. "I've been thinking about

94

ground school and flying lessons I just need to talk it over with my dad."

"And what about you Andy?" asked Reese with genuine interest.

"I'd like to but I can't afford the lessons right now. Maybe later."

Major Reese kept his eyes on the view out the front plane window. "I see. You need a job to earn some money for lessons?"

Andy slumped back into the seat looking rather subdued. "Yeah. But I have no idea what kind of job I could get."

The major nodded his head in understanding. "Is there any type of work you think you might be interested in doing?"

Andy shrugged his shoulders. "I'd be willing to do just about anything, as long as it was legal."

Major Reese turned the plane around and headed back toward the airfield. "Would you want to work at the airport?"

Andy suddenly sat up straight. "Are you serious?"

"Yes, I am."

"That would be fine. What would I get to do?"

The major landed the plane and turned off the motor before he answered. "There's lots of different jobs that need to be done here. Everything from gassing up the planes to maintenance to cleaning up the buildings and answering the phones."

Andy smiled. "I can do all those things except airplane maintenance. But I could learn."

"Well, let me talk to a few people and I should be able to let you know by tomorrow."

"That'll be swell," said Andy happily.

"Okay, let's get out of this vehicle and see what I can accomplish." The major got out, walked around the plane and helped Gracie and Andy back onto solid ground. "Are you planning on being here much longer?"

"Probably not much longer," said Andy. "I left my dog with Gracie's sister and I don't want to burden her with him too long. Besides, I still have to practice my drone flying today."

"Oh yeah, we've been practicing every day," Gracie informed him. "Andy's getting really good. He might even win the next competition."

"Well, that's encouraging to know," said Reese with a smile. "But then, you two are the best drone pilots in the club." He stopped outside the office building. "If I don't see you before you leave, I'll get in touch with you tomorrow Andy."

"Thank you, sir," Andy replied. "I look forward to hearing from you."

Major Reese went back to his desk duties while Andy and Gracie wandered around the tarmac a bit looking at the various airplanes before heading home.

As Gracie and Andy entered the Taylor's front door Rascal raced to Andy and practically jumped into his arms.

"Well, hello there little fella, did you miss me?"

"Did he miss you?" echoed Gwen rolling her wheelchair toward the little group. "I'll say he did. When I let him into the backyard he ran all around the entire yard, sniffing every corner and looking under every piece of furniture. He didn't even stop to chase the squirrel up the tree. The squirrel just sat there watching him. Once he came inside he drank some water and jumped into my lap. He's been there ever since until you arrived."

As Gwen talked, Andy picked Rascal up and sat down on the couch. "I'm sorry he gave you so much trouble."

"Oh, he wasn't any trouble. It was fun to watch him running everywhere. He's so cute!"

"Well then, I'm happy he was able to entertain you."

"Me too. So how was your excursion to the airport?"

Gracie sat in the recliner near the couch watching her sister and Andy. "It was nice. The weather was perfect and Major Reese took us for a ride in his Piper Warrior."

"He even let your sister fly it," chuckled Andy as he scratched Rascal behind his ears.

"Oh really? I bet that was fun!" exclaimed Gwen rolling her chair closer to her sister.

"It was scary," Gracie informed her. "Up in the air like that. I was afraid I'd mess up and we'd crash!"

Andy just shook his head. "That wouldn't have happened. Major Reese would have taken over and everything would have been all right."

"I sure hope so," Gracie remarked.

"I'm sure once you finish ground school and get your private pilot's license you'll make a great pilot," Andy told her sincerely.

"So, you're really going to do it then?" asked Gwen nervously twisting her blonde ponytail. "You're going to get your pilot's license."

Gracie looked at her sister seriously. "I need to talk to Dad first before I decide for sure. I mean I'd like to do it but it will take a lot of time and money. So I want to discuss it with Dad before I make a commitment. Understand?"

Gwen stretched a bit in her chair and stared at Gracie. "Yeah, I understand. But he'll probably give his okay. He knows how much aeronautics means to you." Gwen turned her head to look at Andy. "So, what about you? Are you going to get a pilot's license too?"

Andy shrugged his shoulders and slowly rubbed his arms. "I don't know. If I can get a job to earn the money to pay for the class and lessons I'd like to. Major Reese said I might be able to work at the airport. So we'll see."

Rascal had stretched out on Andy's lap and was soulfully staring up at him with his small brown eyes. He stuck out his tongue trying to lick Andy's hand. Andy looked down at the dog and grinned. He bent down to give the little fellow a hug and Rascal licked his face. Andy laughed and the Taylor's grandmother clock struck five.

"It's getting late," observed Andy casually. "I need to be getting home. I'm sure this little guy would like his supper." He grabbed Rascal's lead from the coffee table, fastened it on his collar and stood up. "Thank you Gwen for taking care of him for me."

Gracie fetched the water bowl, emptied the water and handed him the empty dish.

Gwen smiled at Andy and stroked Rascal one last time before they left. "I was glad to do it. Like I said, he's a cute little guy and a lot of fun to have around."

"Hope that job works out," said Gracie opening the front door. "Maybe we can go drone flying tomorrow."

"Absolutely," stated Andy going out the door. "See you all tomorrow. 'Bye."

"'Bye," said the girls as they watched him cross the street and enter his house.

"Sure hope he gets that job," whispered Gracie to herself and closed the door.

Chapter Nine

Emily and Bridin continued to uncover the horse's skeleton along with the leather reins. There were no saddle or spurs much to Emily's disappointment. She sat on the ground next to the horse's rib bones and watched Bridin remove more dirt from the reins.

"This sure is a big horse," observed Emily rather glumly.

"That it is," agreed Bridin sitting down beside her and taking a rest. "Just think what it must have been like riding such a large animal for any length of time. It's a wonder all the warriors weren't bowlegged." She laughed at the thought.

Emily, however, didn't find any humor in the idea and continued to sit there looking gloomy.

Bridin cocked her head to one side and quietly observed Emily with her light brown eyes. "What's the matter? You look like you lost your best friend."

Emily rubbed her neck and slowly twisted her head from side to side. "Guess I'm just disappointed we didn't find any saddle."

Bridin touched Emily's dirt covered hand and gave her a friendly, understanding smile. "It's not unusual you know. They didn't use saddles back in those days or stirrups. Sometimes they used blankets to sit on."

"I don't understand. How did they get on a horse without a saddle with stirrups."

"They just jumped up on the horse."

"They must have been either very long legged or else had springs in their shoes."

Bridin chuckled. "That's a good one. I'll have to remember that; springs in their shoes." She took a swig from her water bottle and looked up at the sky. "It looks like we may be gettin' some rain. Those gray clouds are gettin' bigger and darker."

"Well, why not? We're making progress so bring on the rain so we have to stop. We're getting so close to the horse's head. Do you suppose these reins will be attached to a bridle and maybe a bit?" She asked Bridin hopefully.

"Oh, aye!" Bridin assured her. "And it will probably be beautiful. I mean look how lovely the shield was and the armband. I'm fairly certain the bridle will be just as gorgeous."

"I hope so," stated Emily firmly. "Well, shall we continue to dig until the rain arrives?"

Bridin smiled and nodded her head. "Absolutely. Let's see how much progress we can make." She picked up her trowel and began to scrape away the dirt.

They had made it to the top of the horse's neck and were getting ready to uncover the jaw when the first raindrops began to fall.

Martin walked down the trench toward them. "Okay girls, that's it for now. Let's get everything covered, and gather the tools then put them in the tool bag." He helped them fasten down the tarp and gather some of the tools before the sky opened up pouring buckets of cold water on everything. "Come along, head for the tent!"

A tent had been set up near this part of the site to put the artifacts they had found. Riley and Ben had been there since after lunch cleaning artifacts and cataloging them. Martin and the girls joined them along with Pat and Paul.

"We might as well stay here for a bit and see if the rain lets up," said Pat. "I'd say though we're finished for the day. Hopefully, tomorrow's weather will be better."

"Well, I think we've made good progress today," offered Martin. "That's the thing about this line of work. The weather has a way of turning a positive day into a lousy day in the blink of an eye."

"Let's get these artifacts into the trunk over here," instructed Pat as he opened the large metal trunk in the corner of the tent.

Within a few minutes the objects that had been found so far were safely stored away and locked in the trunk. As luck would have it the rain had turned to a drizzle just as they finished.

Riley poked his head out the tent flap. "That's Irish weather for you. One minute you have a downpour and the next it's turned into a simple drizzle. By the time we leave it could be a fine little mist or another frog strangler." Everyone laughed.

"Come along," said Pat picking up several of the tool bags. "Let's go home." As they made their way toward the parked cars he greeted the team in the other part of the dig and told them to go home until tomorrow.

When they reached Flanagans they found Mary Jo and Rowena sitting on the living room sofa with Shea resting contentedly on Rowena's lap. As soon as the Parkers and Pat entered the room Shea quickly lifted his head and stared at them. When he realized who it was he sunk his head back on Rowena's lap, flicked his tail and closed his eyes.

Pat strolled over to his wife and kissed her cheek then kissed his daughter's forehead. "Well, how are my lovely ladies this fine afternoon?"

Mary Jo smiled softly. "We're doing fine. How did things go at the dig?"

"Oh, everything was goin' fine 'til the rains came," he told her nonchalantly. "We did manage to uncover most of the skeleton. It's female, by the way. That should make all the women folk here happy. And Emily here along with Bridin have found a horse." He looked at Emily then at Rowena and smiled slightly. "I know, Emily, why don't you be tellin' Rowena and the misses about your find? Go on now."

Slowly Emily made her way farther into the room and sat down on a hassock in front of Rowena and Mary Jo.

"Well, yesterday I uncovered some leather straps; at least that's what I thought. But today Bridin and I discovered they were really horse reins. We've managed to uncover most of the horse. It's really huge! We made it all the way to the neck when it started to rain. If we're lucky maybe tomorrow we'll be able to uncover the horse's head. I'm hoping there will be a bridle. Bridin said if there is then it's possible it will be a fancy one just like the shield we found yesterday." The entire time she spoke Emily carefully observed Rowena just to see how she reacted to her information. She seemed to be interested but Emily wasn't certain.

"It seems like you certainly had an interesting and productive day," remarked Mary Jo. She looked at Rowena and gently squeezed her hand.

"Maybe Rowena will be able to join us tomorrow," speculated Emily brightly. "If the doctor says it's all right, of course. It would be so great Rowena if you could be there when we uncover the horse's head."

Rowena looked at her mother, then at Emily. "I would love to be there. I'm feeling fine and I'd really like to see all the artifacts you've found."

Mary Jo nodded her head slightly. "We'll see how you're feeling in the morning. I imagine it will be all right if you go there for a few hours."

Rowena glanced at her mother and sighed in exasperation. "Honestly, I don't know why everyone is making such a fuss. I am fine. There's nothing wrong with me. Dr. MacDonagh said I was just dehydrated, that's all."

Emily reached out and touched Rowena's hand that was resting on Shea. "If that's all it was then there's nothing to worry about. It's easy to get dehydrated at a dig. We'll just make sure we have plenty of water there for you to drink. No problem." She looked shrewdly at Mary Jo to affirm everything she had said.

Mary Jo briefly closed her eyes in submission. "Okay."

Pat and the Parkers had retreated to the dining room when Emily had sat down to talk with Mary Jo and Rowena. Now Pat poked his head around the corner and into the living room. "Hey, honey, is there anything we can do to help with supper? I know it's still a bit early …"

Mary Jo got off the sofa and walked toward her husband. "Supper is taken care of. I'm making spaghetti. The sauce is on the back burner. I bought some Italian bread at the grocers this morning. I just need to know if you want me to make it into garlic bread or leave it the way it is." She joined the others in the dining room, leaving Emily and Rowena alone in the living room with Shea.

Emily moved from the hassock onto the sofa next to Rowena. Rowena glanced into the dining room and watched the adults leave for the kitchen. She closed her eyes, sighed and leaned back on the sofa. "Thank goodness they're gone. I thought my mum would never leave. She has been right beside me all day long. You'd think I was a two-year-old."

Emily settled into a corner of the sofa and tried not to laugh but a small giggle escaped her lips. Rowena giggled too.

"Oh it's not that bad," said Emily jovially. "You're mother's just concerned about you. So's your dad. That's just the way parents are."

Rowena gnawed thoughtfully on her lower lip. "I suppose."

"I know it can be a pain in the neck sometimes but be thankful they care about you. Not every kid's lucky enough to have parents like that."

Rowena stroked Shea and listened to him purr so contentedly. "I know. I also know the way I behaved yesterday was not due to dehydration."

Emily's eyes opened wide with surprise. "Okay. What was the reason?"

"I know the doctor gave me a sedative to make me sleep. While I was asleep I visualized everything that had happened. It was like I was living through it all again but this time I was just watching, like it was a movie. I saw me walk into the forest looking for the house you told me about. I didn't find it. I did find a woman or rather a woman found me. We talked for a while, she gave me something to drink and then she left but she left a white Connemara pony with me. She said the pony's name was Niamh and it would stay with me until my friends came. The pony and I walked to that pasture where you found me. I tried to find my way out of the forest but I couldn't and the pony wasn't any help. So when we ended up at the pasture I just stayed there. I know the whole thing sounds bizarre."

Emily crinkled her forehead and bit her upper lip thoughtfully. "Actually, it's not as weird as you think. Yesterday evening I went to the park not far from here and I met an elderly gentleman who told me about a girl who had a similar experience." Emily quietly told her the story of the girl and her pony and how the girl didn't remember the incident until quite a while later.

Rowena glanced sideways at Emily trying to decide if she should believe the story. "Do you know the name of this man?"

"He said his name was Shamus O'Keeffe. He was a nice old gentleman," said Emily.

"Do you remember what he looked like?"

"Oh, sure. He wasn't real tall, maybe about five foot seven. He had snowy white hair and bushy eyebrows. And he had the most lovely bright blue eyes. He was really sweet."

"What was he wearing?"

Emily looked at her rather perplexed. "Ah, let me think. He had on a dark overcoat, either black or charcoal gray. His pants were black and he wore one of those flat wool caps."

"Did he have any rings or pins? What about a walking stick?"

"He may have worn a ring or pin. I don't know. I wasn't paying that much attention to his hands and such. He did have a walking stick. It was black." Emily was carefully watching Rowena and her reaction to what she told her. "Do you know this man?"

The color drained from Rowena's face. "No," she whispered and shook her head. She continued to pet her cat and stared at the floor.

Emily frowned. "I don't believe you." She was beginning to get agitated. "You do know this man or something about him. Why won't you tell me?"

"I can't," muttered Rowena. "I just can't."

"I seriously don't understand you. I tell you about the woman in the forest and you get all weird and tell me about Druids. You get lost in the forest and we find you with a pony who just happens to have a Druid goddesses name. Then I tell you about this O'Keeffe guy and you get as white as a snowflake. What is so mysterious and secretive about this guy that you're afraid to tell me about him?"

Shea jumped from Rowena's lap and she stood up and began pacing around the room. "Please don't ask me any more questions. I just don't want to talk about any of this." She paused in front of the living room window and stared at the falling rain. The light drizzle had become a heavy rain again. In the distance there was a rumble of thunder.

Emily walked to the window and looked up at the sky. "Riley is right. The weather here is very unpredictable. For a minute it almost looked like it was going to stop. Now it's pouring down again and there's thunder. I haven't seen any lightening though."

"From the sound of the thunder the lightening is too far away to see," stated Rowena blandly. "If we're lucky it may all drift west toward County Kerry."

"That would be fine. It'll give the ground a chance to dry out by morning," said Emily.

Pat poked his head around the corner. "It's time to eat."

"We'll be right there, Da, we need to wash up," Rowena told him as she and Emily made their way to the bathroom.

"Please don't say anything to my folks about our conversation," implored Rowena. She finished washing and drying her hands and handed the towel to Emily.

"Sure, no problem," Emily agreed. "I've already gotten myself in enough trouble I don't need any more." She dried her hands and hung the towel up. "Let's go. Don't want to keep the grownups waiting."

Chapter Ten

Andy finished his breakfast and took Rascal into the backyard to play. He had made a toy out of one of his old socks and had stuffed it with some rags. He'd also found an old tennis ball in a corner of the garage. Hopefully, the dog would be interested in one or the other.

"Hey there Rascal, look what I have." He held the sock toy up for the dog to see. Rascal cocked his head and looked at the toy, then he spotted the tennis ball laying on the step next to where Andy was sitting. Rascal reached for the ball, put it in his mouth and ran to the back of the yard. He stopped and looked at Andy, then dropped the ball. Andy wasn't quite sure what it was the dog wanted him to do. The two stared at each other for a few seconds before Rascal grabbed the ball and began running around the yard. Andy decided to chase him.

"Is that the game you want to play?" Andy ran and circled around to get in front of the dog. As he ran toward Rascal the dog quickly took off in the opposite direction. "So, that's the way it's going to be is it? Well, watch out 'cause I'm going to get you!" The pair spent the next few minutes running around the yard before Rascal decided he'd had enough and laid down in the grass near the back porch steps. Andy soon joined him. He reached out to pet the dog's head and scratch behind his ears. "Well, that was fun."

Rascal turned onto his side so Andy could rub his belly and he looked up at him with his warm honey brown eyes enjoying every moment.

As they were enjoying their morning quiet time Andy's phone rang. "Hello." He moved from the grass to the bottom porch step. "Oh, hello Major Reese. This afternoon? Yes, I can come to the airport. What time? Two o'clock will be fine. Do I need to bring anything with me? Thank you, sir. Yes, sir I'll see you then."

He watched Rascal laying so peacefully in the grass and smiled. "So far this has been a pretty good week. If I can get a job at the airport it'll be nearly perfect." He called Gracie to see if Rascal could visit with them this afternoon while he was gone. She said it would be all right. "Now, all I need to do is figure out what to wear." He glanced at the dog. "Tell me Rascal, what do people wear to job interviews?"

The dog raised his head and gave him a look that indicated it was a silly question to ask a dog. "You're right," said Andy interpreting the look. "It is a silly question to ask you. Come on, I need to go inside and find something to wear."

Andy gathered the sock toy and tennis ball then headed inside with Rascal.

It was almost 2 o'clock when Andy pulled into the parking lot at the county airport. The palms of his hands were cold and sweaty. He took a quick glance at himself in the car's rearview mirror, removed the keys from the ignition, grabbed his suitcoat and got out of the car. He wiped his palms on his slacks, put the keys in his pocket and slipped on the coat. He couldn't remember the last time he'd felt this nervous. He locked the car and walked to the main building hoping he appeared confident. He definitely didn't feel that way, that's for sure.

Major Reese was standing at the door and opened it to let him in. "Good afternoon, Andy. You're right on time, but then I knew you would be. Come this way." Reese led him down a narrow hallway and into the airport manager's office.

As they entered the room the manager got up from his desk and walked over to greet them. "Hello, you must be Andy Parker, the young man Major Reese has told me about." He extended his hand toward Andy's and shook it firmly. "I'm Dale Kelley, the airport manager."

"I'm very happy to meet you sir," said Andy nervously.

"Please, have a seat, you too Mike," said Kelley pointing to several chairs in front of his desk. He let them get seated and he pulled one of the other chairs around to face them and sat down.

"The major tells me you are looking to earn some money so you can take our ground school class and some flying lessons. Is that right?"

Andy took a quick glance at Major Reese then back at Kelley and swallowed anxiously. "Yes, sir, that's right."

"Have you any past work experience?"

Andy ran his index finger timidly around the inside of his shirt collar. "Uh, most of the work I've done has been at archaeology dig sites. Digging up artifacts, cleaning them, cataloging and things like that."

"Interesting," said Kelley leaning back in his chair and studying Andy. "And where, exactly did you do this?"

"Oh, lots of places. South America, Australia, Java, Israel, Ireland. You see my dad's an archaeologist so we moved around a lot. Up until this past year I helped out at every dig from the time I was old enough to use a trowel and brush."

"I see. The major has told me quite a bit about you but he omitted the fact that you were an archaeologist's son."

Andy's face took on an even more worried look and he sat up much straighter. "I hope my father's occupation won't have any impact on your decision."

Kelley gave Reese a sly look then fixed his eyes on Andy. He shook his head slightly and smiled. "Frankly, I don't care what your father's occupation is. I'm not looking to hire your dad; I'm looking to hire you. I'm interested in what you can do and what your goals are."

"I am willing to do whatever job that needs to be done," said Andy becoming a little more relaxed. "If it's something I don't know how to do I'll be glad to learn."

"All right," said Kelley. "We need someone to help the custodian. We also could use someone to answer phones and help out at the front desk. Do you think you could do that?"

"I can do those things after school and on the weekends. Once school's over in May I'll be available every day."

Major Reese cleared his throat rather loudly. "I believe you neglected to mention the afternoons of the drone competitions."

Andy blushed. "Oh, yes. I forgot to mention that, sorry. But there are only a few more competitions left this year."

"That's all right. We can work around that schedule," Kelley assured him. "Major Reese has told me what an asset you are to the group. So, when would you like to start?"

Andy's eyes opened wide in surprise. "How soon would you like me to begin? We're on break this week so I'm available every day."

Kelley smiled slightly. "How about tomorrow morning about nine? Do you want to know how much you'll be paid?"

Andy grinned. "Ah, sure."

"How does ten dollars an hour sound to start with?"

"That sounds fine to me," said Andy appearing almost giddy.

"You could be making more by summer. Hopefully, you'll have enough to enroll in the summer ground school class."

"Thank you so much, sir. I really appreciate it." he stood up reached out and shook Kelley's hand. "Oh, is there any particular dress code for this job?"

"We're really casual around here. Whatever you wear to school should be fine," stated Kelley jovially as he ushered Andy and Reese out the door and into the lobby. "We'll see you tomorrow morning."

"Yes," answered Andy with a grin. "I'll be here at nine o'clock." He practically ran out the door and into the parking lot.

"Andy, wait up a minute," shouted Reese rushing after him.

"Oh, I'm sorry, sir." Andy stopped and turned around toward Reese. "I want you to know how much I appreciate you taking the time to get me this job. Thank you so much."

"I was glad to do it," said Reese. "There's a few things that Kelley didn't mention that you need to know."

Andy looked at him apprehensively. "Like what?"

"You're going to need to fill out some paperwork. He'll have the forms for you in the morning. But you're going to need to bring your Social Security card with you."

Andy looked a little puzzled. "I don't understand."

"The forms are so you can get paid. They need to let the government know how much you're getting paid so at the end of the year you can file your income taxes."

"You mean I have to pay the government so I can work?"

"Yeah, I guess that's one way to look at it," said Reese smiling slightly. "Anyway I just wanted to make sure you knew what information you needed to bring with you tomorrow."

"Thank you for letting me know. Now I just need to go home and find where my folks keep stuff like that.

It was nearly 3:30 by the time Andy arrived home. He parked his car and ran across the street to the Taylor's house to pick up Rascal. By the time Gracie answered the front door he had calmed down a little bit but he was still grinning from ear to ear.

"Well, from the look on your face I'd say your interview went well," said Gracie opening the door and inviting him inside.

"It was great!" shouted Andy stepping inside and giving her a hug. "I owe it all to Major Reese." He let go of Gracie and walked into their living room where he was greeted by Gwen and Rascal. Rascal jumped out of Gwen's lap and ran over to him. Andy bent down and patted the dog then sat on the sofa. Rascal jumped into his lap as soon as Andy sat down. Gracie sat down next to him.

"So, tell us what happened," said Gwen rolling her chair over to the sofa.

"Well, Major Reese was there. Apparently he had talked with the airport manager, Mr. Kelley, and told him I wanted a job so I could earn money to take the ground school class and flying lessons. Mr. Kelley said the custodian could use help and they could use someone to answer phones and help with office type stuff. So, he hired me. I start tomorrow morning at nine."

"That's great!" said Gracie excitedly. "So you'll be able to attend the class that starts next week."

Andy shook his head dubiously. "I don't think so. I am going to have to wait until the summer class. I won't make enough money for next week's class but I should have enough saved for the summer class."

Gwen watched Rascal curled up so cute in Andy's lap and licking his paw. "So what are you going to do with Rascal this week while you work? Are you going to take him with you?" she asked with curiosity.

Andy's face lost a bit of its joy as he realized the dog could be a problem. He sighed heavily and stroked Rascal's head. "I hadn't thought about him. I can't leave him alone at the house all day. Once my folks get back that won't be a problem but I don't know what to do with him this week."

Gwen glanced at him coyly. "You could always leave him here with us," she suggested. "He's enjoyed himself with us these past few days and he's no trouble. In fact he's fun to have around."

"Oh, I can't ask you to do that," he replied patiently.

"I don't know why not," said Gracie stoically. "We have a nice fenced backyard for him to play in."

"And we can take him for walks to the park," added Gwen cheerfully. "It would be great for everyone."

Andy looked thoughtfully at the sisters. He knew they meant well and he was fairly certain Rascal would be in good hands with them. But he couldn't help but wonder if he wasn't taking advantage of their friendship. He didn't want to do that. He gnawed on his bottom lip trying to think. "Tell you what," he said at last. "I'll accept your offer but you need to let me pay you for taking care of him. Okay?"

Gwen and Gracie stared at each other and shook their heads. "You don't get it," said Gracie determinedly. "We don't want to be paid for taking care of Rascal. We like him. Just letting him be with us is payment enough. Understand?"

Andy scratched his head. "No, I don't, but if that's the way you want it I'm not going to argue with you. Thank you."

"You are more than welcome," said Gwen smiling.

"I need to be at the airport by nine so will it be all right if I bring Rascal over around eight thirty? That's not too early is it?"

"That'll be fine," Gracie assured him. "Dad leaves for the office about eight and I'm always up early."

"All right. I'll see you then." He fastened the dog's lead on his collar and stood up. "I need to get home and call my parents. Apparently I need to bring my Social Security card with me tomorrow and I have no idea what it looks like or where they might keep it."

Gracie chuckled. "Good luck. I hope you find it without any trouble."

"Yeah, me too." He quickly left and headed down the ramp for home.

Once inside he glanced at his watch and realized it was after 9 p.m. in Ireland. He pulled out his cell phone and called his father. "Hi Dad. Yes, everything is fine. I'm calling because I got a job and I need my Social Security card so I can fill out some paperwork. The trouble is I have no idea if I have this card and if I do I don't know where you keep that kind of stuff. Where did I get a job? At the county airport. It's kind of a complicated story and I'll tell you all about it when you get home. Okay, you say everyone has to have this Social Security card thing and mine is in a lockbox in the wall safe in your study. Great," groaned Andy. "And just how do I get into this safe? I mean I don't even have any idea where it's at. Okay, okay I'm going down the hallway right now." He entered the study and turned on a light. "Now, you say it's behind the picture. Which picture? Got it. The painting of the Amazon jungle. All right I moved the picture and I see the safe door. Turn the knob to the right to forty-two, yes, then to the left until I reach eighteen. Got it. Then back to the right to twenty-five." He moved the lever and opened the door. "I found the metal box. So where's the key? Yes, okay. Just a minute." Andy put the box on his father's desk, located the key in the bottom desk drawer and opened the box. "There's all kinds of papers and envelopes in here," he told his dad. "What am I looking for? Yeah, I see an envelope labeled with my name. You say it's in here with my birth certificate." He pulled all the pieces of paper from the envelope and finally discovered the card he was looking for. "Okay, I think I've found it. It's red, white and blue with my name and some numbers. Yes, I understand. Once I'm finished with it tomorrow I put it back in the box and back in the safe." Rascal had followed him into the room and was sitting in the doorway watching his every move. He cocked his head to one side and licked his lips.

Andy took a quick glance at the dog, smiled and gave him a wink before putting the metal box back into the safe.

Martin was still talking on the phone but Andy had put it on the desk while he was closing the safe and wasn't listening. He locked the safe, replaced the painting and finally picked up his phone. "Sorry Dad, what were you saying? I didn't hear that last bit. Oh, the dig. I'm glad it's going well. Like I said, everything is fine here and I'll tell you all about my job when you get home on Saturday. Tell Mom I said 'hello' and that I'm watering her plants just like she told me. You take care now and don't worry about me. 'Bye." He ended the conversation and knelt on the floor next to the dog. He reached out, put his arms around its neck and gave it a hug. "It's a great life Rascal and I'm really glad you found me."

Rascal licked Andy's face several times before Andy released him and stood up. "Come on boy, let's have some supper and then we can go for a walk." Rascal didn't need to be invited twice. He calmly followed Andy to the kitchen and sat patiently for his dinner.

Chapter Eleven

Thursday morning arrived damp and dreary in Blarney. Things weren't any better at the Donoughmore dig site but Pat and Martin decided to not let the weather stop their work, unless a thunder storm arrived. The rain had moved north toward Ulster which was just fine with Pat and his crew.

"I'm so glad you're feeling better. I can't wait to show you what we've found," Emily told Rowena as they tramped across the muddy field toward the area they had been excavating. "I can't wait to uncover that horse's head. I'm hoping Bridin is right and that it does have a fancy bridle to go along with the shield we found."

"Tell me again about that shield," said Rowena stepping around a muddy puddle.

"Oh, it is so pretty," Emily said enthusiastically. "The shield is round. And there were these bronze carvings of horses in a circle on the shield and some kind of plants or maybe trees with the horses. It's fantastic. Oh, yeah, did I tell you the warrior is female?"

Rowena nodded her head. "Dad mentioned it yesterday, remember? So, the warrior is female and she has a shield with horses. And there's a horse buried with her. What else?"

"What do you mean, what else?" Emily was closely watching Rowena process this information. She had an idea of what conclusion Rowena might arrive at. There's a woman warrior buried with a horse and a shield with horses carved on it. "*She's going to decide this is Epona and her horse,*" thought Emily.

"I mean, what else has been found in the grave?" said Rowena inquisitively.

"Oh, well, we found a bronze arm bracelet and I think they might have found some pottery but I'm not sure."

"Interesting," commented Rowena meekly as they reached the edge of the grave.

Bridin was sitting nearby with her legs dangling on the side of the trench, staring at the horse's skeleton. She looked up at the girls. "Morning," she said absently and turned her attention back to the trench.

Emily and Rowena quietly joined her. "So, what exactly are we staring at?" Rowena ventured gently. "I mean, I know it's a horse …"

Bridin glanced at Rowena and smiled thinly. "I was just wondering what it must have been like being a woman warrior back in those days riding this horse and fighting some enemy. Did the woman and the horse die in battle and is that why they are buried here or did they die at some other time?"

"Those are probably questions we may never have answers to," said Rowena sympathetically.

"You're right," agreed Bridin resignedly. She raised her head and looked at the dark cloudy sky. "Well, now that you two are here we might as well get to work. Let's see what we can get done before it starts to rain." She slid into the trench with her trowel and some rags.

Emily grabbed some tools from her backpack, handed some to Rowena and they joined Bridin digging at the ground near the horse's neck.

In some ways digging in the wet earth was a bit easier than digging in the hard dry dirt. It was a tad messier though because the mud liked to stick to the trowels. Slowly the three uncovered the horse's jaw, it's teeth, and made their way to the rest of its skull. Along the way they discovered the bridle Emily was so anxious to find.

"Look at that!" Emily said excitedly as she took a rag to wipe away the mud. "That is so gorgeous!" The more she wiped the more intriguing it became. "Do you see that? It looks like a horse head. And the spirals along the side of the bridle are like the ones on those boulders." She stared at Bridin and Rowena. "This is remarkable. I need to get some water so I can clean it better." She scampered off for water and clean rags.

While she was gone Rowena and Bridin continued to uncover the rest of the horse's skull. "I have to admit I've never seen anything quite like this at a dig," said Rowena.

"Me either," admitted Bridin. "I've seen similar items in some museums and photos in a few books and magazines but I've never found one myself."

Rowena leaned against the side of the trench and brushed the back of her hand across her forehead. She glanced down at the far end of the trench watching her father, and Emily's dad digging. "I don't suppose we have any idea who this woman warrior might be do we?"

Bridin shook her head. "Have no idea. The people weren't exactly noted for keepin' any kind of records ya know?"

"I know," acknowledged Rowena. "It was just a thought."

Emily came running back across the field and jumped into the trench with several bottles of water and some damp rags. "They're making good progress at the other end. They found a headdress to go with the helmet." She began wiping the mud from the bridle and the metal decorations attached to it. "I'd really like to remove the bridle. It would be easier to clean." She looked at Rowena and Bridin and frowned. They were staring uncomfortably back at her. "Don't look at me like that. I'm not going to do it. I know they need to take pictures of all this first. Geez, you'd think I'd never been on a dig before."

Anne was at the other end of the trench taking pictures of the newly found headdress and writing in her notebook. Eventually she made her way toward the girls.

She stood at the edge of the trench and peered inside. "Wow, that is some horse you found," she commented. She began snapping pictures of the horse and the girls.

"Can you get a photo of the bridle?" asked Emily. "It's really unusual. See the horse head? And these spirals too!"

Anne climbed into the trench to take some closeup shots of the horse's head and the bridle. "I must admit everything that's been

116

found so far has been remarkably preserved considering the number of centuries it's been in the ground."

"That it is," remarked Bridin as she attempted to clean dirt and mud from the horse's eye sockets. "This has been a remarkable dig and one of the most interesting I've ever taken part in."

Anne smiled warmly at her. "So I take it you've been on a number of digs around here."

Bridin removed one of her gloves and brushed her light brown hair off her face. "Yes, I went on my first dig in college about ten years ago. I spent my summer holidays on any dig that I could find. Once I graduated I joined Mr. Flanagan's staff and I've been here for the last five years. He's a grand person to work for and most of the digs have been fascinating. I've learned so much about our history, things they don't teach in school."

"I can imagine," said Anne. "Every excavation we've done over the past twenty years has been not only remarkable but very educational as well." She noticed Emily anxiously pacing around the other side of the horse skeleton looking at the bones and then at her. Anne nodded to her daughter. "Emily, settle down. I've finished taking the pictures. So, if you want to remove the bridle and clean it you can." Emily's eyes opened wide in surprise. "Don't look so astonished. Knowing you I'm sure you can't wait to clean it up, so go ahead." She slowly shook her head and chuckled then climbed out of the trench. "Once you remove it you might want to take it over to the tent to clean it. It'll be better than trying to do it in the trench."

Emily let out an exasperated sigh and stared at her mother. "Yes, Ma'am." Rowena helped her remove the leather bridle from the horse's skull and unfasten it from the reins.

"There you go," said Rowena giving Emily the bridle.

"Thanks," she said climbing out of the trench and heading across the field.

As she entered the tent she was surprised to see Paul at one of the tables working on the warrior helmet and headdress. "Hi," she greeted him. "See they have you cleaning things too."

"Oh, I volunteered," he told her pleasantly. "I like digging the stuff up but I want to see what it looks like with all that dirt gone."

"I'm with you on that," agreed Emily. She placed the bridle on another nearby table and walked over to see the progress Paul had made. "You're doing a great job on the helmet. Cleaning the headdress though is going to take a lot of time and patience."

Paul looked up from his work. "That's all right. I like doing this, it's relaxing."

"I guess," said Emily matter-of-factly. "I get a bit impatient sometimes and wish I could get it done faster. When I was little I used to wish I had a magic wand I could use to get it done with one little zap." She smiled and Paul laughed.

"That would be something all right," he stated jovially.

Outside the tent Emily heard something running through some of the vegetation at the edge of the woods. She looked up and saw what appeared to be a small man running into the forest. "I … I just saw a leprechaun!" she shouted and started to run after him. Paul reached out and grabbed her arm to stop her. "Didn't you see him? He ran into the woods. He was wearing brown pants and a tan jacket. He had a short beard and one of those flat caps."

Paul made her turn around to face him and shook his head. "It wasn't a leprechaun. It was just Michael O'Flynn."

Emily stared at him in disbelief. "I don't understand."

Paul took a deep breath and slowly exhaled. "It's simple, really. Michael O'Flynn lives on a farm down the road. He's a dwarf not a leprechaun and quite harmless. I've noticed him here several times. He's just interested in what we've found. He's a nice old guy."

Emily sat on a chair beside the table and ran her fingers through her hair. "This place is definitely strange. First it's Rowena with the Druids, then it's Mr. O'Keeffe, now it's a dwarf that looks like a leprechaun. I just don't get it."

Paul brought a chair over from the other table and sat down beside her. "First of all, Druids are a part of Irish history. Rowena is very interested in them. However, that doesn't mean the woman named Epona you encountered in the woods the other day is a Druid. It also doesn't mean the horse we found with Rowena is connected in anyway with Druids. As for leprechauns, they are a myth, an interesting myth but a myth just the same. Even if they were real they are much smaller than dwarfs."

Emily lowered her head and stared at the ground. Then she raised her head and looked squarely at Paul. "All right, but what about Shamus O'Keeffe? When I mentioned him to Rowena the blood drained from her face and she looked as white as snow."

Paul stared at Emily and closed his eyes for a few seconds. "When did you see Mr. O'Keeffe?"

"That day when we found Rowena with the pony. I met him in a park in Blarney near the Flanagans. He told me about some girl and her pony and her father found her in a pasture, brought her home and the girl didn't remember anything that had happened for quite a while afterwards. He also said they never found the white pony."

"This Mr. O'Keeffe, was he an older gentleman?"

"Yes, and he was very nice."

"I see. Well, if it's the O'Keeffe I'm remembering there was an interesting newspaper article about him a few months ago. He'd seen a banshee warning him that a prominent business man was going to die. And he did. Turned out the man was also a relative of O'Keeffe's he just didn't know it at the time."

"Great," whispered Emily resolutely. "That doesn't explain Rowena's reaction."

"You're right, that one incident doesn't explain her behavior. However, O'Keeffe has been noted to see banshees on more than that one occasion. Usually they just appear when someone in the family is going to die, which was the case with O'Keeffe until this business man incident. But then, it did make sense when someone discovered the man was connected to the O'Keeffe family, Mr. O'Keefe just didn't know it at the time."

"So, Druids and leprechauns aren't real but banshees are, is that right?" asked Emily skeptically.

Paul smiled thinly. "I don't know if banshees are real or not. I've never seen or heard one. My grandmother has, at least she believes she did. She tells the story how when she was about twelve or thirteen she saw a banshee at her window late one night and about twenty minutes later her father got a phone call from his mother that his uncle had died. So, who knows. Maybe they do exist."

"Oh man, that's weird," said Emily.

"Yes, I know." Paul glanced at his watch. "Hey, it's almost twelve thirty and we still have a lot of cleaning to do. Come on let's see what we can get done before lunch."

Emily took a brush and a small bowl of water to the table where she had placed the bridle and began to clean it. Cleaning all the little lines of the carving was a delicate business and she had to be very careful not to damage anything. Slowly the dirt was removed and the intricate lines of the bronze horse head became clearer. It was magnificent. Emily held the bridle up at arm's length just to get a better look at her work.

"That looks good," remarked Paul as he walked over to get a closer look. "Whoever did the artwork for this did a great job. We're lucky to have found this grave and that everything is so well preserved."

"I'm glad we've been here to help," said Emily.

They looked out the tent opening and noticed the crew moving toward the shade of trees near the forest. "Looks like it's time for lunch," observed Paul. "I don't know about you but I'm so hungry I could eat a horse!"

Emily stepped back from him so startled she fell over the nearby chair. Fortunately, Paul caught her before she hit the ground. "What's the matter?" he asked calmly.

"Oh, nothing, nothing at all," replied Emily. "I guess I was just surprised that you'd want to eat a horse, that's all."

Paul laughed. "I would never eat a horse! It's just a silly expression, nothing more. Come on let's go join the others." He gently led her out of the tent and escorted her to the group gathered on a blanket near the woods.

"Glad to see you join us," said Pat. "How's the cleaning going?"

"I've cleaned the helmet and I'm starting on the headdress," said Paul as he grabbed a sandwich from the cooler and a can of soda. He sat down next to Riley and Ben and began to eat.

"What about you Emily?" asked Pat with interest.

"Oh, I'm doing fine. I've managed to get nearly all the dirt off the bridle and the bronze horse's head. It's looking really nice. I figure I'll tackle the rest of it once we finish lunch."

"Ah, good, good. Glad to hear it," said Pat taking a bite of his sandwich.

"We're making good progress at our end of the grave," commented Martin. "We found an interesting statue this morning." He pulled a cloth covered object from a basket near the cooler and began to unwrap it. He soon revealed a small statue of a female standing beside a horse. "What do you think?"

When Rowena saw the statue Emily noticed her dark brown eyes opened wide in shock and she quickly shoved her fist into her mouth to keep from screaming.

No one else noticed Rowena's behavior because they were all engrossed with the statue. Emily scooted close to Rowena and took her free hand as she continued to observe the girl's behavior.

"It looks like a small statue of that Druid goddess Epona," remarked Bridin. "In a way I guess it would make sense to find it here. After all she was supposed to be a protector of horses and donkeys. But I think she was also supposed to help souls into the afterlife."

"That's right," blurted Emily. "She was special for a lot of different things though, not just horses. I read that she was the goddess of dreams not just when you sleep but like a person's hopes and ambitions. I think she was also a protector of families and children and that she liked roses."

Martin glanced at his daughter in surprise. "And just when did you become so knowledgeable about Druids?"

Emily blushed. "I just read about them the other night."

"Ah ha," responded Martin. He wrapped the statue up and placed it back in the basket. "Well, I don't know about the rest of you but I need to get back to work." He put his trash in a bag, got up and headed back toward the trench.

It didn't take long for the others to follow.

Emily stayed with Rowena until the crew left. "Are you going to be all right?"

Rowena stared at Emily and nodded her head. "Yeah, I'll be fine." She stood up and helped Emily and her mother gather the trash and fold the blanket. They took the cooler to the trench just in case people wanted something to drink later that afternoon.

Rowena climbed back into the grave to help Bridin with the horse's skeleton while Emily went back to the tent to work more on the bridle. Anne stood near the trench and took a few minutes to observe everyone at work before walking over to check on the crews in other parts of the dig.

"Well, that was certainly an interesting and educational lunch," remarked Paul when Emily returned to the tent. He had already begun working on the headdress.

"If you say so," replied Emily bluntly. She picked up the bridle and began cleaning the bronze spirals on the side.

Paul watched as she took a brush and began to scrub the bridle in a not too gentle manner and became concerned. He quietly walked to her side and placed his hand on her shoulder. She stopped scrubbing and silently looked up at him. "What's bothering you, Emily. Talk to me."

Emily took in a ragged breath and slowly exhaled. She gnawed on her bottom lip for a few seconds before she put down the brush and turned around to face him.

"I'm worried about Rowena, if you must know. Did you see her reaction when my dad showed everyone that little statue?"

"No, I wasn't looking at anyone. I was just looking at the statue like everyone else."

"Well, *I was* watching her. She looked shocked and scared, like she was ready to scream. That's when she stuffed her fist in her mouth. Something isn't right and I'm concerned."

"You think this has something to do with that little episode that happened the other day don't you?"

Emily shrugged her shoulders. "Honestly, I don't know."

Paul scratched his head. "Tell you what. Why don't you and I see if we can find the answers? Maybe together we can discover who this woman is and solve the mystery. What do you say? Shall we give it a try?"

Emily looked at him in disbelief. "Are you serious or are you just putting me on?"

"I'm very serious. We need to prove to Rowena that this woman isn't a Druid goddess. Okay?"

Emily stared into his light blue eyes trying to be sure he was sincere. She looked at the dig site then at the woods. She stood up and wiped her hands nervously on her jeans. "Okay, let's do this." She checked her pocket to be sure she had her flashlight and her pocket knife and headed out of the tent. She turned to look at Paul. "Well, are you coming?"

"You bet," he said sprinting after her.

Paul wiped the sweat from his forehead and sat down on a nearby log. "I don't know about you but I'm exhausted. We've been tramping around in these woods for a good forty-five minutes and we're no closer to finding this woman and her house than we were when we started. I never thought this place was so big." He watched Emily wandering around the trees and vegetation inspecting every bent tree limb and torn plant leaf. "Come sit down for a bit. We need to come up with a plan."

Reluctantly Emily took a seat beside him on the big old log and stretched her legs. "I sure don't remember these woods being this big when we were here the other day."

"I think we've been walking around in circles," he told her blandly. "That's why we need to take some time to think about where we've been and you need to try and remember what the place looked like when you left that woman's house."

"Don't you think I've been trying to remember? I think I know where I'm going but then I get to walking around in here and I get confused. It's frustrating!"

Paul stretched his back and rubbed the back of his neck. "I get it. Tell you what; come sit over there next to that big tree. Lean your back against it and close your eyes."

Emily apprehensively walked to the tree, sat on the ground and closed her eyes. "Now what?"

"Now, stop thinking about anything and relax." He gave her a few minutes of quiet time before continuing.

She moved her shoulders and back against the tree trunk and folded her legs crossways. She clasped her hands in her lap and took a deep breath. Slowly she exhaled and did her best to relax.

"Okay, now think about Monday. You are at the rocks at the edge of the woods with Rowena and her cat. Can you see that?" Emily nodded her head. "Good. Now, the cat runs into the trees and Rowena goes after him. What do you do?"

Emily furrows her forehead, thinking. "I go after them. But I don't know what direction Rowena or Shea went."

"Fine. Are you walking or running in the woods?"

"Both."

"What does the woods look like? Do you see anything unusual or different?"

"There's lots of trees and bits of sunlight but more dark shadows than light. There's a tree with a hole at the bottom and some birds sitting on the branches."

"Okay, what else do you see or do? Do you stand there looking at the birds or do you go on in the woods?"

"I hear something running in the leaves. I don't know if it's Shea or an animal so I start to run. I step in a hole and fall and hit my head on something; a tree root maybe, I don't know for sure."

Emily's hand reaches for her head then she slowly dropped it. She quickly opens her eyes and stares at Paul. "All right, how do we find this place and once we find it how do we find this Epona?"

Paul scratched his head and blinked his eyes. "I don't know."

"Great," answered Emily getting up from the ground and joining him back on the log. "Well, one thing is for certain, we need to stop walking in circles." She pulled her knife from her pocket and looked up at the sky through the leaves.

"What are you doing?"

"Trying to find what direction to take."

Paul watched as she stood up and studied her pocket knife handle. She looked at the sky again.

"The sun is to our left, so north is straight ahead. At least that's what my compass indicates."

"What compass?" asked Paul rather puzzled.

Emily smiled. "The one in my knife handle. See?" She showed him her knife and sure enough there was a small compass resting there.

"Where in the world did you get that?"

"From my father. He made it for me so I wouldn't get lost."

Paul shook his head. "Unbelievable. But we still don't know what directions to go."

"All right. Let's suppose we've been walking in a circle like you think. How far do you think we are from where we entered the woods? Maybe half a mile or less?"

"I have no idea."

Emily looked at the trees. If she could climb one she might be able to see beyond the forest and see the dig site. Then she could have an idea of where they were. She just had to find a tree. "Ah ha, there it is."

"There what is?"

"A tree to climb. I just need you to boost me up to the lowest branch on that tree. I'll climb it and hopefully get some idea of where we are."

Paul gazed at her dumbfounded. "You've got to be kidding!"

Emily shook her head and scowled at him. "Not hardly. If I can climb high enough I should be able to see the edge of the woods and the dig site. Now, are you going to help me or do you want to stay lost in here until winter?"

"Okay, which tree?"

"That one over there," she said pointing to a large maple tree. She led him to the tree and found a piece of a log for him to stand on. "You stand on this and let me climb up on your shoulders. I should be able to reach one of the lower branches and climb up."

"I don't believe I'm doing this," grumbled Paul as he steadied himself on the log and looked up the trunk to the branches.

"You need to bend down so I can get on your shoulders," instructed Emily firmly.

Paul did as she asked and she climbed on his back and sat on his shoulders. "Now, slowly stand up. You can put your hands on the tree for support," she advised him.

Very slowly and carefully he managed to eventually get his six foot frame upright.

"Good," said Emily. "Now I'm going to need you to stand very still and you may need to help me. I need to get my feet on your shoulders, then I should be able to reach that low branch."

She placed her hands on the tree trunk and carefully managed to get her feet on his shoulders one at a time. She reached for the branch but couldn't quite make it. "Nuts." she looked down at Paul. "I need you to do one more thing."

Paul groaned. "What?"

"Could you put your hand under my right foot and give me a little boost?"

"Look you may be part of a circus acrobat group but I'm not. What happens if you slip out of my hand? We could get hurt."

"Trust me, that's not going to happen. Put your left hand on the tree trunk and my foot in your right hand and just give me a push. You're strong enough to do it."

"Okay, here goes." He did as she told him and before he knew it she was hanging from the branch like a little monkey. She

126

managed to pull herself upright and stand on the branch. Carefully she reached another and eventually made it three-fourths of the way up before she stopped.

"Well, what do you see?!" shouted Paul eagerly.

"Oh, you are not going to believe this! It's great!"

Emily descended the tree much faster than she had ascended it and was on the bottom branch before Paul had time to react.

"Can you help me down?"

Paul gazed up at her and smiled. "Why don't you just jump and I'll catch you?"

"I don't think so, you might drop me."

"All right, grab the branch and start to lower yourself down. I promise to catch you."

Emily watched him very skeptically wondering if he would be able to catch her. "Okay, here I come." Gingerly she clasped the branch and lowered herself. She felt his strong hands grab her calves, then her thighs and finally he grabbed her waist and eased her to the ground. "Thank you."

"You're welcome. Now, what did you see?"

"I think I may have found Epona's house. If I didn't then the woods are on fire."

Paul swallowed nervously. "Well, let's hope the woods are not on fire."

"I saw a small wisp of smoke in the woods over that way." Emily pointed northeast. "It's not very far. Come on." She clutched his hand and began leading him through the woods.

They hadn't gone but about a hundred yards when what little sun that had been visible disappeared. Emily and Paul stopped and turned their faces toward the treetops. A dark gray cloud had replaced the sunshine and it was getting darker by the second. In the distance they heard a rumble of thunder. The tree branches began to sway, slowly at first then more vigorously.

"I think we may be in for a wee bit of rain," commented Paul jovially.

"Ya think?" answered Emily sarcastically.

Nancy Potts

"We have two choices," said Paul calmly. "We can continue on or go back to the dig."

Emily narrowed her eyes and gave him a very determined look. "I don't know about you but I haven't come this far to turn back now. So we get wet, it's not like I'm made of sugar and will melt." She continued to tramp through the forest's carpet of dead leaves toward what she hoped was Epona's home.

Paul stood there briefly speechless. He had known some determined females in his twenty-three years but never a kid Emily's age. It was obvious he couldn't allow her to go on alone. Afterall she was just a kid and a visitor. "Well, I guess we travel on," he said hesitantly. "Hopefully, we'll find this place before we get too wet."

Emily turned around to face him and smiled. "Well, come on then, this way!"

They were making good progress, at least Emily thought they were, when a giant bolt of lightning descended from the sky and struck a tall evergreen tree nearby. The tree cracked and toppled in front of them. Emily managed to jump out of its path but Paul wasn't as quick and tripped over several branches and landed on them.

"Oh my gosh!," screamed Emily rushing over to him. He was laying there with his eyes closed and not moving. "Oh, please don't be hurt or dead." She leaned down on the branches and reached over, grabbing his wrist looking for a pulse. Once she found it she let out a long sigh of relief. "Paul, can you hear me? Are you all right?"

Paul let out a low groan but didn't move.

Tears formed in Emily's eyes and trickled down her cheeks. "What am I going to do? I can't leave him here."

Some bushes rustled behind her but she was too upset to notice. When little Michael O'Flynn appeared beside her she nearly fainted. "Where'd you come from?!"

"Back there," he said pointing to the bushes behind her. "It looks like your friend needs some help."

Emily leaned back on her heels and stared at him. "He needs more than help; he needs a doctor. But I can't just leave him here alone. Look, you know where the dig is, would you go tell them where we are and have them send a doctor?"

O'Flynn scratched his scraggly beard and momentarily studied the situation. "Aye, I kin do that but there's help close by. I'll be right back, so." Before Emily could say another word he was off into the woods.

The tree trunk was still smoldering where the lightening had struck. Emily hoped it wouldn't cause a fire. Quietly she sat beside Paul, watching him breath and wishing he would open his eyes and move.

The sky was getting darker and the wind was picking up. "We should have gone back," she muttered. "This was a stupid idea."

As she continued to berate herself O'Flynn appeared with Epona. When Emily saw her she was both shocked and grateful.

"Hello, young one," said Epona calmly. She carefully approached Emily and Paul then began to check him over. She stroked his cheek and forehead. "Paul, Paul, can you open your eyes?" She continued to run her fingers delicately over his face. He breathed shallowly and opened his eyes for a moment then closed them again. "Can you move your fingers for me?" Slowly he began to move his fingers on his right hand since he was laying on his left side. He blinked his eyes then opened them completely.

"What happened? Where's Emily? Who are you?" he whispered to Epona.

She nodded to Emily and O'Flynn. "I think he's going to be all right." She looked back at Paul. "To answer your questions; a tree fell and it appears that you landed on top of it when you fell. Emily is right here with you and I am Epona. I live here."

Paul reached for his head and felt a lump.

"Do you think you can sit up?" asked Epona.

"I think so," he answered softly. He turned onto his stomach and tried pushing himself up onto his knees but the tree branches just wouldn't let him.

"Can you turn onto your back?" asked Emily. "If you can then maybe we can help you up."

Slowly and carefully he managed to get himself turned around. "That was more difficult than I thought," he stated breathing shallowly.

Emily and Epona each took one of his hands and held on to his upper arm while O'Flynn stood at his head just in case they needed help to lift his shoulders.

"Okay, let's do this," said Epona standing on the tree branches. Emily did the same. Paul managed to bend his knees and place his feet on the ground between some of the branches. "Everyone ready? On the count of three. One, two, and three!" Paul stood up a bit unsteady among the branches but Epona and Emily helped to keep him upright.

He put his hand on his head. "Man, I feel dizzy."

"It's all right," said Epona. "Put your hand on my shoulder and we'll get you out of these branches."

Carefully the three guided him away from the tree and onto solid ground. "Maybe you should sit down for a minute," suggested Emily looking for a place for him to sit.

"Good idea, my legs feel like rubber."

"I have a better idea," said Epona. "I'll take you to my place and you can lie down for a bit. O'Flynn, bring the wheelbarrow here won't you?"

O'Flynn pushed the wheelbarrow behind Paul and Epona helped him in. There was another crack of lightning followed by a very close boom of thunder.

"My place is close. We should make it before the storm."

Paul held onto the sides of the wheelbarrow until his knuckles turned white and tightly closed his eyes. *Who'd a thought a simple walk would end up like this*, he thought.

Emily followed close beside Epona carefully observing everything along the way. She wanted to be sure she could find her way out when Paul was able to leave.

They reached Epona's residence just as the first raindrops made their way through the treetops.

The place was just as Emily remembered. It did look like a giant tree trunk with a flat roof. It reminded her of pictures she'd seen of the giant sequoia trees in California. Epona maneuvered the wheelbarrow into the one room dwelling, over to the cot and helped Paul onto it. She handed the wheelbarrow to O'Flynn who took it outside and turned it upside down to keep it from filling with rain.

She went to a cupboard and returned to Paul with a blanket. "Now you just relax, stay warm and I'll make some tea." She covered him up then filled her teakettle with water and placed it on her woodburning stove.

"Emily dear, come sit over here near Paul and keep him company." Epona had placed a dark green wing backed chair near the cot.

Emily's eyes darted around the room. "Are you sure there isn't something I can do to help you?"

Epona smiled kindly. "I'm sure. You just keep him company for now. You've had a rough afternoon. You need to relax for a while."

Reluctantly Emily did as her hostess suggested and sat down next to Paul. She kept an eye on her as she made the tea. She was anxious to see what the lady actually put in it.

"You have a very nice place here," observed Emily making a mental note of everything she saw.

"It serves its purpose," said Epona nonchalantly.

"And what purpose is that exactly?"

Epona thoughtfully scrutinized her young visitor. "The purpose is to give me a place to live in solitude. It's a place where I can do what I want when I want and I don't have to deal with people who don't want people to think for themselves. I like thinking for myself."

"So do I," said Emily. "Even though I get myself in trouble sometimes, like today."

Epona smiled slightly. "You are a very unusual young lady."

Emily shrugged her shoulders. "I guess. But I've had an unusual life."

"Yes, so I understand. Spending your life on archaeology digs isn't normal. It's given you an opportunity though to learn things most people don't know and your parents have taught you to think for yourself. You're very lucky."

The teakettle began to whistle and Epona set about brewing the tea. Emily carefully scrutinized the lady and wondered how she knew about her life. She certainly didn't recall telling her anything about herself.

Emily quietly leaned over and took Paul's hand. "How are you feeling?"

"I'm feeling fine, a little sore but that's to be expected when you land on an enormous pine tree." He pushed the blanket off and sat up on the side of the cot. Emily gathered the blanket, folded it neatly and placed it at the foot of the cot.

Epona moved the small coffee table over toward her guests then set a tray with the tea on it. "Come join us Michael. There's no need for you to be sitting on the other side of the room."

He joined the group and sat on a small sofa near the coffee table. "Thank ya kindly."

"You're more than welcome Michael, you know that," said Epona. "Who knows what would have happened to these two if you hadn't found them."

"Yes, we're very grateful to you. Without your help I'd probably still be out there getting soaked," said Paul as he noticed the rain beating down on the roof.

Epona handed each of her guests a cup of tea. "There's milk and sugar for whoever wants it. Just help yourselves."

"Thank you," said Emily taking some of each. "You do make very good tea. I don't think I've ever had tea that tastes like this."

"It's a special herbal tea, an old family recipe that's been passed down in my family for several generations."

Paul finished his tea and glanced at his watch then at Emily. "It's getting late and with all this rain they probably decided to close things up and send everyone home early."

Emily swallowed her mouthful of tea and began to cough. "Are you okay?" asked Paul very concerned.

She waved her hand in front of her face and finally stopped coughing. "I'm all right. It just went down the wrong way." She took a deep breath. "You're right they probably did but I can't leave until I get the answers to the questions I came for."

Epona cocked her head to one side and gave Emily a very puzzled stare. "What questions?"

Emily squirmed uneasily in her chair. "Well, I guess my main question is did you find Rowena Flanagan in these woods earlier this week?"

Epona twisted her long light blondish red hair thoughtfully. "Maybe. What does she look like?"

"She's sixteen, about five foot five with dark red shoulder length hair, brown eyes and freckles."

"Sounds familiar."

"Okay. Well, did you take her to a pasture, along with a white pony named Niamh and leave her there?"

Epona's eyes brightened up. "Oh that girl. Sure I remember her. I found her wandering around in the woods. She was lost and not talking very coherently. She was looking for the Druid horse goddess Epona. For some reason she thought that was me just because that's my name. I told her I wasn't that goddess but she wouldn't believe me. Then she saw my pony and thought it was a horse that belonged to another Druid goddess, Niamh. She was a peculiar young woman."

"But did you take her to a field near here and leave her there with the pony?"

"Eventually, yes. I tried to give her something to drink because I thought perhaps she was dehydrated from wandering around in the woods and that's why she was acting so strange. But she only took a small sip then threw the rest away. So I walked around with her for a while and when we came to that field she decided to sit down and refused to move. Anyway I left my pony with her figuring someone would come looking for her and I knew she would be safe with my pony."

"Well, what would you have done if we hadn't found her?"

"I probably would have sent Michael here over to the dig to let them know where she was. Now, I'm a little curious. Is she all right?"

"Yes, she's fine," answered Paul. "In fact she's at the dig today helping out."

"But we were worried about her," stated Emily tersely. "She was dehydrated. The doctor gave her IV fluids and she had trouble remembering what happened. I think she's still thinking you are this Druid goddess."

"I am sorry but I'm glad the doctor was able to help her. As for her thinking I'm some Druid goddess, well I can't do anything about that. My parents named me without asking for my permission or opinion."

"I understand. But then there was this man I met, Shamus O'Keeffe. He told me about some girl who had a pony just like yours and how her father found her in this field with the pony and afterward the girl didn't remember how she got there or even anything about her pony and how someone named Epona promised to look after it so it wouldn't get sold to some nasty little girl."

"Wow, that's quite a story," said Epona truthfully.

"Sure, but then O'Keeffe might a made it up, 'specially if he thought it would make you feel better," said Michael.

"Were you upset when he saw you?" asked Epona.

"Yeah, I was worried about Rowena and I told him what happened."

"Well, there ya have it," said Michael. "Shamus is a great guy an' we know he's had some strange things happen in his life, but he also likes to help people with their troubles."

"Oh," murmured Emily. "Well, I guess that's that. You've answered all my questions. Thank you." She looked at Paul. "I know it's still raining but would you like to see about getting back. My parents are probably going nuts wondering what happened to us."

"Yes, we should get going. I just hope we don't get lost again."

"Don't be worryin' none," said Michael. "I'll get ya back without no trouble. Come along." He headed for the door and Emily and Paul quickly followed.

"Thank you for everything Epona," said Emily.

"Yes, thank you," echoed Paul.

O'Flynn left Emily and Paul in the woods right before they reached the boulders. "Good to be meetin' ya both. Be careful," he advised them and jogged back into the trees.

Emily looked at Paul and wiped rain from her face. "I hope you're not in too much trouble. And I'm really sorry about the tree and everything."

Paul just looked at her and smiled. "You've got nothing to be sorry for, okay? I agreed to go with you. And it's not your fault lightning hit the tree and caused it to crash. As for being in trouble; I'm more concerned about the trouble you're going to be in."

"Oh don't be. I get myself in trouble all the time. I'm like a magnet that just attracts trouble. I don't need to look for it, it just finds me. You know, I've been thinking about our meeting this Epona. She never told us her last name."

"Well, we never told her our names either," said Paul.

"We didn't, but she knew them, didn't she?" said Emily suspiciously. "She also knew things about me that I never told her."

Paul arched an eyebrow. "She probably just heard us talking to each other that's all. What I am curious about though is how she earns any money to buy food for her pony, which we never saw, and for herself. And I wonder if the people who own that property know she's there. It's all rather strange don't you think?"

"I never thought about any of that," stated Emily. "It would make sense though. Even though she lives like a hermit she does need food. I didn't notice any electricity. The stove burned wood. Did you see a well where she might have gotten water? She must get it from someplace. There isn't a stream or pond around is there?"

"Not that I'm aware of. Just between us, I think there's more to this woman that we need to discover," Paul said with a wink.

"I agree," said Emily happily.

When they entered the clearing they noticed Emily's parents, along with Pat and his daughter Rowena gathered in the tent where the artifacts were cleaned and cataloged.

Emily looked at Paul and grinned. "Looks like my folks, Rowena and Mr. Flanagan are still here. Well, guess we'd better get this over with!" She shrugged her shoulders, grabbed his hand and headed for the tent.

Chapter Twelve

Andy's alarm clock went off at seven. He rolled over to shut it off and go back to sleep when he suddenly remembered he had a job to go to. Rascal was snoring peacefully at the foot of the bed and twitched his ears when he heard the alarm buzzer but didn't open his eyes.

Quietly Andy showered and dressed before eventually waking Rascal and making him move. "Come on boy. You need to move so I can make the bed."

Rascal slowly raised his head to look at Andy as if to say, 'you have to be kidding.' He reluctantly moved and jumped to the floor waiting patiently for Andy to finish so they could go outside.

Andy rubbed the dog's head and took him into the backyard. "Boy you're going to have fun for the next few days. Did you know that? Just think, you get to spend the day with Gracie and Gwen. Won't that be fun?" He followed Rascal around the yard and brought him back inside. He grabbed the dog's food, bowls, toys and a donut for himself then headed for his car.

"Get in Rascal. That's a good boy." Rascal jumped into the passenger seat and sat down. Andy got behind the steering wheel, closed the door and backed out of the driveway and over to the Taylor's. He picked up the dog's things and took the very energetic Rascal to the front door. Gracie opened it before he even had a chance to ring the bell.

"Hello Rascal," Gracie greeted him taking all his belongings from Andy. "Don't worry now, we'll take good care of him for you. You just have a good day at work."

"Thanks. His food and toys and bowls are in the bag." Andy bent down and gave Rascal a final scratch behind the ears. "You be a good boy now and I'll see you later." He ran down the ramp, got into his car and was on his way. As he finished his donut he realized he didn't have anything to drink. "Brilliant Andrew," he muttered, "you've got a mouth full of food and nothing to drink."

As he continued down the road he heard something rolling around in the back of the car. When he stopped at the traffic light he took a quick look to see what it might be. It was a can of Coke. He couldn't remember how or when he put it there. He figured it must have rolled under one of the seats at some time. It didn't matter. He was just glad it was there. He was able to reach it just before the light turned green and he set it in the cup holder. "It's better than nothing," he said. He decided to let the can sit for a while before opening it. He didn't want to get a Coke shower all over his clothes. He'd made that mistake once before.

It was ten minutes before nine when he pulled into the airport parking lot. He figured the soda can had time to settle down but just to be careful he put an old paper napkin over it before he popped the lid. No shower, thank goodness. He took several large gulps emptying half the can before returning it to the cup holder. *That should last me for a while*, he thought as he got out of his car and headed for the office building.

The airport manager, Dale Kelley, was behind the check-in desk when Andy entered. "Good morning Andy. I was just getting things organized so I could show you around and get you familiar with our operation."

"Good morning, Mr. Kelley. Thank you." Andy joined Kelley behind the desk and took mental notes on where everything was located, who they might expect to be flying today and how to answer the phone. As he was concluding his instructions Major Reese showed up along with a middle-aged lady dressed in jeans and a black t-shirt with a giant eagle's head decorating the front.

Kelley raised his head as they entered the room. "Morning Mike; Angie." He nodded his head toward them as he greeted them. "Angie, I'd like you to meet Andy Parker, Andy, this is Angie Phillips one of our flight instructors. She helps out around here in the office too. Andy is going to be helping here after school and weekends. He wants to earn money for ground school and flying lessons."

"Nice to meet you Andy," said Angie pleasantly. "Flying these prop planes will be helpful if you decide to become a pilot for the military. Have you given any thought on joining the Air Force after school?"

Andy took a step backwards, surprised at the question. "I really haven't decided," he admitted nervously.

"Andy is one of my drone pilots at the high school," Reese told her stepping into the conversation. "In fact he's one of the best on our team. His father is Martin Parker, the new archaeology professor at the university. Maybe you've heard of him. He and his students excavated that cave in Kirksborough in January."

Angie tilted her head to one side and stared at Reese. "You mean the one with the sarcophagus and where those boys were trapped in that cave-in?"

"That's the one," Reese assured her smiling thinly.

"I see," she said. "Well, I hope you enjoy working here, Andy. Mr. Kelley's a good manager and if you need any help just let us know." She made her way down the hallway and entered one of the offices.

Major Reese joined Kelley and Andy behind the desk. "So, what are you teaching him to do Dale?"

"Just the everyday things. Keep track of who has checked out what plane, when they're going to be flying, how to answer the phone and transfer calls, stuff like that. Then I was going to take him out to the hangars, show him how to fuel the planes and wash them down. Once Gary gets here I figure he can show him how to clean the offices and toilets."

"Sounds good. If you want I can take him to the hangars and show him the ropes out there."

"Sure, that'll be fine. I'm done here so he's all yours."

Reese looked at Andy and winked. "Come along young man and I'll show you the rest of the operation. You're going to love it." He escorted Andy out the door and over to the nearest hangars. They opened the hangar doors and walked inside.

"These buildings sure are well organized," observed Andy as he began to walk around the airplane. "The mechanics shouldn't have any problem locating the tools or parts they need."

"We try to keep things in order," said Reese. "It makes everyone's job easier. Of course not everyone understands that. Some of the mechanics get a little sloppy so we need to always check everything when they're done and put things back where they belong. Right now there are two guys that are a bit careless with things and we always need to check the place once they're finished."

"I don't understand," said Andy. "If they are irresponsible why doesn't Mr. Kelley fire them?"

Reese shook his head and quietly chuckled. "It's not that easy. They don't work here; they keep their plane here. As long as they pay their hangar rental fee they can work on their plane and use the facility."

"Oh. Guess I've got a lot to learn. Still, I don't see why you couldn't make it a rule or something that people need to put the equipment back where it belongs."

"It would make sense, that's for sure. Some people though just don't want to obey rules."

The major showed Andy around the hangar and where things were kept. Afterward he climbed up the side of one of the planes to check its fuel gauge.

"A pilot is supposed to check the fuel gauge before and after each flight. You might recall this is my plane we flew in the other day."

"Yes, sir, I do."

"I flew several people that day and I didn't take the time to fill the tank afterward. There were a bunch of people gassing up their planes and I just didn't feel like waiting around to take care of mine. Anyway, it gives me an excuse to show you how, unless you already know."

"No, sir, I do not," replied Andy.

"All right, we're going to take the plane over to the pumps. You can hop in and ride over with me or you can just meet me over there on the other side of the runway."

Andy smiled. As tempting as it sounded he really didn't want to climb into that plane right now. "I'll meet you over there."

While Reese climbed into his Piper Warrior Andy strolled to the gas pumps and watched the major slowly taxi toward him. He stopped near the pumps and climbed out. "Now, one of the things you learn when you fly one of these planes is how to fill the gas tanks. So, the pilots will know how to do this, at least they should. However, some of the student pilots might need your help, especially those first time flyers. Their instructors are supposed to teach them but sometimes they like to let the students figure things out for themselves. I never thought that was a good idea. Anyway, if you're going to be a student it won't hurt to know how things operate. The fuel cap is here in the wing. You unscrew it and check the color of the fuel and the quantity in the tank. This fuel should be blue and the quantity should match the indication on the fuel quantity gauge." Major Reese continued to run through all the steps of fueling the plane with Andy and then he ran through some of his post flight checks before returning the plane to the hangar.

"There sure is an awful lot to learn," observed Andy as he followed him back to the office building.

"You're right but no one expects you to learn it all in one day. It'll take time but I know you'll get the hang of everything in a little while." Reese walked him back to the check-in desk. "Now, over here is the list of people planning to go flying today. It has their name, the plane's number and maybe their destination. Not everyone knows where they're going, sometimes they just want to fly around to fly."

"What if someone comes here and they haven't called ahead what do I do then?" asked Andy.

"Well, you have them fill out one of these forms, check it against those that are scheduled and if it's a rental take their money and give them the key to the plane." He showed him the board with various plane numbers and hooks with the keys for each plane. "Over here is a rental list for each of the planes, the cost of gasoline and so forth."

Andy looked the list over. "Seems fairly simple. What do I do when they bring the plane back?"

"Well, you hang the key back on the hook, and take their paperwork and put it in this stack. If they had any problems with the plane they are supposed to let you know so our mechanics can fix it and they should fill the gas tank on the plane too."

"I noticed this airport doesn't have a tower. So am I correct to presume they have a radio frequency so traffic can talk to each other?"

"That's right. But you need to understand, this is an uncontrolled airport. Normally no one is there to tell pilots they have permission to land unless there is a hazard or they expect an unusual amount of traffic. Today things are a little different because it's spring break and we're expecting some student pilots to be flying. So Angie's going to be in the radio/com room to monitor things for a while."

"Oh, that's good. So I only need to answer the phones and don't have to try to tell people where to land and stuff."

Reese chuckled. "No, you're not responsible for telling people where to land."

"Do you know what we didn't do out at the hangar?" asked Andy sheepishly.

"Ah, no. What did we forget?"

"Mr. Kelley mentioned something about showing me how to wash down an airplane."

Reese laughed and patted Andy on the back. "I think it's something that can wait until another day."

Andy smiled. "All right, if you say so."

"I most certainly do," said Reese cheerfully. "Have you filled out your paperwork yet?"

Andy slowly shook his head. "He was so busy telling me about everything I guess Mr. Kelley forgot about it."

"That's all right. I need to see him anyway I'll just get it for you."

"Thank you."

"You're welcome." Reese quickly walked down the hall and entered Kelley's office.

Andy sat down at the desk and began to sort through the forms and get the desk organized. He had to admit he hadn't known what to expect when he took this job. One thing was certain, it wasn't anything like working on one of his father's excavation sites. He had finished filing the last piece of paper when Major Reese came back with the paperwork for him to fill out.

"Kelley said he was sorry he forgot to have you do this when you got here this morning. He was just so anxious to get you started it slipped his mind. Anyway, once you're finished you can just run it down to his office. No problem."

"Thank you. I'll get right on it."

"Okay, I'll see you later." Major Reese was out the door before Andy had time to pick up a pen.

Most of the day was uneventful. People came in to pick up the keys to the planes they had scheduled to fly but that was about as exciting as things were until 3:35.

Andy had been listening to the little prop planes take off and land at irregular intervals during the day and occasionally a jet would pass by but not very often. All that changed at 3:35 p.m.

Andy was just leaving Mr. Kelley's office and was passing by the radio room when he heard "…county traffic, November seven niner six niner Foxtrot Papa ten miles southeast of the airport, landing runway seven, Greene county traffic."

"Greene county traffic pattern is clear. Go ahead six niner Foxtrot Papa," answered Mrs. Phillips.

Within a few seconds there was an earsplitting sound and the building began to vibrate.

At first Andy couldn't believe what was happening. Sure he'd heard jets take off and land at various airports over the years but

143

this one sounded like it was going to land right on top of the building. More importantly why was a jet landing here?!

Kelley ran down the hall and out the door onto the tarmac. Andy wasn't far behind.

Fortunately, the jet managed to come to a stop just a few feet from the end of the runway and turned left, to park on the ramp.

The pilot had turned the engines off and was climbing out of the cockpit by the time Mr. Kelley and Andy arrived.

As he approached the ground Kelley was right there to greet him. "Hello, I'm Dale Kelley, the airport manager. It isn't often we get jets landing here. We mostly deal with small prop planes."

"Well, I'm glad you're able to handle small private jets. I really didn't want to land at the large airport in Vandalia. Oh, by the way, I'm Eric Murphy." He reached out and shook Kelley's hand. "And who's this young man?"

Kelley turned to look at Andy, not aware that he had followed him. "Uh, this is Andy Parker. He's just recently joined our staff."

"Nice to meet you Andy," said Murphy. "I must admit it's been quite a while since I've been here." He pulled his phone from his pocket. "I need to call my daughter to let her know I'm here and she can come pick me up."

Mr. Kelley and Andy gave him some space to make his call. They didn't want him to think they were eavesdropping on his conversation. Andy discreetly observed the man and tried to think of where he'd heard that last name. Andy decided the guy looked like he might be in his late 60s or early 70s and he probably didn't get much exercise judging by the bulge around his middle. He probably had a lot of money, especially if he could afford his own jet. He watched the man slide his hand over his thin silver hair and slip his phone back into his slack's pocket.

The man joined Kelley and Andy. "It's going to be a little while before my daughter can get here. She's coming from Kirksborough. Would it be all right if I wait for her in your building?"

"Absolutely," said Kelley. "We have a nice lounge where you can relax. Do you have any luggage?"

Murphy snapped his fingers. "I knew I forgot something. My suitcase is in the plane." He started to walk back down the runway.

"I'll be happy to get it for you, sir," offered Andy.

"Well, thank you young man. The door is unlocked and the suitcase is behind my seat."

"All right. You go on and I'll bring it to you in the lounge." As Andy jogged over to the ramp he wondered what they were going to do with the guy's plane. They sure couldn't leave it there. Guess he'd ask Mr. Kelley.

It didn't take long to retrieve the suitcase and bring it to Mr. Murphy in the lounge. As he entered the area he suddenly remembered where he'd heard that last name. It was the name of the guy he and Gracie had found in the cemetery.

"Here you go sir," said Andy placing the suitcase next to the chair the man was sitting in. "Is there anything else I can do for you?"

"Thank you but I'm fine."

Andy hesitated for a moment. "Could I ask you a question?"

The man looked at Andy and nodded. "Sure."

"You said your name was Murphy. I was wondering if you were related to Mr. Fanin Murphy."

"I'm his son."

"I thought you might be. I'm awfully sorry for your loss."

The man blinked in surprise. "Did you know my father?"

Andy stared at the floor and rubbed the toe of his shoe across the tile before raising his head. "Not really. My friend and I are the ones who found him in the cemetery next to your mother's grave."

"I see," said Murphy solemnly. "My family and I are very grateful to you and your friend."

"I also found his dog."

"His dog?" Murphy asked surprised.

145

"Yes, Doc Schafer, he's the veterinarian, he checked the dog's microchip just to be sure. It was registered to your father. He's a real nice dog. Doc said he didn't think you or your sister would want him so I've been taking care of him." Andy paused not quite sure what to say or do. "But if you want him I'll understand."

Murphy frowned and shook his head. "No, son, I don't want him and neither will my sister or my daughter. Doc was right. You may keep him."

"Thank you. Like I said he's a real nice dog. We call him Rascal." Andy left and started back to his desk duties but stopped by Mr. Kelley's office along the way.

He stopped outside the office and knocked on the door frame. "Could I talk with you for a moment?"

Kelley glanced up from the paperwork he was working on. "Sure, what's up?"

"This is probably none of my business but what are you going to do with the jet? I mean it can't just sit on the ramp can it?"

Kelley smiled. "You're right. It can't just sit on the ramp. I'll have Mr. Murphy move it to one of the hangers. We want to make sure we have plenty of space for other planes to land."

Andy went back to his desk duties and waited for Mr. Murphy's daughter to arrive. He glanced at his watch. It was almost a quarter to five and he was anxious to get home to Rascal. He sure hoped the dog had behaved and that they all had a good time. Even though daylight-saving time had gone into effect he was worried he might not have enough daylight left to fly his drone this evening.

As he was thinking about all these things Mr. Kelley came down the hall. "I think you've spent more than enough time here today Andy. Why don't you go on home? We'll see you tomorrow."

Andy's face brightened at the thought. "If you're sure you don't need me any more today."

Kelley slowly shook his head and smiled. "I'm sure. Go on now, tomorrow will be another busy day."

"Thank you. I'll see you then." Andy grabbed his jacket and headed for the door just as Mr. Murphy's daughter arrived.

Chapter Thirteen

It was still raining when Emily and Paul entered the tent at the excavation site. They were both soaked of course from head to toe and were prepared to be greeted by very upset and angry individuals.

The Flanagans and Parkers were at the other side of the tent having a quiet discussion about something, about what Emily and Paul didn't know. As soon as they stepped inside all heads turned in their direction.

"Oh thank God!" shouted Anne rushing over to her daughter and Paul. She gave them both a hug then stepped back to take a good look at them. "We were so worried. Where have you been?"

Emily glanced at Paul then at her mother. She sighed deeply and gave her mother a very worried look. "Is it all right if we sit down for a minute? We're really tired." She walked over to a couple of metal chairs and had Paul sit next to her. She suddenly realized the air was cold and began to shiver.

Anne gave her raincoat to Emily and looked around for something to give Paul. Pat pulled a slicker from one of the backpacks and silently gave it to him.

Martin gave them each a cup of tea and patiently waited while they drank it.

"Okay Emily, answer your mother's question. Where have you been?" demanded Martin vigorously.

Emily stared at her father and tried to remain calm. "We were in the woods looking for the woman who helped me when I fell the other day and the woman Rowena had been searching for."

"I see," her father said patiently.

"Anyway, while we were there lightning struck one of the trees, it fell and Paul got hurt." She briefly glanced at Paul. "I was going to try to come back to get someone to help but I was kinda lost. That's when Michael O'Flynn showed up, saw we were in trouble and brought Epona to help us. She took us back to her place, took care of Paul and then it started to rain. Well, we knew it was getting late and since it was raining you would probably send everyone home so we thought we'd better be getting back here even in the rain. Luckily, Mr. O'Flynn was able to guide us through the woods and, well, here we are." She took a deep breath, exhaled and took a sip of her tea.

Anne, Pat and Rowena stood nearby staring at Emily and Paul in disbelief.

"Emily Marie, you've come up with some pretty farfetched stories over the years but this one is one of your best," said Anne shaking her head. "Do you really expect us to believe this?"

Paul sat up straighter in his chair and looked directly at Emily's mother. "It's the truth Mrs. Parker. Every word of it. I know we should have told someone what we were doing but it was just a spur of the moment thing. I went with her because I didn't want her going into the woods alone, especially after what happened to Rowena. I didn't want to take the chance she might get lost and truthfully I really didn't think we'd be gone very long."

"Okay, so you found this Epona and her house," said Pat joining the discussion. "What can you tell us about her?"

"Well, she lives a fairly simple life," stated Paul candidly. "Her house, if you can call it that, does look like the inside of a hollowed out tree with a roof."

"It's basically one room with a wood stove, a table, some chairs and a bed. It's very sparce but nice," added Emily. "We didn't see any electricity, you know, no electric lights, no refrigerator or anything like that. She did have candles though."

"She had water but we don't know if she had a well or where she got it. She's got a lot of herbs. She made us some herbal tea that was delicious," said Paul with a smile.

"All right, and who is this Mr. O'Flynn?" asked Anne stoically.

Emily started to giggle then noticed the no nonsense look on her mother's face and abruptly stopped.

"Mr. O'Flynn or Michael as he is known around here, is a dwarf who lives in Donoughmore," stated Paul. "He likes to visit our dig site to see what we've found. He's a nice old man. When Emily first saw him in the woods she mistook him for a leprechaun."

"You didn't!" squealed Rowena suddenly and laughed.

Emily looked at her uncomfortably. "Yeah, I did."

"Oh leprechauns are much smaller than O'Flynn," said Rowena grinning. "They only come up to his knees."

Pat stepped over to his daughter and put his hand on her shoulder. "That'll be enough of that." He quickly looked around the tent. "Let's finish cleaning things up and go home. It's supper time. Hopefully, the weather will be better tomorrow." He began to place the most recent artifacts in the trunk while the Parkers tidied up the rest of the tent.

That evening Emily really wanted to talk with someone about her conversation with Epona. The trouble was, all the adults were too busy to talk with her. She thought about talking with Rowena but she wasn't sure if that would be a good idea. The girl seemed to be doing better and she didn't want to risk her having a relapse or worse. Besides, they would be leaving the day after tomorrow and she would probably never see any of these people again.

Emily looked out the living room window. The rain had stopped. She noticed Rowena curled up on the couch with a book and Shea was lounging by her side.

"I don't suppose you'd like to go for a walk or something," Emily inquired innocently as she walked over to the couch.

Rowena glanced up from her book. "Sure, why not."

Emily grabbed her jacket. "Just let me tell my folks we're going. I don't want to get into any more trouble."

"Sure," giggled Rowena softly and took her jacket from the hall closet. "I'll meet you by the front door."

Emily found her parents and the Flanagans at the dining room table looking through old photos. "Sorry to interrupt," she apologized, "but Rowena and I thought we'd take a little walk now that it's stopped raining. Is that all right?"

Mary Jo looked at Pat then back at Emily. "It's fine with us."

Martin glanced at his daughter and gave her a small smile. "Sure, take a walk, just don't get lost."

"Very funny, Dad." She twisted her mouth from side to side then abruptly turned around and left.

As she passed the living room she noticed Shea was still snoozing comfortably on the couch and she quietly joined Rowena at the front door. "Come on let's go."

They made their way through the front garden and Rowena twirled around breathing deeply. "Oh it smells so grand after it rains, don't you think?" she asked Emily.

Emily observed her for a few moments then looked up at the sky. "Yes, it does smell good. That's one of the nice things about this country. It's a beautiful green and it smells so fresh and clean. I'm going to miss it when we leave on Saturday." They had moved out of the grass and were walking down the sidewalk toward the park.

"Well, maybe you can come back this summer."

Emily slowly shook her head. "We're going to Arizona. My dad is taking his class out west on a dig. They haven't decided where exactly because there's lots of places he'd like to explore. So, I'm afraid all I'll be smelling is the dry desert sand."

"What about the Indians?" asked Rowena. "Won't it be dangerous digging out there?"

"You've been watching too many cowboy movies. We're friends with the Indians. They're nice people."

"I guess my knowledge of Indians is like your knowledge of leprechauns."

"Well, maybe, but Indians are real."

Rowena stopped walking and stood in front of Emily. "Are you saying leprechauns aren't real?"

Emily took a small step backwards. "Of course they aren't.

They're just like fairies, ghosts, Big Foot, the Loch Ness monster and other mythological creatures."

"Next you're going to tell me Druids don't exist either."

Emily just shook her head sadly. "Of course Druids existed. They were a religious group, just like Christians, Jews, Muslims, Hindus and Buddhists. Whether their gods and goddesses existed is another question entirely. That's like saying the Viking, Greek and Roman gods were real. They weren't."

"And what about Epona?"

"What about her?"

"Well, you and Paul said you saw her and talked to her. She's real." Rowena bent her face down toward Emily. It was obvious she was becoming agitated.

Emily stayed silent and continued walking down the street to the park. Once there she found a bench and sat down. Rowena didn't sit. She simply stood there watching Emily. "Will you please try to calm down. Have a seat." She patted the bench.

Rowena paced back and forth in front of Emily a few times but finally decided to sit.

Emily looked at her and gently patted her hand. "I know you would very much like this woman to be the Druid goddess Epona. I wish I could tell you that it is so, but the truth is, even after Paul and I spent all that time with her this afternoon she is still a mystery. She did not tell us her last name, how she came to live in the woods, or even how she supports herself. She did tell us how she found you and left her pony with you. She may practice Druidism but she's just a real person. Besides, didn't you tell me you really don't believe in those gods and goddesses?"

Rowena stared at Emily then shifted her eyes to the ground. Emily leaned back on the bench looked up at the sky and listened to the crickets chirping. To her, the sounds they made were almost like music and she found it relaxing. She briefly glanced at Rowena then closed her eyes. She wished she could help the girl but she didn't know what more she could do. The Epona could very well be a Druid but she wasn't a goddess, a recluse maybe but not a goddess. Emily took a deep breath of the fresh damp air. It smelled so good she thought she could stay right where she was forever.

The quiet, relaxing interlude was eventually interrupted by the sound of shuffling footsteps entering the park. Emily sat up and looked around. It was Mr. O'Keeffe. Rowena spotted him about the same time as Emily and when she did she jumped off the bench and nearly ran into the nearest tree.

Emily calmly motioned for the man to come and sit beside her. "Good evening, Mr. O'Keeffe, how are you?"

"Oh, I'm fine," he answered warmly. "I am sorry if I frightened Rowena. I didn't' intend to." He glanced at Rowena and smiled politely.

Emily looked at Rowena standing next to the tree. She appeared to be shivering although it wasn't very cold. Emily figured she just must be scared or nervous. "Excuse me a moment," Emily said to Mr. O'Keeffe and she walked over to Rowena.

"Please come back and sit down. Mr. O'Keeffe isn't going to hurt you. He's a very nice old man." She gently touched Rowena's arm. "Come on."

Rowena looked hesitantly at Emily and nervously stuffed her hands into her jacket pockets.

"It's all right, honest," Emily encouraged her as she slowly led Rowena back to the bench. Emily sat down next to Mr. O'Keeffe and Rowena timidly sat next to Emily.

"That was some rain we had this afternoon," said O'Keeffe just to make some conversation.

"Yes, it was," replied Emily. "They had to stop work early at the dig because of it."

"I imagine this weather does interfere with the excavation, for sure," said O'Keeffe. "I think it's supposed to be better tomorrow and most of the weekend. That should help make progress easier."

"That'll be good. My folks and I will be going home on

Saturday but I know Mr. Flanagan and his team will welcome the dry weather."

"So, did ya find anything interestin' today?"

Emily shrugged her shoulder's and smiled. "We found a horse skeleton and its bridle. The bridle was decorated with a horse's head made of bronze. It was very pretty and unusual. I'm not sure what else they found because I was in the tent cleaning the bridle." She turned toward Rowena. "Did you find anything else before it rained?"

"N … no, we just uncovered the rest of the horse," answered Rowena apprehensively.

"Well, now I'm sure that was interestin' to find. Was there a warrior in this grave?" inquired O'Keeffe pleasantly.

Emily perked up quite a bit with his question. "As a matter-of-fact there was a warrior; a female warrior and you should see her shield and headdress. The shield has these beautiful bronze horse carvings and the headdress that fits on the helmet is so lovely. I can't wait to see what it looks like once it's all cleaned up."

Rowena turned sideways and looked a little perturbed at Emily. "Well, maybe if you and Paul would have stayed in the tent cleaning things instead of running around in the woods it would be cleaned by now."

Emily eyed Rowena and smirked. At last she was getting a reaction from her which was good.

"You went into the woods?" asked Mr. O'Keeffe.

Emily nervously looked at her feet then at Mr. O'Keeffe. "Yeah, I did but I didn't go alone. One of the guys helping at the dig went with me."

"So, what happened? Were ya there during the storm?"

"Yes, we were there during the storm. Lightning struck one of the trees, it fell and the guy I was with, Paul, was hurt a little. But Michael O'Flynn got Epona and we took Paul to her house and when he was feeling better Michael helped us find our way back to the dig and we went home."

O'Keeffe laughed hardily and slapped his knee. "O'Flynn, you say. Saints preserve us, little Michael O'Flynn. It's been ages since I've seen him. How's he doing?"

"He seems to be doing fine," answered Emily. "Apparently he likes to spend some time at the dig to see what they find."

"Oh aye that he would." Shamus O'Keeffe's bright blue eyes sparkled and he ran his thin boney hand down his firm jaw. "And you say Michael was with Epona."

"Yes, that's right," said Emily affirmatively.

"Tell me, does this Epona have sort of long strawberry-blonde hair and she's rather thin?"

"Yes. Do you know her?"

"She has a pretty white Connemara pony too, doesn't she?"

"That's what she said but we didn't see it. She said it was the one she left with Rowena the day we found her in the pasture."

"Well now, all of what you have told me about meeting Epona the other day and Rowena's encounter with her is making sense, so it is."

"So, you know who this lady is?" asked Emily hopefully.

"Aye, that I do. Her family owns a nice size farm in Donoughmore. She's had a good education but has always been a bit strange, if you can understand that. She's into meditation and herbal medicine, things like that. She's nice enough but she's rather shy, doesn't like to be around a lot of people. They make her nervous."

Emily gave Rowena a smug sideways glance as if to say, 'I told you so.' She changed her attention back to O'Keeffe. "So, how is it that you know this woman and her family?"

"Like I said, her family owns a fairly large farm and they raise racing horses. When I was much younger I liked to spend time at the racetrack. I got to know the O'Briens and their horses. They have a son, Alexander, who runs the farm now for his parents."

"So, does Epona live on her parents' farm?"

"Yes, they built her a cottage there in the Druid Forest and they provide for her. They understand her idiosyncrasies."

155

Emily rubbed the back of her neck thinking about the last few days. "You know, all of this makes perfect sense about everything that has happened to us. When I hurt my head she helped me feel better. She tried to help Rowena and when she couldn't she left her pony to keep her company until we found her. She helped Paul when he got hurt too." She clutched Rowena's hand and looked at her. "You see Rowena, there's nothing so mysterious about this lady after all."

Rowena still looked rather dubious as she watched Emily. "I suppose it does explain things. I just don't understand though why anyone would name their daughter Epona and why they call it the Druid Forest."

Mr. O'Keeffe smiled and chuckled softly to himself. "Darlin' that's like asking why someone would name their child Mary, or Peter or John or Patrick. Granted you're not going to find many people named Zeus, Thor, Aphrodite, Neptune or even Vulcan. But here in Ireland people do name their children after some of the Druid gods and goddesses. It's just what they do. As for the forest, their daughter named it."

"Besides, if they raise horses it might make sense to name their daughter after the horse goddess," Emily suggested brightly.

"That it might," said Mr. O'Keeffe. He looked thoughtfully at Emily as though he'd just remembered something important. "Now, I may be expectin' way too much but if I'm rememberin' correctly you said you were living in the States, correct?"

"Yes, that's right," answered Emily. "We live in Ohio."

"And what town might that be?"

Emily sort of smiled. "Kirksborough. We moved there in June. Remember? My dad teaches at the university."

O'Keeffe scratched his snowy hair under his cap for a minute. "I don't suppose you'd be knowin' a Mr. Fanin Murphy. He used to be on the school board, but he retired maybe fifteen or twenty years ago. Long before you moved there."

Emily shook her head. "The name doesn't sound familiar, but then I don't know many people. I know mostly teachers, newspaper people, some of my dad's students and the police. I'll be happy to look him up for you when I get home. Is he a friend?"

"He was married to my younger sister Brigid. They met during World War Two. She was an aide at one of the hospitals and he was a mechanic with the Eighth Army Air Corps." He looked at the ground, and fiddled with his walking stick before continuing. "It's kind of you to offer to look him up but I'm afraid you won't be able to do that. I just found out he passed away over the weekend and he's to be buried tomorrow next to Brigid."

"Oh, I'm so sorry," said Emily as she patted his hand in sympathy.

"How did you find out about his death?" asked Rowena as she joined the conversation. "You didn't see a banshee did you?"

Emily thought she noticed a bit of sarcasm in Rowena's voice and wanted to pinch her but she decided to ignore it.

Mr. O'Keeffe shook his head sadly then touched a pin in his coat lapel. It was shaped like a Medieval shield with a tree and a horse on it. "No, you only see banshees if it's a direct family member. Murphy was family by marriage only." He glanced sorrowfully at Emily and then at Rowena. "Fanin's son sent me an email this morning to let me know."

"You know what I could do?" Emily asked trying to sound cheerful. "I could go to the cemetery and take a picture of the grave for you when I get home. Then I could either mail you a copy or send it to you in an email."

O'Keeffe smiled slightly acknowledging her offer. "That would be very nice," he whispered. He found a piece of paper in his pocket and a pen and wrote both his home address and email address. "Thank you."

"Oh, you're very welcome," said Emily as she folded the paper and placed it in her jeans pocket. She looked at her watch and then at the sky. The moon was up and some of the stars were beginning to sparkle in the dark gray sky.

"It's getting late," observed Mr. O'Keeffe. "You young ladies should probably be gettin' home."

"Yes, you're right," agreed Emily. She stood up and subtly had Rowena do the same. "It's been ever so nice meeting you Mr. O'Keeffe. I've enjoyed the time we've been able to spend together." She unexpectedly gave him a hug and kissed his cheek. "You take care of yourself and I'll send you those pictures just as soon as I can. Good-bye."

"Good-bye dear, have a safe trip back to the States." He waved and watched them leave the park and head back to the Flanagans house before heading to his own home.

Rowena was silent the entire walk home. In a way Emily was grateful because she wasn't sure how she might have reacted if the girl had made a nasty comment.

Their parents had moved from the dining room to the living room while they had been gone. They were still discussing old times and more recent excavations when the girls entered the house.

"Hello, girls, how was your walk?" asked Mary Jo looking up from one of the photo albums.

Emily and Rowena entered the living room and sat down on separate chairs. "The walk was fine," said Rowena. "We just went down to the park. It was good to just sit and enjoy the evening."

Emily watched Rowena to see what else she would say or do. Shea wandered from behind the couch and jumped into Rowena's lap curling into a snuggly little ball. It only took a few seconds before he began to gently purr.

"So, Emily," said her mother, "we were wondering if you wanted to go to the dig tomorrow or if you'd rather go sightseeing, maybe visit Blarney Castle and do a little shopping at the Woolen Mills."

Emily quickly shifted her gaze from Rowena and her cat to her mother. "I'm sure the castle and the woolen mills are wonderful tourist sights but if it's all the same to everyone I'd rather go back to the dig. I'd like to help clean the headdress and see what else we might find. After all it'll be our last day here."

Martin leaned his head back against the sofa and slightly smiled to himself. He was fairly confident he knew his daughter would choose the dig over visiting the castle and he wasn't disappointed. "You know Anne, maybe you could visit the castle and the mills with Mary Jo. You can take some pictures and even buy a few things. Get something for Andy so he can see what he missed by not coming."

Anne squinted at her husband and sighed. "I suppose I could do that if you're sure you don't need me at the site."

"I think we can get along without you tomorrow."

"I would love to show you around," said Mary Jo.

"Well, I'd love to go Mary Jo. I've always wanted to see the castle and the Blarney Stone."

"All right, that's what we'll do. It'll be fun. The castle grounds are beautiful and the guides are nice and friendly. And wait until you see the Woolen Mills. You won't believe the things they have for sale there."

"What about you Rowena?" asked Pat. "Do you want to help at the dig or go with your mom and Anne?"

Rowena looked at her dad and shrugged her shoulders. "I don't know. I'll let you know in the morning."

"Okay." He glanced at the television sitting silent in the corner of the room. "Hey, you two feel free to turn on the telly and watch whatever you want."

"Thanks but I'm really not in the mood for TV," replied Emily. She pulled her phone and earbuds from her pocket and began watching a video.

Rowena let Shea down on the floor and stood up. "If you'll excuse me, I'm really kind of tired and think I'll just call it a day. G'night." Slowly she made her way to her bedroom with Shea following silently.

Emily watched her go. Things were definitely not going well between them and she just didn't know what to do. She wanted to be friends and thought they would be but now she just didn't know if that would happen. One thing was certain, she wasn't going to the bedroom until Rowena was asleep. She continue to watch the video for a few more minutes then decided to text Gwen. It was 7:30 in the evening here but only 2:30 back home.

She briefly watched her parents and the Flanagans then stood up. "I'm going out on the front porch for a little while." She put her jacket on and went outside. She sat down and sent Gwen a text. *Yt? Need to tlk asap.*

Emily stared up at the now inky black sky with its sparkling diamonds and moon brightening the night. This was a beautiful country but she was missing her friends in Kirksborough and was anxious to see them. Just then her phone began to jingle. It was Gwen. "Hi Gwen! How are you? Are you over at Ted's? Well what's that barking? Wait a minute let me put you on speaker. I'm outside and there's no one else around so it's okay." She pressed the speaker button and put the phone on the porch table. "Tell me again about the barking."

"I said it's Rascal. Gracie and I are dog sitting this afternoon. So what's going on? Find anything exciting?"

"Wait a minute. You're dog sitting. Whose dog?"

"Yours of course."

"We don't have a dog."

"Yes you do. I guess you haven't talked with your brother lately. Maybe it's supposed to be a surprise so don't tell your folks. He's a cute little guy. Let me send you his picture." Gwen quickly snapped a photo of Rascal and sent it to Emily.

As soon as she saw it she began to laugh. "Oh my goodness. He is one funny looking dog. Kinda reminds me of a furry Yoda. When did Andy get this little guy?"

"It's rather complicated and it would be better if you heard the story from him once you get home."

"So where's my brother that you and your sister need to dog sit? Is he out flying his drone or something?"

"Actually, he's at work."

160

"What? Andy, working. When did that happen and where's he working?"

"He's working at the county airport and today's his first day. Major Reese arranged it for him when Gracie and your brother were out there the other day."

"I can't believe this. My brother working at an airport of all places. I can't wait to see my parents reaction to all of this. It'll be interesting, that's for sure."

"So, how's the dig going?"

"Oh fine. We found a horse skeleton and a warrior."

"Cool. Hope you took lots of pictures. I can't wait until you get home and you can tell me all about it."

"Yeah, I can't wait to get home either. There's so much to tell you and for you to tell me too."

Rascal began barking rather loudly. "I'd like to talk more but Rascal needs to go outside. You take care and we'll see you this weekend."

"You take care too. See ya soon!" Emily put her phone into her pocket and continued to enjoy the spring evening thinking about tomorrow's dig and flying home on Saturday. Home. Well, things were going to be different there, that's for sure. *A dog, my brother got a dog. Sure hope he's friendly and he likes me,* she thought as she leaned back in the chair and closed her eyes trying to imagine what it will be like to actually have their own pet.

Chapter Fourteen

Andy pulled into the Taylor's driveway anxious to see Rascal and to let Gracie know about Mr. Murphy's son. He heard Rascal barking before he even got out of his car. Just as he reached for the doorbell Gracie opened the front door.

"Guess you don't need a doorbell with Rascal around," he told her cheerfully.

"That's for sure," she agreed letting him inside.

Andy reached down to scratch the dog behind his ears but Rascal turned his head around and licked his hand. Andy knelt down and gave the dog a hug. "I'm happy to see you too, boy." Rascal then decided to lick Andy's face. He laughed and sat back on his heels. "I hope he didn't give you any trouble."

"He was a perfect gentleman. We took a stroll over to the park. Ted and Jasper were there so the dogs played for a while. On the way back we met Mac and Archie out for their afternoon walk. You know how laidback that little old basset hound Archie is, well he got very excited when he met Rascal. I was surprised. Rascal just seems to get along with all the dogs in the area."

"Well, I'm glad for that. He did meet Jasper before and they had a good time at the park but he's never met Archie." Andy got off the floor and sat on their living room couch. "You aren't going to believe what happened at the airport this afternoon."

Gracie joined him and the dog followed her like a shadow. "I'm not good at guessing games so just tell me; what happened."

"Fanin Murphy's son arrived. He landed his jet on the runway. Can you imagine landing a jet at that airport? Anyway, he thanked us for finding his dad and said I can keep the dog. He seemed surprised to know his father even had a dog."

"Well, I guess it's good that you can keep the dog," said Gracie. "I did read in the newspaper that Mr. Murphy's funeral is to be tomorrow. I wonder if his daughter will be here. It's a long flight from Hawaii to Ohio."

"I don't know. He didn't mention his sister except that she wouldn't want the dog and neither would his daughter. I did sort of bump into his daughter when I left work. At least I assumed she was his daughter. She came to pick him up."

"The obituary did mention a granddaughter. She teaches at the grade school."

"Do you know her?"

"I know her," Gwen chimed in as she rolled her wheelchair into the living room. "She's Mrs. Maguire, Molly Maguire. She was my third grade teacher."

"Is she about five foot six with dark brown hair and wears glasses?" asked Andy curiously.

"Yep, that's her," said Gwen. "She was a good teacher."

Rascal was sitting at Andy's feet staring dramatically at him and ready to go home. Andy patted the dog's head. "Okay, I get it, boy, you want to go."

Gwen handed him Rascal's dishes, toys and dog treats that she had gathered before entering the living room. "Here you go. We'll see you tomorrow."

"Thank you Gwen. Don't know what I'd do without you and your sister."

Gracie just smiled and shook her head. "I'm sure you'd think of something." As soon as Andy had the dog's lead fastened she opened the door and walked them to his car. "See you tomorrow."

"Yes, tomorrow. Thanks again for helping me out."

"Sure, no problem." She watched him back out of her driveway and into his then she walked back inside to help her sister fix dinner.

Andy fed Rascal his dinner then went into the backyard to practice with his drone. He spent the next 20 minutes flying around obstacles, through some hoops and doing a few loops before the battery died. He gathered his drone and went inside to fix his supper.

As he heated his microwave dinner he glanced at the kitchen calendar. Just one more day of freedom and then his life would once again be invaded by parents and his little sister. He watched Rascal stretch out on the dining room rug and couldn't help but wonder what his life had been like with Mr. Murphy. Probably nice and quiet just like things were right now. Lucky dog.

Rascal casually watched Andy eat his supper and took a little snooze while the boy washed up the few dirty dishes. Andy dried the last dish, stashed it in the cupboard and headed for the family room. He turned to look at Rascal. "Hey, boy, let's go watch T.V."

Rascal raised his head slightly then got up and followed Andy. They spent the rest of the evening watching boring programs and trying to stay awake. By 10 o'clock Andy decided to call it a night. "Come along boy, let's go out so you can pee and we can go to bed." Rascal didn't need to be asked twice. It took him less than five minutes to take care of business and then he was racing up the stairs and curled up at the foot of Andy's bed. Soon both Rascal and Andy were sound asleep.

Chapter Fifteen

Emily rolled out of bed early Friday morning anxious to make the most of her last day in Ireland. She was looking forward to exploring the rest of the site and hoped she might be allowed to help clean the headdress Paul was cleaning yesterday. Quietly she gathered her clothes so she didn't wake Rowena and headed for the bathroom to dress.

The girl was asleep when Emily went to bed last night. If she wasn't asleep, thought Emily, she had done a good job of pretending, that's for sure. Once she was dressed she made her way to the kitchen for breakfast. Her parents and the Flanagans were already up and Mary Jo was fixing pancakes and bacon. There was a rich aroma of freshly brewed coffee mixed with the bacon.

"Good morning," Emily happily greeted everyone and sat at the table. "Everything sure smells good."

"I'm glad for that," said Mary Jo. "Everything should be ready in a minute."

"Would you like milk or orange juice?" asked Anne as she took a glass from the cupboard.

"Milk will be fine Mom, thank you."

Pat stirred the cream in his coffee and glanced at Emily. "So, young lady, is there anything special you'd like to do at the site today?"

Emily looked at him and smiled brightly. "I'd like to see some more of the other things your team has uncovered if I may and I'd like to help clean that warrior headdress we found."

Pat leaned back slightly in his chair pretending to contemplate her request. "Well, I think we might be able to arrange that. What do you think Marty?"

Martin glanced at his daughter then gave his friend a solemn look. He rubbed his jaw. "Well, I don't know. After yesterday I don't think she should be left on her own. I think someone responsible should be with her."

Pat somberly nodded his head in agreement. "That's probably a good idea. We don't want her wandering off somewhere. Do you have anyone in mind?"

"Well, I was thinking maybe Riley or Ben or even Vince. They all seem to be very responsible men. Definitely not Paul. You saw how much trouble they got themselves into yesterday."

"True, true. We can't be havin' that, that's for sure."

Emily sat quietly watching the men trying to decide if they meant what they were saying or if they were just teasing her. She tried to get a clue from her mother when she set the glass of milk in front of her but her face revealed nothing. Finally she saw a mischievous glint in her father's eyes and knew what they were up to.

She took a small sip of milk and put her hands in her lap. "You know, you are absolutely right. I shouldn't be wandering around the dig on my own. I mean who knows what might happen to me. Someone should be with me and it definitely shouldn't be Paul. I think Vince would be a good person. He's been supervising some of the other parts of the dig and I'm sure he knows exactly what's been found and where." She lowered her head and smirked before raising it again to look innocently at her father and Pat. She coyly blinked her eyes, tilted her head slightly and smiled ever so faintly.

The men looked at her and began to laugh loudly and Emily joined them.

Mary Jo placed the bacon and pancakes on the table. "What is so funny?" She had been so engrossed in preparing the food that she hadn't been paying attention to the conversation.

Anne turned to Mary Jo stifling a chuckle. "The guys were trying to play a joke on Emily but she caught them."

"Well, good for you," said Mary Jo. "Now dig into the food before it gets cold." She turned toward Emily. "Is Rowena still asleep?"

"Yes, Ma'am. At least she was when I left the room."

"Wonder if I should wake her or let her sleep?"

Pat swallowed a forkful of pancake and took a sip of his coffee. "Let her sleep. She's had a busy week. So just let her rest."

Everyone was nearly finished eating when Rowena showed up in the kitchen doorway dressed in jeans and a work shirt. "Good morning." She moved into the kitchen, poured herself a cup of coffee and leaned against the kitchen counter watching everyone.

"Good morning Rowena," said Emily warmly. "Come join us. There's still pancakes and bacon left."

"Yes, join us," said her father. "We figured you were tired so we were letting you sleep."

Rowena took a plate from the cupboard, some silverware from the drawer and joined the others at the table. The only chair left was the one next to Emily. She put her cup on the table, sat down and helped herself to breakfast.

"So, have you decided if you're coming to Blarney Castle or are you going to the dig?" her mother asked.

She sighed and observed the demeanor of those at the table. Everyone seemed rather neutral. "I've decided to go to the dig. There are a few things I'd like to continue working on."

"Fine," said her father. "Well, eat up then so we can get going. The rainy weather has put us behind a bit."

While she finished eating, her mother and Anne cleared the dirty dishes from the table and loaded the dishwasher. Emily watched Shea sneak into the kitchen, get a drink of water and then sit near the cabinet where his food was stored. Anne noticed the cat, got his food from the counter and filled his dish.

"There you go kitty," she told the cat as she placed the dish near him on the floor. Shea quickly devoured the food.

Once the dish was empty Emily watched the cat race to the basement and its litter box. She shook her head and smiled then got up from the table to help clean things up.

Martin and Pat continued to sit at the table as Rowena finished her breakfast. "I think we've made fairly decent progress on the area we've been excavating," noted Martin.

"Oh, for sure," agreed Pat. "I just wish you'd be able to stay longer. Finding the female warrior and her horse were something I never expected to find. Your being here has definitely brought us good luck."

"You would have found it even if I hadn't been here and you know that."

"Maybe, but it would have taken us much longer to get to that spot. I only went there because you were here and I wanted to dig someplace new with you." He watched his daughter as she finish eating and took her empty dishes to the sink. "Maybe you can come back this summer."

Martin sadly shook his head. "Wish I could but I'm already committed to taking my students to Arizona."

"You could bring them here instead."

"That would require them to get passports and I'm not sure everyone would be able to do that in time. Staying in the States makes it more affordable for them and the university."

Pat slowly nodded his head. "Yeah, you're right. Still it would be great if *you could* come back."

Martin chuckled. "Tell you what, I'll think about it and see what I can do. Of course you could always come to the States and help us this summer you know."

"Right!" Pat glanced at the wall clock. "It's twenty to eight. We need to get going. Come along girls, get in the car. We're taking Martin's car today so the ladies can have the other one."

In no time at all they were pulling into the parking area at the dig. It wasn't quite 8 o'clock so not many cars had arrived yet which suited Pat and Martin just fine.

Vince Walker was busy at one of the trenches near what had been determined to be someone's hut. "Hi Vince, how's it going this morning?" asked Pat as they approached the top of the trench.

"Hi Boss, I'm just sortin' through some things we found before the rains came yesterday."

Emily studied the man who she thought might be in his mid-30s. He wasn't as tall as her dad who was six foot. She figured this guy was maybe five foot seven. He wasn't too bad looking in spite of his two-day old beard and super short hair. His haircut reminded her of some of the military guys she'd seen from the Air Force base, that's how short it was.

"Have you found anything interesting?" asked Martin as he stared into the trench.

"Just some cooking pots and utensils and this figurine. It's a horse." He showed them a small statue carved in stone. "We also found some tools made from chert and a couple of baskets."

"Have you found any more skeletons?" asked Emily, curious to know how many other people were buried here besides the warrior they had found and the few skeletons in the grave site.

"As a matter of fact we've found some pig, goat and even chicken bones over there where we think they did their cooking."

Emily frowned and twisted her mouth into a pucker. "I meant human skeletons."

Vince's hazel eyes twinkled mischievously. "Aye, that we have darlin' but they're over in the burial hill there." He pointed to a mound over toward his right. "We've found just one more since the ones I showed you at the beginning of the week. Of course what we've found doesn't begin to compare with that female warrior you've found with her horse. That's some discovery for sure."

"Yes, it was," agreed Pat happily. "It's the first we've found here, thanks to the good luck Martin brought us."

Martin just shook his head drearily. "Like I told you, I am not responsible for you finding that skeleton and horse. You would have found it eventually."

"Ah, yes, but it's because of you that we found it when we did," said Pat amusingly.

As the guys continued their silly conversation Emily's eyes roamed over to the site they had been working all week. At first she thought the woman she saw might be Bridin but then she noticed there was a white pony standing there and the woman looked like she was wearing some kind of long dress or coat with a hood.

Emily bumped Rowena with her elbow and nodded in the direction of the woman and pony. Rowena's dark brown eyes nearly popped out of their sockets and the color drained from her face so fast that her freckles looked like someone had sprinkled cinnamon on a marshmallow. Emily nodded again, grabbed Rowena's hand and began to briskly jog toward the site. The men were so engrossed in their discussion they didn't even notice them leave.

The woman's back was turned toward them and she was so focused on what she was doing she didn't hear them approach the area. The pony, however, had been watching their every move and when the girls were a few meters away the pony began to scratch the ground and whinny.

The woman scampered out of the trench, jumped on the pony and raced for the woods. Emily started to run after them but Rowena wrapped her arm around Emily's waist and stopped her.

"Let go of me!" shouted Emily struggling to get free. "They're getting away!"

Rowena clutched Emily's arm and turned the girl around to face her. "Let them go," said Rowena quietly.

"But she took something from the grave. Didn't you see that?" Emily stated vigorously.

"I saw her leave but I didn't see her take anything."

"Well, she did and we need to get it back!"

Rowena glared at her. "How can you get something back when you don't even know what she took? You don't even know who she is!"

"Of course I know who she is and so do you. It's kind, sweet, crazy, Epona and her charming Connemara pony," uttered Emily scowling at Rowena.

"You don't know that for sure," retorted Rowena.

Emily walked to the edge of the trench. "Look at these footprints. These were made by Epona. She wears a pair of boots that make this same footprint."

Rowena stared at the indentations and frowned. "It just looks like footprints to me."

"Well, they aren't. She wears these square toed boots and the heal of one of them has a small groove in it, just like this." Emily pointed to the left footprint. "She also had the same long strawberry-blonde hair. And did you see how she moved? She moved like a ballet dancer and she's skinny just like Epona."

"You're nuts!" snapped Rowena.

It was during this dramatic discussion that Martin and Pat showed up. "Just what are you two arguing about?" demanded Pat glaring angerly at his daughter.

"Nothing," muttered Rowena lowering her head and staring at the ground.

"You know that's not true," said her father as he grasped her upper arm. "Now, I'll ask you again. What were you two arguing about?"

Rowena raised her head and stared irritatingly into her father's flashing brown eyes. "There was someone, a woman, in the trench here when we arrived. We didn't see who she was before she got on her pony and rode into the woods. Emily thought it was Epona and that she took something from the trench. Emily tried to go after the woman but I stopped her."

Pat stared at Rowena and took a deep frustrated breath.

Martin walked over to Emily who was standing at the edge of the trench. "Is this true?" he asked her.

Emily solemnly nodded her head. "Yes. I don't know what was found in there that didn't get removed to the cleaning tent. Maybe she was there digging on her own and found something. I just know she took something. It couldn't have been very big or heavy because she was able to jump on the pony and ride away."

"You're sure it was Epona?" he asked.

"It looked like her. The footprints look like those made by her boots and the pony looked like the one we found in the field the other day when we found Rowena."

"Okay," said Martin rationally. He turned toward Pat. "Well, what do you want to do? Do you want to find this woman and see what she took or do you just want to forget about it?"

Pat stuffed his fists in his jeans pockets and paced back and forth beside the trench. "I'd like to recover whatever she took," he said at last. "But after everything that's happened I'm very hesitant about sending anyone into those woods."

Cautiously Emily walked over to him. "Mr. Flanagan, I think I understand your concern. Our meetings with Epona have been a little strange, to say the least. But I don't think she means harm to anyone. She's just unusual. Anyway, I'm willing to find her and see what she took and get it back." She glanced at her father hoping he would agree to let her go. She noticed he didn't look very receptive to the idea.

Pat gave Martin a very dubious glance then focused his attention back to Emily. "I appreciate your offer but I can't allow you to go out there alone even if your father agrees."

Martin stared at both Pat and his daughter. "I'm willing to let Emily go looking for Epona but I will not allow her to go on her own. One of us must go with her." He looked at Emily to make sure she understood.

"I don't know what you guys are making such a fuss about," said a frustrated Emily. "I think I can find my way there and back. If I get lost I can use my compass to get back."

"No," said her father. "Someone must go with you."

As they were debating the issue Riley showed up to begin work on the trench. "Someone must go with who, where?" he asked with some interest.

Martin shook his head in frustration. "With Emily into the woods to find Epona and whatever she took from the dig."

Riley stroked his honey-brown moustache in thought and his light blue eyes lit up his rugged tan face. "Are we talking about the weird chick that lives in the forest there?" he asked pointing toward the woods.

"Do you know her?" asked a surprised Martin.

"Nah, I've never met her, just heard about her from some people down at the pub and places." He methodically rubbed his chin then hooked his thumbs through his beltloops. "Her family owns a farm nearby and they raise horses, race horses."

"That's what Mr. O'Keeffe said too," added Emily enthusiastically.

Martin looked at Emily with concern. "Who's this Mr. O'Keeffe?"

Emily smiled. "Just a guy I met in the park near the Flanagans. He's a nice old man. His sister and her husband lived in Kirksborough."

"Where do they live now?" asked Martin skeptically.

Emily gave him a very somber stare. "In the cemetery. They're dead."

Martin took a step backward surprised at her answer. "I presume you got this information from this Mr. O'Keeffe."

"That's right, last evening when Rowena and I were in the park. His brother-in-law's funeral is today."

Riley watched this interaction between father and daughter with curiosity before loudly clearing his throat to get their attention. "Well, now that we've established who this woman is and where we might find her, what exactly did she take from the dig?"

"We don't know what she took," said Pat joining the group. "Emily and Rowena just saw her leave the site when they arrived."

"She got on her pony and rode into the woods," added Rowena impassively.

Riley nodded his head in understanding. "Got it. So you just want to get whatever she took back."

"Right," said Emily. "I offered to go but my dad and Mr. Flanagan don't want me to go alone."

"I see," said Riley earnestly. "Well, how would it be if I went with you?"

Emily looked pleadingly at her father. "Would that be all right Dad? Please."

Martin skeptically observed his daughter and Riley. He knew from past experience she wasn't going to let this go. If he said no she would find a way to do it anyway. "Okay, you and Riley can go but if you aren't back in an hour the entire team will be combing those woods for you and you will spend the rest of the day sitting on the edge of this trench and you will not leave my sight. Understand?"

"Yes, sir," said Emily with a smile. She glanced at Riley. "Shall we go?"

"At your service Ma'am," said Riley with a deep bow.

Before anyone could utter another sound the two were off into the woods.

Emily went to the area she saw Epona enter the woods and began looking for the pony tracks. She motioned to Riley. "This way. See the tracks made by the pony?"

"Clever girl. Do you think she'll be goin' back to her house?"

Emily looked at him with a smile in her eyes. "That's where I'd go unless I had some secret place to hide."

Riley put his hands on his hips and studied the hoof prints. "Do you think she might have such a place?"

Emily looked at him and shrugged her shoulders. "I haven't any idea. Her house is pretty secluded as it is so I don't think she'd really need some secret hideout. But she is a strange person so anything is possible."

"Right," agreed Riley with a grin. "Well, let's follow the trail my all-knowing scout!"

"Okay, the trail goes over there!" Emily cautiously studied the ground following the prints left by the pony until they were deep into the woods. There were more dead leaves and vegetation on the ground which made tracking the pony more difficult. Suddenly she stopped and looked around.

"What's the matter?" asked Riley looking around the gloomy uninhabited area.

"I can't find anymore hoof tracks." She gave him a worried look. "I'm sure there must be more around but I just can't see them because of all these dead leaves and stuff." She noticed a spot where the leaves appeared to be more trampled than the others. She knelt down and brushed the leaves away. "I found a shoe print," she told him. "Come see. It belongs to Epona. She must have gotten off her pony here but where did she go and what happened to the pony." Emily continued to scout the area while Riley studied the print and took a picture of it with his phone.

A few yards away Emily noticed a fairly large tree that had fallen. "I wonder…" she remarked with curiosity as she made her way toward it.

"You wonder what?" asked Riley following her.

She gave him a surprised and astonished look. "It's the tree that fell when Paul and I were here yesterday. You know, when that storm came through. Lightening hit this tree, it fell and Paul got hurt. I can find her house from here. Come on!" She began racing through the woods.

When they got to within 500 yards of Epona's house Emily stopped. She knelt down on the ground and Riley joined her. "Well, now what?" he asked with uncertainty.

"I'm trying to see if she's home," Emily told him. "I don't see any lights on and there's no fire going. Everything sounds super quiet. It's almost too quiet."

"Maybe she took the pony out to pasture," suggested Riley.

Emily slightly nodded her head. "Yes, that's possible." She was about to say something more when they heard someone in the distance softly singing. Emily and Riley stared at each other in amazement. Soon they witnessed Epona enter the garden in the front of her home. She was dancing and singing and in her hands she held a small statue. But they were too far away to have a close look at it. Emily gave Riley a questioning look and he gave it right back to her. They watched her pick a few herbs from her garden and then go into her house.

"Do you want to go talk to her or do you want to get your dad and Pat and bring 'em here?" whispered Riley still with a shocked look on his face.

Emily shifted her mouth from side to side in thought. She knew she should probably go get her father but at the same time she didn't want to leave Epona unsupervised. She didn't know what to do. While she was trying to make up her mind a visitor arrived at Epona's door.

Riley watched as the man knocked loudly on the door and shouted, "Open up Epi it's me!" Riley ran his hand over his light-brown hair and blinked his pale blue eyes in disbelief. "What in the world is little Michael O'Flynn doin' here?"

"It looks to me like he's making a social call. He and Epona are friends," explained Emily. "You didn't know that?"

"No, I did not."

"He helped get Paul to her house yesterday."

"Well, this could be trouble," said Riley glumly.

"How so?"

"O'Flynn likes to spend quite a lot of time around archaeology digs."

"So I've heard," said Emily unemotionally.

"Yeah, well he's been known to walk off with bits and pieces now and then, if you get my meaning."

Emily slowly nodded her head. "We've had people at every dig we've done try to steal things. It's just something people do so I'm not surprised."

"Yes, well he could be part of this. He could've had her find whatever it is she's got. Then again she may have done this on her own. If that's the case and he sees it he's going to want a piece of the profits when she sells it."

"You think she'll sell the statue?"

"Isn't that what most thieves do, sell what they steal?"

"Yeah, they do, but sometimes they keep it. Well, we need to get it back. Everything we've found needs to be in a museum, not in someone's illegal collection."

"I agree. So, shall we go get it?"

"Absolutely. Let's go." Emily stood up and walked purposefully to the cottage with Riley right beside her. She loudly rapped her fist on the door and waited for a response. There was none. She pounded again and called out, "Epona, please open up, this is Emily Parker. I need to talk to you." There was still no answer. Emily looked determinedly at Riley. "We know they're in there. Why aren't they answering?"

Riley peeked inside the window near the door. The room appeared to be empty. "I don't see anyone," he whispered. Slowly he turned the doorknob. The door wasn't locked. Cautiously he slightly opened the door just a crack. There was no response so he opened it a little wider. Finally he opened it all the way and stepped inside.

"Should we be here?" whispered Emily nervously as she quickly scanned the room. "Where'd they go?"

"Have no idea," Riley replied. He carefully surveyed the area and noticed a small area rug was rumpled. When he walked over to straighten it he saw that it was slightly covering a door in the dirt floor. "That's strange," he said and pointed out the door to Emily.

"Do you suppose they went underground?" she asked.

"Well, that would be my logical conclusion," he stated.

"Should we just stay here and wait for them to come up?"

Riley looked at his watch. "Your father gave you one hour to find her and get back, remember? By my watch we have only twenty minutes to return before he sends everyone into the woods to locate you. As much as I would like to wait here for their return I don't think it would be the prudent thing to do. Do you?"

Emily sighed reluctantly and pouted. "No, it wouldn't."

"Then let's go. We can go back to the dig and tell them what we found and where. Then we can let Pat and your father decide what to do. All right?"

Emily unenthusiastically nodded her head. "Yeah, all right." Very quietly they left the cottage and headed back to the site.

When Emily and Riley left the woods and entered the dig site Emily's father was organizing teams so they could begin the search of the forest.

She ran up to him from behind and vigorously wrapped her arms around his waist. "Hi Dad! Did you miss me?"

To say Martin was unprepared for this sudden encounter would be an understatement. He was shocked and nearly lost his balance with her impulsive embrace. He grasped her arms, disengaged himself and turned around to face her. "I'm glad to see you made it back in time."

"And with an entire two minutes to spare," she said.

Martin took a quick glance at his daughter then fixed his attention on Riley who was standing several feet away. "Well, did you find this woman?" he inquired with authority.

Riley moved closer to Martin and Emily before answering. "Yes, sir, we did. She has a statue. Whether it's a statue from here or not we can't be certain because we only saw it from a distance. She took it into her home. We attempted to make contact with her but couldn't."

Martin appeared a bit frustrated. "What do you mean you couldn't contact her? Didn't you go to her house?"

"Yes, Dad we did, right after she let Michael O'Flynn inside. We knocked on the door but no one answered. We even went inside but no one was there. It was like they'd just disappeared. There wasn't a trace of them to be found. So we decided to come back and tell you and let you and Pat decide what to do."

"We can guide you back to the cottage," Riley stated helpfully. "We thought about waitin' around for them to return but we were running out of time and we didn't want you to be worrin' none. You understand."

Martin ran his long tan fingers over his short dark brown hair in exasperation. "Yes, I understand." He turned around and looked at the people gathered around the field near the trench he had been excavating and wearily shook his head. "I'm sorry. It appears we won't be needing your help after all. Thank you. Please go back to your work."

As the workers dispersed Pat joined Martin. "Well, are we goin' after this statue or not?"

"Of course we're going after the statue," replied Martin. "The question is where do we go?"

Riley hesitantly stepped forward. "If I might offer a suggestion. We think there's a trap door in the cottage and that might be where they went. We're not one hundred percent sure you understand but it's a good possibility."

"Fine, it's a start. Please, show us the way," said Pat.

By the time they reached Epona's home it was late morning. Everything appeared to be calm and quiet except for the faint sound of music coming from inside. Emily, Riley, Pat and Martin discreetly approached the door. Pat gently rapped on it and patiently waited for a response. They could definitely hear movement coming from inside and the music was silenced. Eventually Epona cautiously opened the door and looked outside.

"Wh ... who are you?" she stammered, stunned to see so many people gathered in her garden.

Emily made her way through the men to the front of the group. "Hello Miss Epona. We're sorry to disturb you but we need your help."

"My help? With what?" Emily definitely thought the woman looked not only perplexed but frightened.

"We've lost something and we thought perhaps you might be able to help us find it," said Emily smoothly and offered her a small smile. "May we come in please?"

Epona guardedly scrutinized the men standing on her doorstep. "I don't know."

"There's nothing to be frightened of," Emily assured her. "This is my father, Martin; his good friend Pat; and our friend Riley."

Epona opened the door a little wider and after more thought let the group inside. She did not offer them a seat but stood there in the small entrance way. "Now, what is it that you've lost exactly?"

"We're archaeologists and we're excavating a site on the other side of the woods," stated Pat. "We know how kind you were this week helping Emily here when she fell and my daughter Rowena when she became lost earlier this week and then yesterday one of our students, Paul. Anyway, it seems a small statue that was in one of our trenches was taken this morning. It's rather important that we find it because everything we find will go to a museum here in Donoughmore.

"Well, if I see your little statue I'll let you know," stated Epona tersely.

Emily carefully stepped in front of the woman, touched her hand and looked sadly into her face. "Miss Epona, I know you have the statue. I saw you take it from the warrior's grave early this morning when you rode off on your pony. Later Riley and I saw you with it here in your garden right before Mr. O'Flynn arrived."

Epona ripped her hand away from Emily and stumbled backwards. Her emerald eyes sparkled like they were on fire. "How dare you spy on me after all I've done for you!"

"Maybe you shouldn't go around robbing graves," advised Emily contemptuously. "So what have you done with it? Did you give it to O'Flynn? Is he going to sell it for you or something?" Emily was very agitated and losing her composure. She wanted to wallop this woman but knew that wouldn't be a good idea. Still she clenched and unclenched her fist several times.

Martin stepped over to his daughter and laid his hand firmly on her shoulder. "That's enough young lady. Calm down."

Emily looked up at her father and tears began to run down her cheeks. She gulped nervously then turned, wrapped her arms around him and gave him a hug. "I'm sorry Daddy, I'm sorry," she sobbed.

Martin stroked her short curly hair and hugged her. "There, there, sweetheart, everything's going to be okay. You just need to practice controlling your temper." He lifted her chin and kissed her forehead.

Epona timidly stepped farther back into the room as she watched everything unfold.

"Miss O'Brien," said Riley stepping beside Martin and Emily. "We mean you no harm, truly we don't. We just want our statue back. That's all. You give it to us and we'll be leavin' you alone. We won't bother you anymore."

"Wh … why did you call me O'Brien" she stammered.

Riley smiled coyly. "Because that's your name. Epona Elizabeth O'Brien. Your family owns a horse farm here. These woods, the Druid Forest, are part of their property."

She stared at him with a startled expression. "No, you're wrong. I'm Druid goddess Epona! I protect horses and heal people. And that statue is mine!"

Now it was Martin's and Pat's turn to be shocked. They gawked at Epona then at Riley. Pat shook his head in confusion. "Excuse me but I'm a wee bit confused. Riley, you say this is the O'Briens' daughter. The O'Briens who raise the race horses and the Connemara ponies."

"Yes, sir, the very same."

"That's what Mr. O'Keeffe said too," piped in Emily.

"And just what would old Mr. O'Keeffe be knowing about the O'Briens?"

"Well, he said he used to spend a lot of time at the racetrack when he was younger and that's where he got to know them. He said they built this cottage for Epona and now that they are getting older their son Alexander is running the farm," stated Emily helpfully.

Pat looked at her and quietly rubbed the side of his face. "You certainly have managed to learn a lot these past few days darlin' that's for sure."

He turned his attention to Riley. "And Mr. Riley Morgan, how is it that you happen to be knowin' so much about this woman? You said you just knew about her from what you heard at the pubs."

Riley looked shyly at the ground before looking back at Pat. "Well, you see, my Uncle Sean, works at different racetracks. Anyway, when I was a kid my dad and me would visit him at the Cork Racecourse, you know near Mallow, and I got to meet some of the horse owners, trainers and jockeys and such. That's where I met the O'Briens. They're real nice."

"And what, if I may ask, does your uncle do at the race-track?" asked Pat with interest.

"He's a trainer. Not for the O'Briens, for another guy. He's trained quite a few winners," said Riley smiling.

Pat turned his attention to Epona. "Well, my dear, it seems you are not a Druid goddess, as much as you would like to be. So, let's stop playing games and just give us the statue."

Riley and Emily watched as she quickly flicked her gaze toward the covered trap door and then back toward them. "I don't have your statue," she stated insistently. "Look for yourselves if you don't believe me."

Emily gave Riley a conspiratorial nod. "I don't believe we will find it in here," he said smiling slyly and moving toward the small area rug near the sitting area. He kicked the rug to reveal the trapdoor. "But we may find it down here!"

Epona collapsed onto the floor. "How … how did you know?"

Riley opened the door and looked to Pat and Martin. "Would either of you care to have a look?" he asked gesturing toward the opening.

Emily slid over to Epona and knelt on the floor beside her. "Sorry Epona, it was just a guess." She took a pillow from a nearby chair and placed it under Epona's head. "We saw the door earlier when we were here. We tried to get you to answer your front door when Mr. O'Flynn was visiting with you and when we didn't see either of you we saw the trapdoor and figured that you must be down there."

Epona blinked. "How could you do this to me?"

"How could you do what you did to Ireland?" Emily asked calmly. "Don't you understand? Whatever is found at the excavation site belongs to Ireland. It doesn't belong to Mr. Flanagan or anyone working on the dig. It belongs to everyone in Ireland. It's part of the country's history. That makes everything that is found important."

Epona quietly looked at Emily and slowly sat up. She smoothed her dress around her legs and stood up as she watched all the men in the room closely. She sighed reluctantly. "Okay. The statue's down there, go get it."

"Thank you Miss O'Brien," said Pat, happy to have an end to the ordeal.

Martin pulled a small penlight from his pocket and handed it to his friend. "It looks awfully dark down there. You may need some light."

"Thanks, I could always count on you to always have whatever kind of tool we needed." He turned on the thin flashlight and descended the stone steps into the underground chamber. He returned a few moments later with the stone statue.

He held it up for everyone to see. "Well, what do you think?" he asked them.

"I think it's beautiful!" exclaimed Emily stepping closer to get a better look. "It's very similar to the other one you found but this one is prettier. Just look at the details on the carving. The horse is so sweet and look at the face of the woman riding it and her clothes." She looked inquisitively at her father. "Do you think this statue is supposed to be the woman warrior we found in the grave? I know it doesn't have the headdress or the helmet but do you think it could represent that woman?"

Martin studied the statue and shrugged his shoulders. "It's difficult to say. It could be or it could be the goddess Epona put there to help guide the warrior to the other side."

Emily's face brightened. "I didn't think of that. I remember the Celts did believe in an afterlife and there were gods and goddesses that were supposed to help them get there." She glanced at her father and smiled. "That makes perfect sense."

Riley closed the trapdoor and replaced the area rug over it. He walked over to Epona. "I am very sorry, Miss O'Brien, for all the trouble we've caused you today. I hope you can forgive us, eventually. And I just want to say it was very nice to finally meet you." He moved toward the door ready to leave.

Pat noticed this and looked at his watch. "Thank you for your time miss but we need to get back to work."

"Yes, yes we do," said Martin heading for the door along with Pat and Emily. "It's been a pleasure making your acquaintance. Thank you also for helping my daughter the other day when she fell. That was very kind of you."

"You're very welcome for my help. You have a fine young lady there, take good care of her," said Epona. "I look forward to seeing that statue in a museum, so I am."

"We'll let you know when that happens, I promise," said Pat. "Come along now. We need to get back. You know how lazy those people can be if someone isn't there all the time to keep an eye on them."

The little group eagerly left and shut the door behind them. "Well, I'm glad that's all taken care of," Martin said with a sigh of relief. "She is one strange woman, that's for sure."

"Well, what do expect when your parents name you after a Druid goddess," Emily said with a laugh and ran ahead through the woods to the excavation site.

After lunch Emily spent the afternoon in the cleaning tent with Rowena and Ben Nolan. Paul had been reassigned to another area digging up village dwellings.

"I see you've been given the pleasure of cleaning the statue we retrieved," noted Emily kindly as she entered the tent and watched Rowena.

Rowena smiled plainly and gazed at Emily. "I understand there was a bit of a problem getting it back."

"Oh just a little. I'm sure you, your dad and Riley would have been able to do it without my dad and me."

"I suppose so," said Rowena as she continued cleaning the dirt from the stone.

Emily strolled over to Ben who was cleaning bits and pieces of jewelry that had been found on the skeleton. "Nice job," she told him.

"Thanks," he said. "It always amazes me at some of the things we find at these places. I look at this jewelry and wonder how they even came up with the idea in the first place let alone where they found the metal and how did they make it." He rubbed the back of his gloved hand over his scrawny brown beard and smiled at her.

Emily cocked her head to one side and smiled back. "It is amazing that's for sure. They were definitely talented people." She saw the helmet's headdress laying on a far table, untouched since yesterday. "Is anyone taking care of this?" she asked pointing at the item.

"It's all yours if you want it," said Rowena. "With all that fine frilly work all over it that will be a right tedious job to clean, it will. You're welcome to it."

Emily picked up a pair of gloves, along with the cleaning supplies then walked to the table. She carefully began the delicate task of gently cleaning all the frail little circles and lines that held the headdress together. She knew she would not get it finished today but she didn't mind. This was a project that would take days, maybe weeks to complete. Someone else would get to finish it. But for some reason, today, this seemed like the perfect task for her.

Chapter Sixteen

It was nearly 8 o'clock when Andy woke Friday morning. He glanced at his alarm clock and jumped out of bed startling Rascal. "Sorry, boy, I forgot to turn on the alarm last night and I've overslept." He rushed to take his shower and dress. Meanwhile Rascal just sat on the bed cocking his head from one side to the other like he was trying to understand what all the excitement was about.

Finally Andy headed out his bedroom door and Rascal ran after him. He gathered his phone, the dog's food, treats and bowls then headed out the backdoor. He jumped in the car and the dog scooted into the backseat. It wasn't until he was nearly at the airport that Andy looked in his rearview mirror and noticed Rascal sitting behind the passenger seat looking out the window.

Andy slapped the palm of his hand against his forehead. "Stupid! Stupid! Stupid! Now what are you going to do? How could you forget to take the dog to Gracie's?" He pulled into the airport parking lot and turned the car engine off. Rascal promptly jumped up front into the passenger seat, breathing heavily and looking at Andy. He stretched his head toward Andy and licked his face.

Andy laughed and gave the dog a hug. "Well, I can't leave you in the car so you're going to have to come with me. I don't know how much trouble I'm going to be in and if I can take time to take you back home. Maybe Gracie can come here and pick you up." He took Rascal's lead from the bag and put it on him then gathered the bag with all the dogs things before heading for the office building.

Mr. Kelley was standing in the lobby talking with Angie Phillips when Andy entered. "Good morning Mr. Kelley and Mrs. Phillips. Sorry I'm a little late. You know how traffic can be this time of the morning." He quickly guided Rascal beside him to the desk hoping they were too busy talking to notice. He signaled Rascal to lay down under the desk and placed the dog's bag on the floor on the other side.

Andy began going through the papers on the desk to get things organized and to look busy. Kelley slowly strolled toward Andy and stood pleasantly at the corner of the desk. He looked at Andy half smiling. "So, who's your little friend?" He tilted his head to glance at the dog.

Andy swallowed nervously. "Ah, that's Rascal. He's Mr. Murphy's dog … I mean he was Mr. Murphy's dog before he died, now he's mine. I'm sorry about bringing him here but I didn't have time to take him to the dog sitter."

"I see," said Kelley leaning closer to get a better look at the dog.

"I am going to call the dog sitter and see if she can come and get him. He's really very nice. Likes everyone and won't cause any trouble. I promise." Andy fumbled in his pants pocket for his phone.

Kelley put his hand on Andy's shoulder. "It's all right. The dog can stay here today. He looks like he's a friendly guy. He didn't bark or try to attack me. Just keep his leash on him to play it safe. Get him his food and water and whatever else he needs. There's an old blanket in my office closet. I'll get it for you, that way he won't need to lay on the cold linoleum floor."

While Kelley went to fetch the blanket Andy began to call Gracie, then he noticed Mrs. Phillips was still in the lobby. "May I help you with anything Mrs. Phillips?"

She looked at him and slightly shook her head. "No, I just need to talk with Dale about this summer's ground school class and some of my students."

"Oh, all right." Andy stroked Rascal's back then filled his dish with his breakfast food. "You eat and I'll get you some water." He walked to the nearby water fountain, filled the bowl half way then placed it beside the desk by the time Kelley returned.

Kelley placed the blanket on the floor between the desk and the wall. "He should be comfortable on that," he told Andy as he watched the dog finish his breakfast. "When he needs to go out there's plenty of places for him to relieve himself. Just make sure you clean up after him if he needs to take a dump. You'll find some plastic bags in the bottom desk drawer. You can throw them in the trashcans outside."

"Thank you, sir. I appreciate this," said Andy still a little nervously.

"Glad to help. I've always liked dogs. Having them around here once in a while is all right. We just don't want to make it a habit."

"Yes, sir. Once my folks get back this won't be a problem. Someone will always be there to look after him."

"That's fine." Kelley turned his attention back to Angie who had been patiently waiting for him to conclude his business with Andy and the dog. "How about we go to my office Angie," he suggested indicating for her to lead the way down the hallway. "After you."

Andy watched the two go into Kelley's office before attempting to call Gracie again. "Hello, Gracie? It's me, Andy. I know, that's why I'm calling. I overslept and when I left I forgot to bring Rascal over. No, no, he's not at the house. He jumped into my car and I brought him with me to work. I was concerned that Mr. Kelley might be upset about it but he's been really nice. Said Rascal can stay and even gave him a blanket to lay on. I just didn't want you to worry because I didn't come over. Anyway I'll need you to take care of him again tomorrow because my folks won't be back until tomorrow night. Will it be all right? Your dad won't have a problem with it will he? Good. Okay, I'll see you later. Maybe we can fly our drones this evening. Great. Gotta go, 'Bye."

As he ended his conversation his friend Simon Gallagher entered the lobby with Major Reese. "Good morning Major Reese. Hi Simon. What can I do for you?"

"I just thought I'd check in to see how you were doing before I take Simon, here, for a ride," said Reese adjusting his cap. He looked over the top of the desk and noticed Rascal. "Nice looking dog. Is he the new airport mascot?" He took a second look at the dog and began to laugh.

Andy looked at him and smirked. "No, he's not the new airport mascot. Maybe he can be the mascot for the drone club." He chuckled and shook his head. "His name is Rascal and I admit he does look a bit strange but he's very friendly."

"Where did you get him?" asked Simon staring at the animal.

"I found him in my backyard a few days ago and he's attached himself to me like glue."

"Do you think he's lost? Have you tried to find his owner?" Simon was beginning to get rather stressed.

"Calm down Simon. I found his owner. It's Fanin Murphy. He's dead. Gracie Taylor and I found the man in the cemetery earlier this week at Mr. Murphy's wife's grave. Anyway, no one in Mr. Murphy's family wanted the dog so they said I could keep him. You want to pet him?" Rascal stared at Simon with his sweet brown eyes and licked his mouth.

Simon took several steps away from the desk. "No, that's all right." He glanced apprehensively at Major Reese. Andy could tell his friend was anxious to leave.

"That's a shame about Mr. Murphy," said Reese sincerely. "I did read his obituary but didn't know you and Gracie found his body in the cemetery."

"We'd just been out flying our drones and discovered it by accident. It's no big deal. Gracie said his funeral is today. His son Eric arrived yesterday. Mr. Kelley found him a hangar for his jet while he's here."

"Jet?!" gasped Simon. "The man landed a jet here?"

Andy grinned at him. "Yes, the man landed a jet here. Do you find that unusual?"

Simon was looking rather shocked. "I thought this airport was just for small prop planes."

"No, it handles jets too," said Reese with a smile. "It can't handle the large passenger jets of course but your average corporate jets are no problem. This Eric Murphy must have a bit of money if he can afford his own private jet."

"I wouldn't know," said Andy. "He seems to be a nice enough guy. I talked with him a little yesterday while he was waiting for his daughter to arrive. I left before I had a chance to meet her."

Reese looked at Simon. "Well, we better get going if you want that ride before lunch."

Andy watched them leave then gathered up Rascal's empty breakfast bowl. "Good job, boy." He put it in his bag so he could wash it when he went home.

Mr. Kelley came down the hallway with several yellow legal size pieces of paper. "Do you know how to use a computer to type stuff?" he asked Andy laying the pages on the desk.

Andy looked at him and blinked his eyes in confusion. "Yes, I know how to do that. Do it all the time in school. What do you need typed?"

"Mrs. Phillips needs these typed up for her class this summer. Mostly it's just information on when class starts, what books people will need and things like that. Once you have it done we'll put it on our website. Okay?"

"Ah, yeah, sure. The only thing is I've never put anything on a website before."

"Oh, don't worry about it. We have someone to do that. You just need to type the stuff up and email it to me."

Andy slightly scratched his forehead. "Be glad to but I don't have your email address."

"Don't worry, I'll send it to you as soon as I get back to my office. I gave you the info on how to log into the airport email. It should be somewhere in that stuff I gave you yesterday."

Andy nodded his head. "Right, no problem." As soon as Mr. Kelley headed back to his office Andy began to sort through the pile of papers Mr. Kelley had given him when he arrived yesterday morning. "Great, a piece of paper with login instructions. Okay dummy where'd you put it?"

As if things couldn't get any more complicated Rascal decided he needed to take a trip outside. "Wonderful. I need to find someone to mind the phone so wait a minute."

Luckily for Andy and Rascal Mrs. Phillips showed up and noticed his dilemma.

"I'll take care of the desk and phone," she told him. "Go take care of the dog. It'll be all right."

"Thank you," said Andy as he grabbed Rascal's leash and headed out the door.

When he returned he noticed Mrs. Phillips had placed a piece of paper on top of the information she needed typed. It was the log-in and email address information he needed. Andy looked at her and smiled slightly. "Thank you for finding this for me."

"You're welcome," she replied. "After you finish with the typing Mr. Kelley wants you to police the runways."

Andy gave her a confused look. "Police the runways? What exactly does a policeman do on the runways?"

Mrs. Phillips laughed quietly. "I guess I should have used a different term. What he wants you to do is to go out on the runways and pickup any litter, we call it FOD, foreign object debris, not just trash paper and such but any metal, like nuts, bolts, screws, things that might get caught in engines especially jet engines. We don't want any debris to get sucked into Mr. Murphy's engines when he leaves."

Andy's face brightened up. "Oh, I get it. Do we know when Mr. Murphy will be leaving?"

"Haven't a clue," Mrs. Phillips replied. "I just know the funeral is this afternoon. If he has to take care of any of his father's estate he may be here until next week or later."

Andy nodded his head in understanding. "Well, I'll get all of this taken care of right now," he told her. He sat down, logged into the computer and began typing.

Mrs. Phillips left for the lounge and returned a few minutes later with a couple of donuts and a cup of coffee. She placed them on the desk. "You look like you could use something to eat. I have a feeling you probably didn't have any breakfast. Hope you like coffee. There's cream and sugar if you use them."

Andy was taken completely by surprise. He started to dig in his pocket to pay her but she put up her hand to stop him. He tilted his head to one side. "Thank you. You're right, I didn't have any breakfast. But you really should let me pay you."

"Nonsense, I'm happy to do it. Now, I'm going to let you get back to work." She left the building and Andy got back to typing.

It was a bit messy, eating chocolate covered donuts and typing but he managed to complete the task and clean the keyboard with a minimal amount of difficulty. He emailed the information to Mr. Kelley and put all his trash in the nearest trash container.

Andy stopped by Mr. Kelley's office. "Ah, sir, I just sent you the information you asked me to type and I was getting ready to go cleanup the runways. Is there a trash bag or something I can use to put stuff in?"

Kelley got up from his desk and walked over to Andy. "Come along and I'll show you where things are." He led Andy to the lounge. "We keep the trash bags and things over here in these drawers." Kelley guided him to the counter where there was a sink, a small cabinet and drawers underneath the counter. There were also cupboards above the counter. "The trash bags are in the bottom drawer. There's different odds and ends in the drawers, things like plasticware, napkins, dishrags and dish towels. In the cupboards up here," he said pointing to the upper cupboards, "are paper plates, plastic glasses, paper towels and such. Okay?"

"Yes, sir," said Andy making a mental note on where to find various items. He took one of the plastic bags from the drawer and closed it.

"Oh, you might want to bring some work gloves with you tomorrow, keep them in your car just for future jobs."

"All right," said Andy.

"If you want to take your dog with you while you cleanup the area that will be all right. Just be sure to keep him on his leash and out of the way of any aircraft landing on the runway."

"Yes, thank you." As they left the lounge Andy stopped and turned toward Mr. Kelley. "Oh, one more thing. Who's going to answer the phone while I'm out there?"

"Oh, don't worry about that. The phone will just ring in my office." Kelley stopped at his office door. "I was planning on making a run to the local sub shop for lunch. I noticed you didn't bring any lunch with you this morning so I'll be glad to bring something back for you if you want."

"Thank you, that'll be great." Andy dug his wallet out of his pocket. "Do you know about how much it'll be?"

Kelley just smiled. "You can pay me when I bring it back. Do you have an idea what kind you want?"

"An Italian sub will be fine, and maybe a bag of chips."

"Will do."

Andy continued down the hall, grabbed Rascal's lead and they headed out the door. He glanced up at the sky and was thankful for the clouds because he'd forgotten his sunglasses. He was wondering about picking up the litter when he noticed a long grab stick leaning next to the door. "Guess this is what you use to pick up the trash." He looked at Rascal then out at the runway. "Well, come on, old boy, let's get this done."

He and Rascal had been cleaning up the area for nearly an hour when Major Reese and Simon finished their flight and landed. Rascal, of course, got excited and wanted to chase the plane down the runway. "No, boy, no!" shouted Andy firmly grasping the dog's lead. Rascal wasn't having any of that 'no' business and continued to pull forward dragging Andy along. "You are one strong dude. Maybe we need to take you to Alaska and let you pull a sled."

Rascal quit running once the plane stopped and parked at its hangar. Andy and the dog trotted over to greet the major and his friend.

Major Reese climbed down from the cockpit and Rascal tried to jump up on him. Luckily, Andy was just a fraction quicker than the dog and scooped him up off the ground. "One thing's for sure, that's one energetic dog," said Reese. To Andy's amazement Rascal quieted down just as soon as he picked him up. The dog looked first at Andy then at the major. Andy could have sworn the dog was smiling but realized that wasn't possible. Dogs didn't smile, at least he didn't think they did. He stroked Rascal's head and the dog stuck out his tongue, turned his head and licked Andy's hand. Both Andy and Major Reese chuckled.

By now Simon had also disembarked from the cockpit and had made his way to where the others had gathered. "Are you and the dog the airport greeting committee?" he asked Andy cynically.

Andy eyed his friend warily. "No, we were just cleaning the runways and Rascal got excited when the major landed, that's all."

"Oh," answered Simon quietly.

"So, how was the flight?" asked Andy with interest.

Major Reese casually shrugged his shoulders and glanced at Simon. "It was just a normal flight. Nothing unusual or remarkable about it."

"Well, I guess that's a good thing." Andy put Rascal back on the ground and picked up the trash bag. "If you'll excuse me I need to get back to work. The runways won't clean themselves." He gently pulled on Rascal's leash. "Come along boy, let's see how much more we can get done before lunch." He and the dog turned and continued on their way. He thought Simon was acting a bit strange and wondered why. Was it the dog or something else? He hadn't a clue.

They had made their way down the second runway and were on their way back to the office building when Mr. Kelley came out to greet them. "Looks like you finished just in time," said Kelley. "Put the trash over there in the can and come inside for your lunch."

"Thank you," replied Andy following Mr. Kelley's directions. "I never knew a runway could collect so much junk."

"It is extraordinary isn't it?" Kelley held the door while Andy and Rascal entered then he followed. "Get yourself something to drink then go on to the conference room."

"All right." Rascal, however, wasn't waiting to enter any old conference room for a drink. He stopped by the desk and helped himself to a nice long drink of water. Andy thought the dog was never going to finish. As soon as he had slurped his fill Andy took him to the lounge and got himself a Coke before entering the conference room.

To say he was surprised to see Major Reese, Mrs. Phillips and Gracie's grandfather, George Taylor there would be an understatement.

"Come on in and have a seat," said Kelley and handed him his sub and potato chips.

Andy took his lunch and sat down hesitantly.

"Thank you." Rascal laid down at Andy's feet and closed his eyes, exhausted.

"Please, go ahead and eat," said Kelley. "That's why we're here, to have lunch." He unwrapped his sandwich and the others did the same. "I imagine you're wondering why all of us are here."

Andy blinked trying to not look so stunned but the look would not leave his face. He swallowed uneasily and whispered. "Yes, sir, I am."

"There's nothing to be nervous about," stated Mr. Taylor. "We have some good news for you, that's all."

Andy opened his Coke and took a sip. "You do?"

"Of course," answered Mr. Taylor with a smile. "We know one of the reasons you came to work here was to earn money for ground school and flying lessons. Isn't that right?"

"Yes, sir." Andy's eyes opened wider as he wondered where this conversation was going. "I've always enjoyed flying, especially on the small planes and helicopters we took when we traveled from one excavation site to another. I thought it might be fun to learn how to fly one."

"I don't imagine you've ever thought about joining the military," ventured Mr. Taylor.

"Not really. Sir, you understand that I have spent most of my life in other countries. I haven't even lived in the United States a whole year yet. There's a lot I still need to learn about this country."

Major Reese politely cleared his throat. "George, what career this young man plans to pursue is not the reason we're here."

"Humph, I know that. I was just curious that's all."

"Can we get to the point please?" asked Mrs. Phillips looking intently at the men. "Andy, we want to help you earn your private pilot's license by the end of the summer. This means I am willing to give you one on one instruction for ground school starting Monday and every day you are here. And Major Reese has agreed to give you flying lessons on the weekends and during the summer, several days a week."

Andy looked at her dumbfounded. "I don't know what to say. Why do you want to do this for me? I don't even know that I'll have earned enough money to do all of this."

"You don't need to worry about paying for this," said Mr. Kelley.

"I can't let you do this for free. I want to pay for it."

"Payment will be you working here," explained Major Reese. "That's what you wanted to do with the money anyway. Right?"

"Well, yeah, sure, but there's no way I would be able to cover the cost of all this on the amount of money I'm earning."

"Exactly," said Mrs. Phillips. "That's why we want to help."

Andy rubbed is forehead and still looked confused. "I don't understand."

Major Reese bit on his bottom lip and thoughtfully looked at Andy. "Okay, it's like this. The kids like Simon and Gracie will have their parents pay for the school and the lessons. Their parents can afford it and the kids figure why earn money for this when I can get mom and dad to foot the bill. You're different. You want to earn your own way and we respect that. We want to help you out. That's all. This way you can use the money you earn to help pay for college or tech school, or whatever you decide."

Andy slowly ran his fingers up and down the moisture covered soda can as he glanced at everyone gathered around the table. "All right, we can try this but I want to pay for something. Can I at least pay for the books and the fuel for the airplane when I fly?"

Mrs. Phillips and Major Reese exchanged glances. "Okay," said Reese, "you can pay for the books and fuel."

"Thank you. Now, where do I get the books?"

"They're in my office," answered Kelley with a smile. "I'll get them to you before you leave this afternoon and you can pay for them tomorrow."

"All right. Thank you." He looked at Mr. Kelley. "Speaking of money, how much do I owe you for lunch?"

Kelley laughed. "Seven bucks."

Andy dug his wallet from his back pants pocket and gave Mr. Kelley $8. When Kelley tried to give him change Andy stopped him. "The extra's for the gas to pick it up."

Kelley just shook his head and put the money in his pocket. "Oh, before I forget. Some of the planes need to be washed down this afternoon. Tomorrow will probably be busy; it usually is on Saturdays. The major here can show you which ones to clean and where to do it. All right?"

"Sure," answered Andy as he devoured his sandwich.

Rascal lazily raised his head to look around as most of the people got up and left. Only the major remained.

"There's only two planes that need washed," said Reese. "The custodian should be here about three and should be able to help. And as soon as you finish your lunch I'll meet you over by the hangars and I'll help you get started."

Andy swallowed the last of his sandwich and took a large gulp of soda. "Thank you. I think I'm ready now." He gathered his trash and threw it away, grabbed his soda and Rascal's lead then followed the major outside.

"I thought we'd start with this Piper Cub," said Reese. "We'll hook it to this golf cart and bring it over to the hose. You'll find a bucket, a couple of brushes, and a stack of towels over there next to the wall." While Reese hooked the plane to the cart Andy gathered the bucket and other supplies and joined the major. "Hop in."

Reese stopped at the washing station and they got out of the cart. "Okay, washing an airplane is different than washing a car. First we need to cover various areas like static ports, tubes, sensors and things so the water doesn't get sprayed into them. We need to be sure the doors are closed and latched. So, we'll take this orange tape and use it to cover those areas." As he spoke he removed a couple of rolls of bright orange banner tape from a bag he had beside him in the cart and handed one to Andy.

"Is there a particular reason you use this color of tape?" asked Andy.

"It's easier to spot for removing when we're finished."

"Oh, I guess that makes sense. I imagine it could cause a problem if you missed removing them."

"Yes, it could." Reese proceeded to show him what areas needed to be covered. When they finished he stepped back to make sure they hadn't missed anything. "Okay, now we're going to spray the plane down then go over it with our hands to make sure we get all the bugs and stuff off. Start at the top and work our way to the bottom. And go from the tail to the nose. The last thing to clean is the underside of the plane. Got it?"

"I think so," said Andy. "What about the windows? I heard once that you can't just wash them with regular soap and water or window cleaner, you have to use some special kind of cleaner."

"That's right. You'll find that cleaner in this bag also," said Reese indicating the bag he'd removed the orange tape from. "Okay, let's get going. You take the right side and I'll take the left. It'll take a couple of hours to get this thing clean."

It was nearly 3 o'clock by the time Andy and Major Reese finished with the Piper and the custodian arrived.
Andy stepped out from wiping down the belly of the plane and noticed the man standing near the wheels talking to the major.

"Oh, Andy, I don't think you've had a chance to meet our custodian yet. This is Gary Ames. Gary, this is Andy Parker. Andy's helping out around here for a while. He's one of my drone club students. In fact he's one of my best."

Andy wiped his wet dirty hands on one of the rags and offered his hand to Ames. "Nice to meet you Mr. Ames."

Ames shook Andy's hand and smiled. "You don't need to be so formal. Just call me Gary."

"All right."

"Gary is also a great mechanic," said Reese. "Whenever we have a problem with a plane we can count on him to fix it."

Gary shook his head slightly. "I'm an okay mechanic. We both know I can't fix everything."

"All right, have it your way," agreed Reese pleasantly. "I still trust you with my plane." He looked at the plane they had just finished washing. "Looks like we're done with this one. We just need to remove the tape and take it back to the hangar."

Andy walked to the bucket he'd left near the plane and dropped the towel he was holding on the ground, then he began to remove the orange tape from the plane. Gary stepped in to help and soon the plane was ready to return to its hangar.

Reese hooked the plane to the golf cart. "I'll take this one back and bring out the Cessna. You two can stay here and get acquainted. Tell Andy about your great-grandfather and the Tuskegee airmen." Reese climbed in the cart and drove off.

"So, was your great-grandfather a pilot with Tuskegee airmen?" asked Andy with fascination.

Gary shook his head and ran his fingers through his curly black hair. "No, he was with the flight crew. Not everyone was a pilot with the group. They needed mechanics and a ground crew to keep the planes repaired."

"I'll bet it was interesting even if you weren't flying. It was probably safer too."

"Maybe, I don't really know. My great-grandfather didn't talk about the war too much. I know he talked a little about the flight chief, a Staff Sargent Leslie Edwards, I think his name was. And he talked about some of the pilots, especially a guy named Charles McGee. McGee was inducted into the National Aviation Hall of Fame a few years ago. A nice guy. I got to meet him once."

"So, how did you become interested in aviation? Was it because of your great-grandfather"

"Maybe a little bit. I've just always liked fixing things and I've been interested in aviation ever since I discovered the word. I liked to build model airplanes as a kid and my grandfather would take me to the park to fly them. Sometimes my great-grandfather would come along."

"Is he still around?"

Gary shook his head and rubbed his jaw. "No, he passed away last year, not long after his one hundredth birthday. But I'm lucky I had him in my life for twenty years."

Andy nodded his head and stared at the ground then looked at Gary. "Yes, you're very lucky. I've never even met my grandparents let alone my great-grandparents."

"They're all dead then?"

"I suppose. I don't really know. My folks don't talk about any of them."

"I'm sorry to hear that."

"Yeah, me too." He heard the golf cart motor and looked toward the hangar to see Major Reese coming in their direction with the Cessna. "Looks like our next plane is arriving." He picked up the orange tape rolls and handed one of them to Gary. "Never realized until today how much effort went in to cleaning an airplane."

"It does take time and lots of elbow grease," stated Gary. "But it's important for the plane's safety. People who don't pilot a plane don't understand how dirt can affect how a plane flies."

"I'm beginning to understand that," said Andy.

Major Reese parked the plane near the water hose, and detached it from the cart. He drove the cart a safe distance away, parked it and walked back to Andy and Gary. "Okay guys, it's all yours. And Andy, I'll see you Monday, after school. We need to talk about the next drone competition."

Andy wrinkled his brow. He had no idea what he needed to talk with the major about concerning the competition. He shrugged his shoulders and figured he'd find out whatever it was about on Monday.

"Times a wasting, let's get this taken care of," said Gary with a smile, his dark brown eyes twinkling. "Do you want the right or left side?"

"It doesn't matter. Whichever side you don't want I'll take," said Andy. He took the orange tape and began taping the ports, tubes and sensors. He checked the doors then picked up a soft brush and clean cloth.

Gary finished taping the other side then turned on the hose and aimed it at the plane. "Okay, I'll take the right and you can have the left."

"Sounds fine to me." He watched the water flow over the fuselage and run down the sides. He looked over toward the trees where he had left Rascal snoozing. He'd stayed in the shade the whole time Andy and Major Reese had cleaned the other airplane. He was thankful that the dog had been so good all day.

When Gary finished hosing down the plane he filled the bucket with fresh water and some soap. He laid the hose on the ground and before he could turn off the water Rascal raced for the nozzle and began lapping up the liquid. When he was done he took the hose in his mouth and began spraying water everywhere.

Gary quickly shut the water off and began chasing the dog. "Get out of here dog, go home!"

"Stop!" yelled Andy as he chased after Rascal. He caught his leash and stopped him from running. He scooped the dog up in his arms and walked back to Gary and the plane. He stroked Rascal's head and gave him a hug. "This is my dog Rascal," he explained. "Guess I should've told you he was here. But he's been so quiet all day and he was resting under the trees that I just didn't think about it."

Gary blinked and stared at the dog. "Sorry, I just thought he was some stray that had wandered over here. He looks like a nice guy. May I pet him?"

"Sure, he's pretty friendly."

Rascal looked curiously at the man and closed his mouth. Gary held out his hand and stroked the dog's back. "I'm sorry there little guy." He continued to rub his hand over the dog's back and apologize until Rascal opened his mouth licking his nose with his long tongue.

"I should've brought his water bowl out here with me but I didn't think about it."

"Here, let me turn the water back on and see if he wants more to drink," suggested Gary. Andy put the dog on the ground then held the end of the hose so Rascal could get a drink. Once he'd had his fill he wandered back to the trees and laid in the shade again watching Andy and Gary wash the plane.

By 5 o'clock they had the plane washed, dried and back in the hangar. Andy helped Gary clean things up and took Rascal back to the office building.

"Well, how'd things go?" asked Mr. Kelley when Andy entered the building.

"I think everything went fine," replied Andy. "Both the Piper Cub and the Cessna are clean and ready for anyone who needs them." He went to the desk and gathered Rascal's bowls and treats and put them in his bag. He picked the blanket up off the floor. "Shall I take this home and wash it for you?"

"Thanks but I don't think that'll be necessary. I'll just shake it out and it'll be fine," Kelley assured him taking the blanket from him. "Major Reese said your parents are coming home this weekend. Is that right?"

"Yes, sir, sometime tomorrow night, I'm not sure the exact time."

"Well, if there are things you need to do before they arrive and don't want to come in tomorrow that will be all right."

"No, that's okay, I'll be here, no problem."

"Fine. I'll see you tomorrow morning then." He stopped and placed the ground school books on the desk. "Here are the books you need. The price is on the back. You can pay for them tomorrow if you want. Have a good evening."

"Yes, sir, thank you. You have a good evening also." Andy picked Rascal up and headed out the door for his car.

He opened the back door and put the dog and his belongings inside. "This has been some day hasn't it boy? I'll be glad to get home. Hope I'll have time to practice with my drone before it gets dark." He slid into the driver's seat, buckled his seatbelt and headed for home.

When Andy pulled into his driveway he was surprised to see Gracie sitting on the back porch steps. He took Rascal's leash off and opened the car door. Within seconds the dog was racing around the yard, watering several trees as well as fertilizing the grass. Andy watched Rascal's escapades as he gathered the dog's bag from the car and put the leash in his pocket.

"Hello Gracie," he greeted her as he headed toward the porch. "To what do I owe this wonderful visit?"

"I was out flying my drone this afternoon down by the old McAllister place and I found this. I thought you might want it." She held out an orange dog collar and leash. There were several tags attached and one shaped like a bone had the name Taliesin engraved on it.

Andy gently took the collar from Gracie's hand and examined the tags. "This is unbelievable. Where did you find it over there?"

"Near some bushes close to the woods."

"There's his dog license, his Home Again tag, his name tag and this other little tag. I don't think I've ever seen anything like this before. It's a tree with a horse and it sort of reminds me of some ancient shield. Kind of like the ones knights used in Medieval times."

Gracie looked at him, nodded her head and smiled slightly. "I did some research, just a little. The symbols look like they might be Irish. The tree looks like it's supposed to be oak. I found similar pictures on the Internet. I'm not sure about the horse but it probably has some connection to Ireland too."

Andy turned the item over to examine the back. "Well, it does say it was made in Ireland and Murphy was Irish so I guess that makes sense. Thank you. Want to come in?"

"Thanks, but I need to get back home. My grandfather is taking us out for supper." She stood up and stepped onto the grass. "Try not to over sleep tomorrow. Gwen and I missed having little Rascal around today."

"I'll do my best to remember to turn on my alarm clock when I go to bed," he told her and laughed.

"You do that. See you tomorrow."

"Yep, see you tomorrow." He watched her walk down his driveway and cross the street before he turned around to call the dog. He searched the yard but didn't see him. "Where did that silly dog go? Here Rascal! Rascal where are you?!" Andy started walking to the back of the yard hoping the dog hadn't gone down to the creek. "Come on Rascal where are you?!" Suddenly Rascal came racing out of the trees and bushes at the back of the property. He was soaking wet. "Where have you been?" The closer Andy got to the dog the worse things smelled. "Phew! Boy do you stink and you're all wet and dirty. You were in the creek weren't you?" He took the leash from his pocket and hooked it onto the dog's collar. "Come along. You're getting a bath before you have any supper, before I have any either. Just what I want to do, give a bath to a stinking dog before I eat. Yuck!"

Chapter Seventeen

"Well, this last day in Ireland has certainly been interesting," remarked Emily to Rowena as she opened her suitcase to pack for the trip home. "In fact, this entire week has been interesting from the discoveries at the dig to all the people I've met."

Rowena sat on her bed petting Shea and watching Emily. "I imagine you'll be glad to get home," she replied mildly.

Emily turned to look at Rowena. "Yes, and no. I've missed my friends and some of the things that have happened there this week. On the other hand I'll miss not having the chance to help with the excavation here. Some of the things we've found have been wonderful. I've really enjoyed it and I'd like to be able to finish but Spring Break is over and I have to go back to school on Monday." She turned back to her packing.

"Going to school does put a damper on helping at the dig sites."

Emily folded her shirts and put them in the suitcase. "It's never been a problem before."

Rowena stared at Emily and wrinkled her forehead. "I don't understand. You have to go to school and if you're in class you can't be at the dig."

"That's the thing," said Emily looking at her and smiling coyly. "We didn't go to school; not like you do. We attended classes online. If there wasn't any computer access we had classes on DVD's and either our parents or a tutor taught us. It was cool. We could help at the dig during the day and do school work in the evening. I liked it. This is the first year I've ever gone to a real school with other kids. It's been different and took a bit of getting used to but I'm enjoying it. I've actually had a chance to even make some friends. Never really had much of an opportunity to do that before."

"That must have been some life," commented Rowena. "My dad's only done excavations here in Ireland. Sometimes I'd get to

Nancy Potts

help. We'd usually rent a house near the site, like we did here, and
sometimes we'd be there a year or so. It just depended on how big
and how complicated the excavation was."

"You've moved around a lot then too," said Emily as she
folded her last piece of clothing and put it in the suitcase.

"Not nearly as much as you. I know my dad said you've been
to some pretty exciting places."

"They have been fascinating, for sure and I've enjoyed doing
all of it."

"But your brother hasn't," said Rowena removing the cat from
her lap and placing him on her bed.

"You've got that right. He can't stand archaeology even
though he's good at finding stuff and digging it up." Emily
gathered her toothbrush and other items from the bathroom,
stuffed them in a small zippered case and slid it into her backpack.
"I'm sure he has enjoyed his time away from us this week. I know
I haven't missed him."

"Really?" asked Rowena with some hesitancy.

"Well, maybe I've missed him a little bit," she answered with
a giggle. "But he can be such an awful tease and pain in the neck
sometimes."

Rowena laughed also. "Even if he can be a nuisance
sometimes at least you have a sibling. I never have. At times it can
be a little lonely."

Emily stopped giggling and looked somberly at Rowena. "I
guess I never really thought about what it would be like without
him around. If he goes away to college this fall I suppose I'll find
out."

"Suppose you will," she agreed. Rowena looked around the
room. "Have you got all your things? Take a good look around to
make sure you haven't forgotten anything."

Emily walked around the bedroom and the bathroom just to be
certain she hadn't missed anything. "I've got everything," she told
Rowena as she closed and locked her suitcase. As soon as she sat
down on the other bed the cat jumped up and stretched out beside

her. She softly stroked the cat and thought about the week. Rowena seemed to be in a fairly agreeable mood tonight, which was good. She carefully observed her roommate. They had certainly had their ups and downs this week and she wanted to leave on pleasant terms with the girl. "I'm glad we were able to get that little statue back today. You did a wonderful job cleaning it. It looks great. I'm also glad you allowed me to work on the warrior's headdress. It is going to be beautiful once it's finished, don't you think?"

Rowena nodded her head. "Yes, I think it will be, but it's going to take time to clean because it is so delicate."

"I was wondering if I could ask a favor?" asked Emily carefully.

"Sure."

"Well, once the headdress is cleaned could you or your dad or mom, take a picture of it and send it to me? I'd love to see what it looks like when it's all finished."

Rowena smiled. "Sure, we can do that. Does my dad have your address?"

"I think so. I know he has our phone number but I can give you our address and you can have my email address too. That way if you just want to email it to me you can do it that way."

"All right." Rowena handed Emily a notepad and pencil from her desk. "Just write it all down."

"Thanks." Emily carefully printed the information on the page and handed the pad back to Rowena. "It's been nice getting to know you this week. I've learned a lot about things I'd never known before." She glanced at her watch. It was almost 9:30. "I suppose I should get some sleep before we have to leave in the morning. Four o'clock is awfully early."

"You're right. It is," agreed Rowena. "I'll let you sleep and if I am not awake when you leave I want to wish you a good safe trip back home. It's been a pleasure."

"Thank you, Rowena, I've enjoyed visiting with you and your family." Emily laid down on the bed, Shea jumped onto the floor and Emily covered herself with the quilt that was folded at the foot of the bed.

"Pleasant dreams," said Rowena as she and Shea left the room and she turned off the light.

"Good night," said Emily as she snuggled under the quilt. In less than ten minutes she was off to dreamland.

"Emily," whispered Anne, "it's time to get up." She gently touched her daughter's shoulder to wake her. "Come along, we need to get going."

Emily rubbed the sleep from her eyes and sat up on the bed. The room was dark but there was a faint glow coming from down the hallway toward the living room. "What time is it?" she murmured still trying to wake up.

"It's a quarter to four. Come along. We need to leave in fifteen minutes." Anne helped Emily out of the bed and folded the quilt, placing it back at the foot of the bed. Emily grabbed her suitcase and backpack then headed out the door and down the hallway.

Martin and Pat were waiting in the living room with the rest of the Parker's luggage. As soon as Emily and Anne arrived the men took everything out the front door and loaded the car.

Emily and Anne silently followed, closing the door behind them. They got into the backseat while the men finished loading the bags. Anne looked at her daughter and smiled. "Just think, in a few hours we'll be home. I'm really looking forward to sleeping in my own bed tonight and to seeing Andy. I hope he didn't miss us too much."

"Oh, I'm sure he's fine," said Emily smiling slyly.

She leaned back in the seat and began to think about everything Gwen had told her. Boy, were her parents going to be surprised. Andy working and having a dog. She could hardly wait to see their reaction, especially when they saw the dog. It was something for sure. It was definitely the funniest looking dog she'd ever seen.

Pat and Martin slid into the front seats. "Everyone ready?" asked Pat. "Got your seatbelts fastened?"

"Yes and yes," answered Anne. "Let's get going, shall we?"

"Yes, dear," said Martin condescendingly. "We have plenty of time. There's hardly any traffic this time of the morning and it's less than an hour and a half to get to the airport. So, just sit back and relax. Close your eyes and take a nap, why don't you?"

Anne sighed in exasperation, then leaned back in the seat and closed her eyes. Emily glanced at her mother then turned her attention to her window and watched all the scenery pass by. Her father was right about the traffic. There were hardly any cars or trucks on the streets. It reminded her of a deserted ghost town, very spooky.

It was almost five thirty by the time they reached Shannon Airport and Pat had parked the car. The men grabbed the luggage but Emily rescued her backpack from them and they headed inside the terminal. Things weren't very busy here either and soon they were through customs and their bags were checked.

"Well, old man, I think you can find your way from here," said Pat with a grin. "It's been grand seein' ya and I hope we can get together again before another ten years go by."

"I hope so too," replied Martin. "It's been great and I think I can speak for Anne and Emily when I say we enjoyed every minute. We are thankful to you for having us. You've got quite a dig going and a wonderful crew working it."

"Aye, I think so too. Some of them have been with me since their college days. They're a good group of kids." He shook Martin's hand and gave a hug to Anne and Emily. "You have a safe trip now and give us a call when you land in Ohio." Martin began to protest but Pat just stared at him. "I know it'll be late but do it anyway. Okay?"

"Okay," agreed Martin. "Now, you have a safe drive back to Blarney and tell Mary Jo and Rowena again thank you from us." The intercom interrupted the conversation when they began announcing flight numbers and boarding gates. "Guess we better get going, don't want to miss our flight. So long." He turned, waved to Pat and ushered Anne and Emily toward their departure gate.

"So long!" shouted Pat as he watched them leave. "I'm going to miss you," he whispered and headed out the door.

The Parkers got on the plane and found their seats near the center of the jet. "Well, I think we've got pretty good seats," stated Martin. "Who wants to go first?"

"I will," said Anne. "Emily can sit between us." She made her way to the window seat; Emily took the middle and Martin got the aisle seat.

"Do you think I'll be able to watch a movie?" asked Emily hopefully.

"We're only going to London," said Martin. "That's about an hour and a half flight. So, no you won't be watching a movie. They should feed us breakfast, however."

"Oh," said Emily disappointedly. "How long will we be in London?"

"A little over three hours," said Anne calmly. "We leave there about twelve fifteen and reach Washington D.C. around three twenty."

"Considering the time difference that'll be the longest flight, about eight hours and a bigger plane," said her father. "And they'll feed us lunch. I believe you'll be able to watch several movies right at your seat. You did this in December, right?"

"Yeah, I did but the movies weren't all that interesting," admitted Emily looking at the screen in the back of the seat in front of her. "How long will we be in Washington before we leave?"

"We have a few hours there," Martin told her. "We leave there about five forty if everything's on time and we should get to Dayton by seven thirty. I suppose we need to let your brother know when to expect us."

"We can call him when we get to Washington," said Anne.

"Right," agreed Emily smiling to herself. "No need to call him any sooner." She settled into her seat getting ready for the long boring flight.

Chapter Eighteen

Saturday morning Andy dropped a very clean Rascal off at Gracie's a little before 8:30 and headed for the airport. He never knew bathing a dog could be such a challenge. He certainly got an education last night. Just getting the dog into the bath was a problem. Rascal hid under Andy's bed as soon as he heard the tub filling with water. It took half a hamburger simply to get him out from under the bed. Once Andy got him in the bathroom he shut the door so the dog couldn't escape. Thinking about this now on his way to work made him laugh. Once Rascal was in the water he sat down, which was good, but when Andy tried to wash the dog's backside he refused to stand up. It was a struggle but eventually he did accomplish the task.

The important thing is that today, Rascal is clean. In fact he even smells like lemon tea because that's the only shampoo Andy could find to use. As he parked his car he was still thinking about the dog and wondering how his folks would react to him. He hoped they would like him and that Rascal would like them too.

It was a few minutes before nine when he entered the office building and headed for Mr. Kelley's office. He wanted to pay for the ground school books. As he reached the office he heard Kelley talking on the phone in a rather loud voice. "I don't care how much money he has we don't have a spare hangar. Tell him to check one of the other airports maybe they have a spare he can use. No! Absolutely no!" When Andy heard Kelley slam down the telephone receiver and pound his fist on his desk he decided to back away from the door and head for the lobby.

Andy was sitting at the desk arranging papers and sorting the mail when Kelley came down the hallway and walked out the front door. He watched Kelley walk toward the hangars before he was out of his sight. Andy finished with the mail just as Mrs. Phillips arrived.

Andy looked up from the desk when he heard her enter. "Good morning Mrs. Phillips, how are you this morning?"

"I'm fine," she replied, "which is more than I can say for Kelley. I just saw him outside and he looks like he's ready to bite the head off of the first person who even says hello to him. What's got him so upset?"

Andy gave her a wide eyed bewildered look and shrugged his shoulders. "I honestly don't know. When I arrived he was on the phone with someone and he sounded pretty upset. What little bit I heard it sounded like someone wanted a hangar here but apparently there aren't any to be had. They're all full. Mr. Kelley told whoever he was talking to he should tell the guy to try another airport. That's all I know." He fiddled nervously with a pencil that had been laying on the desktop. "He doesn't know I heard him, at least I don't think he does." He put the pencil down and looked uneasily at her.

Mrs. Phillips nodded her head slowly in understanding. "Don't worry, I won't tell him." She noticed the ground school books on the desk. "I see you have your books."

"Yes, Ma'am. Mr. Kelley gave them to me yesterday before I left. I was going to his office this morning to pay for them when I overheard the conversation."

"Why don't you put the money in an envelope and I'll put it on his desk for you. He can give you a receipt later."

"Thank you," said Andy. He found an envelope in one of the drawers, wrote a note on a piece of scrap paper and put it all in the envelope and sealed it. On the outside he put Mr. Kelley's name and handed the envelope to Mrs. Phillips.

"Okay. Now, are you going to be here Monday after school?"

"I plan on it," said Andy.

"All right. If you can, please read the first two chapters of this book, *Private Pilot* by Jeppesen. Then we can discuss it."

"Okay. I'm really looking forward to this and I appreciate you taking the time to teach me."

"Good," said Phillips. "And don't be concerned by people like Taylor asking you if you're going to join the military. Not everyone who gets a private pilot's license flies for the military.

213

Some people just like to fly for fun. You will find out though that a good many of us connected to MacAir were once with the aero club at the base."

Andy studied her for a few seconds not sure he understood what she said about MacAir and the base aero club. "I didn't know the base had an aero club."

"Oh yes. Anyone connected with the base could be a member, including Air Force dependents and civilians working there. A few years ago the base had us move so now we are here. In a way it was good because we aren't limited to base restrictions and anyone can join us here."

"I see," said Andy. "So you became involved with the aero club because your husband was with the Air Force."

Mrs. Phillips just smiled. "No, I joined the aero club because I was a pilot with the Air Force."

Andy's face took on a shocked appearance and the blood of embarrassment slowly crept from his neck, up to his cheeks and ended at his hairline. He swallowed nervously. "I'm sorry, I didn't know," he whispered.

Her brown eyes smiled mischievously. "Don't worry. A lot of people don't. I was a cargo plane pilot for most of my career and during the little war we had with Iraq I also flew helicopters. My husband was with the Air Force for a while also as a nurse. He's a PA (physician's assistant) now with a local doctor."

"So, how long were you with the Air Force?" asked Andy regaining his composure.

"Thirty years," she answered. "I just recently retired. Now I spend my time teaching people about flying here and at several of the local colleges and universities."

"Do you enjoy doing that?"

"You bet. I wouldn't do it if I didn't. One of the things I discovered a long time ago was that if you want to be happy find a job that you love. I love flying. Being up there is like being in an entirely different world. It gives you a sense of freedom you don't experience down here on the ground." Phillips looked at him and grinned. "Look, I've wasted enough of your time. I'll let you get back to your work and I'll deliver this envelope to Kelley's desk. Let's hope his mood improves before the end of the day." She walked down the hallway to Kelley's office and then to the lounge.

Several people stopped by to check out various airplanes over the next half hour. Kelley was right when he said things were usually busy on the weekends. As long as the weather stayed clear and calm he imagined they would stay that way.

Kelley came back into the building about 11 o'clock and stopped by the check-in desk. He seemed to be a little calmer than when he left several hours earlier for which Andy was grateful.

"How are things going?" he asked matter-of-factly. Andy could tell he really wasn't all that interested in the answer he was just trying to make conversation.

"Things are going well, sir," Andy replied formally. "About half a dozen planes have been checked out. You were correct when you said things are busy on the weekend, especially with the weather being so nice."

"Tomorrow will be different," said Kelley. "We're supposed to get rain most of the day, plus it's Sunday. Not as many people fly on Sunday." He started for his office.

"Oh, sir," said Andy quickly turning toward him. "The money for the ground school books is in an envelope on your desk."

"Fine, fine. I wasn't concerned about it but thank you." He started down the hallway again but stopped. "Oh, if you see Mrs. Phillips would you send her to my office?"

Andy smiled politely. "She's in the lounge, sir."

"Thanks." Kelley continued down the hall toward the lounge and Andy gave a long sigh of relief.

Things were quiet for the moment so Andy decided to open the private pilot book to get an idea of what the first two chapters were about. He only made it to the second page before Major Reese strolled through the door. Andy closed the book and stood up. "Hello Major, can I help you?"

"I was wondering if you would go help at the fuel pumps. Ken and Gary could use some help. It seems like everybody and his brother have decided to go flying today."

Andy glanced at the phone which had been silent all morning, then down the hallway. "I suppose I can but who will take care of the desk and phone?"

"Kelley can do that."

Andy looked at him dubiously. "I don't know. Right now he's with Mrs. Phillips and he hasn't been in a very good mood this morning."

"Ah ha, well tell you what, I'll take care of the desk for you. They'll just need your help until about twelve thirty. Things usually quiet down for a bit after that. Okay?"

"Sure. That'll be fine." Andy grabbed his jacket before heading out the door because even though it was calm and sunny it was only April and the weather was still a little cool.

Andy noticed several planes were in line waiting for fuel when he arrived. "Hi, Major Reese said you needed some help," said Andy.

"Yep, we sure do," acknowledged Gary. "Oh, by the way, this is Ken, Ken this is Andy Parker. Andy's here to help out wherever we need him. Yesterday he got to wash planes and tidy up the runways."

"And today I get to help fuel the planes," Andy said with a grin. "It's been a real learning experience."

"I'll bet it has," said Ken pleasantly.

"Ken's been here for a few years," stated Gary. "He's a great mechanic. He's taught me quite a lot."

"Maybe you'll be able to teach me about airplane maintenance," said Andy cheerily. "I imagine it's helpful to know how to fix one if you're going to fly. Sort of like knowing how to fix a car when you drive."

"Well, it can't hurt that's for sure," said Ken readjusting his ballcap on his bald head.

As each airplane tank was filled Andy watched the pilots

return the planes to either a hangar or to one of the tiedown areas. The more he experienced working at the airport the more impressed he became at how efficiently it was run.

When the last plane in line pulled up Andy was surprised to see Gracie's grandfather climb out of the cockpit. "Hello Mr. Taylor. It's good to see you again. Shall I fill the plane or would you prefer to do it?"

"Thank you Andy I would like to do it myself," said Taylor. Andy waited for him to open the tank then handed him the gas nozzle.

"Have you been flying already or are you just getting ready?"

"Oh, I've been up already. It's a wonderful day for flying."

"I agree," said Andy watching Mr. Taylor. "Tell me sir, how long have you been a member here?"

George looked at Andy with some interest. "I've been a member of the base aero club for over thirty-five years. But I've been flying for almost forty."

"What kind of planes did you fly for the Air Force?"

George stared at Andy and chuckled. "I flew a desk."

Andy looked confused. "I don't understand. I thought you were in the Air Force."

"I was young man. But not everyone is a pilot."

"I guess I just presumed everyone had something to do with airplanes. Either flying them or fixing them. So, if I might ask, what did you do?"

"I was a lawyer of course. The only planes I've ever flown are these. Got my private pilot's license in my early thirties and after I was stationed here I joined the aero club. They're a nice group of people." He finished filling the plane's tanks and handed the hose back to Andy.

"So was this your last assignment?" asked Andy becoming more interested in Mr. Taylor and his past.

"Yes, we ended up here in the late eighties and when I retired from the Air Force we just stayed and I opened my own law firm. After nearly twenty-one years with the military it was nice to stay in one place." He climbed into the plane so he could taxi it back to its hanger. "Keep up the good work young man." He waved at Andy, started the engine and rolled away.

Gary made his way over to Andy. "I think that's the last of them for a while. Thanks for helping."

Andy smiled slightly. "I was happy to do it. Just let me know if you need help with anything else."

"Will do," Gary assured him.

Andy made his way back to the office building where Major Reese was still manning the desk and telephone.

"Well, how'd it go?" asked Reese ending a call and hanging up the phone.

"It went fine. We filled all the planes that needed filling. I even had a chance to talk with Gracie's grandfather."

"Nice. George is a great guy. A bit straight-laced and proper sometimes but we're glad he's on the board."

Andy walked around to the back of the desk. "I wonder if he's the reason Gracie is so interested in aeronautical engineer."

Reese just shook his head. "I can't say for sure but I don't think so. This is something she's discovered on her own. You'd think with both her dad and grandfather being lawyers they would have guided her in that direction, not toward aviation."

"I guess," said Andy slightly scratching his jaw. He glanced around at the empty lobby. "Have you been very busy?"

"Naw, it's been fairly quiet." Reese straightened some of the papers on the desk and folded his newspaper. "Look why don't you go have some lunch? I can stay here for a while longer."

Andy slowly shook his head. "No, you don't need to do that. I just brought a sandwich and some water. If there hasn't been much traffic I can just eat here, can't I?"

"Well, I suppose so," said Reese agreeing reluctantly.

"Okay then," said Andy. He looked at the major and lowered his voice. "Before you go, how's Mr. Kelley? He was kinda upset this morning when I arrived."

Reese gave him a slight questioning glance before he answered. "He's doing all right. The problem's been resolved."

"Well, who was the guy that wanted a hangar here?"

"Just some bigshot from the East. It's nothing we need to be concerned about." He patted Andy on the shoulder. "Eat your lunch and enjoy the rest of your day. Bet you're looking forward to your folks getting home tonight."

Andy swallowed apprehensively. "Ah, yeah. It'll be good to see them." He sat at the desk and retrieved his lunch bag from the bottom drawer as the major left. He still didn't recall what time his mother said they would arrive at the Dayton airport. It really didn't matter much since he didn't have to pick them up. His dad had driven them to the airport and just left the car there. Still he figured he needed to tidy the place up before they arrived. And he couldn't stop wondering how they would react to finding a dog living in the house. He really hoped they would let him keep it.

The afternoon was just as uneventful as the morning had been. There were a few planes that needed refueled but Gary and Ken were able to take care of them without his assistance. He was going to cleanup the runways but Mr. Kelley asked him to take care of some paperwork instead. Once he finished he opened the private pilot's textbook and began to read. By 4:30 he'd finished the first chapter and was ready to start on the second when Mr. Kelley stopped at the desk.

He paused for a moment before looking directly at Andy. "I went over the paperwork and you did an excellent job. Thank you. We don't seem to be very busy this afternoon so I think it'll be all right for you to leave. I'm sure there are a few things you need to take care of before your parents get home. Also, we're not going to need you tomorrow. Spend it with your family and reading your pilot's textbook. We'll see you on Monday after school. All right?"

Andy had already closed the book and was paying close attention to everything Mr. Kelley was saying. "Thank you, sir. If you change your mind about tomorrow just call me. I'm sure my folks won't mind. And I'll be here Monday right after school. Thank you."

"You're very welcome. Enjoy the rest of your weekend. I'm certain your parents will be happy to see you." Kelley turned and walked back to his office while Andy gathered his lunch bag and made his way to the parking lot and his car.

When Andy got home he parked his car in the garage then walked across the street to fetch Rascal. As he walked up the Taylors' drive he noticed the dog was racing around their backyard. He also noticed Gracie, Gwen and their father were all there with him. Everyone looked to be having a good time. He watched Mr. Taylor throw the old tennis ball and Rascal ran across the yard to retrieve it.

"Hello," said Andy as he approached the fence. "Looks like Rascal's having a great time and so is everyone else."

Everyone stopped and turned to look at Andy. "Hello Andy, it's good to see you," said Mr. Taylor walking to the gate and letting him in. "I'd say we've all had a wonderful afternoon out here. You have quite a talented little dog." He closed the gate and the dog trotted over to Mr. Taylor with his ball then dropped it at Taylor's feet. "Good boy. Now sit." Rascal obediently sat. Mr. Taylor took a dog treat from his pocket and knelt on the ground in front of the dog. "Shake," he told him and Rascal quickly offered his paw which Mr. Taylor accepted and shook. He then gave Rascal a treat and stroked the dog's head. "Good boy."

Andy slowly shook his head. "I didn't know he knew how to do that. Or did you teach that to him today?"

Mr. Taylor glanced at Andy and smiled. "I think he already knew how to do that. He can also roll over, beg, and find moles hiding under the grass." He pointed to a small mound of dirt in a corner of the yard.

"Oh no, he dug up your yard," Andy said in shock.

220

"Don't worry about it," said Mr. Taylor. "That mole's been tunneling around our yard for years. He's a speedy little rodent and he managed to escape your dog."

"I'm still sorry Rascal tore up your yard." Andy looked at the dog and frowned. "I think I better take him home before he does any more damage."

He started for their back door when his phone rang. He stopped and pulled it from his pocket. "Hello, Dad. Yes, everything's fine. I'm over at the Taylors. Oh, okay. Yep, I'll see you then." He looked at Mr. Taylor. "It was my dad letting me know they were in D.C. and should be home around eight tonight."

While he had been on the phone Gracie had gone into the house to get Rascal's bowls, treats, food and toys. She brought them into the backyard along with his leash.

"Here you go," she said handing everything to Andy.

"Thank you," he said fastening the leash onto Rascal's collar. He looked at Gwen, Gracie and Mr. Taylor. "Thank you, all of you, for taking care of Rascal for me. I really appreciate it."

"You're welcome," said Gwen rolling her chair over toward him. "We were happy to do it. Now, you need to go home. Rascal will be wanting his supper."

Andy smiled at her. "You're absolutely right. Besides, I should probably make sure everything is clean and tidy before they show up. Thank you again."

Gracie walked to the gate and opened it. "You're very welcome. As my sister said, we were happy to take care of him." She watched them cross the street and enter the house before closing the gate and latching it. She walked toward her dad and sister. "It's getting late. Shall I fix supper?"

"How about if I just order pizza?" asked their dad. "It's been a while since we've had any."

Both Gwen and Gracie looked at him and grinned. "Sounds good to me," said Gwen.

"Me too," agreed Gracie as she helped push Gwen up the ramp and into the house.

Andy walked into his kitchen with Rascal, took off his lead, filled his water dish and fixed the dog some supper. Rascal glanced at Andy, then at his food dish. "Go ahead and eat Rascal," urged Andy with a smile. "The rest of the family is coming home soon and it's going to be an interesting evening, for sure."

Rascal didn't need to be urged to eat. He quickly began to devour his supper and cleaned his dish before Andy pulled his own dinner from the microwave. "I'd say you were one hungry doggie."

While Andy ate at the kitchen table Rascal stretched out on the kitchen rug nearby and took a nap.

As soon as he finished Andy washed the few dishes he and Rascal had dirtied. He swept the kitchen floor then walked through the rest of the house to make sure everything was nice and neat. He didn't want to give his folks any reason to be upset over leaving him here on his own. He figured introducing the dog to them was enough for them to object to, he didn't need to add any other problems to his life. Once he was satisfied he walked to the kitchen and woke Rascal. "Come on boy, let's take a walk around the yard." Rascal raised his curly blondish brown head and stared at Andy. Slowly he got to his feet and walked to the back door and sat down while Andy attached the leash to his collar. "Okay, let's go." Andy opened the door and Rascal raced down the porch steps and into the yard. He wandered around sniffing the trees and flowers before stopping beside the old maple tree and watering it. Andy and Rascal watched a pair of squirrels playing in the oak tree. They jumped from its branches to the garage roof before scampering across to another tree and running into the bushes and down to the creek. Rascal of course barked at them and he would have chased them if Andy hadn't had a tight grip on the leash. Once the squirrels were out of sight Rascal sat in the grass cocking his head to the right then to the left like he was trying to figure out where they had gone. He looked at Andy then turned around and headed back to the house. Once inside Andy gave him a treat, hung up his leash, picked up his private pilot book and they headed to the family room. Andy turned on the radio to the classic music station then settled down on the sofa to read.

Chapter Nineteen

On the flight from Washington D.C. Emily managed to persuade her parents into allowing her to have the window seat. They had been traveling for over fifteen hours, she was tired and anxious to get home. She stared out the window at the cotton white clouds and thought about the dog her brother had found. She pulled her phone from her pocket and found the picture of the dog Gwen had sent her. He was one strange looking animal, that's for sure with his curly blondish brown hair and his little teddy bear face, and those teeth. Some of them were very long. *Sure hope he's as friendly as Gwen said*, thought Emily. *Because I bet those teeth could do some serious damage.*

Emily leaned back in her seat and closed her eyes. She learned a long time ago that trips are shorter if you take a nap. She listened to her parents as they talked about the trip and how glad they would be to get home. She couldn't help but wonder how they would react when they discovered her brother not only had acquired a dog while they were gone but also had a job. *Yep, it was going to be an interesting evening.*

It was a quarter after eight when Andy heard the back door open. Rascal's ears perked up at the sound. He began to bark and raced down the hall and toward the kitchen. Andy ran after him and scolded himself for not putting the dog's leash on him. When Martin stepped inside the house Rascal jumped up on him and barked even louder.

Andy rushed over and picked the dog up. "Hush Rascal. Be quiet. They live here." Rascal quieted down and began to quiver. Andy stroked the dog's head and back to help calm him down. Finally he looked at his parents and sister who had all managed to make it into the house without any more problems. "Hi, glad to see you all made it back. I'd like you to meet Rascal."

Emily stood out of the way in the kitchen grinning, watching her parents reaction to the dog. Both her mother and father were standing there staring at Andy and Rascal. She thought her father's eyes were ready to pop right out of his head. Her mother though just appeared to be curious and began to smile.

"Well, he certainly is an unusual little guy," said Anne moving toward Andy and the dog. "I take it your dog sitting for someone. So, who does he belong to?"

"To us," answered Emily gleefully.

Anne was about to pet the dog but quickly withdrew her hand as soon as those words left Emily's mouth. "To us?" she asked twisting around to look at her daughter. "Did you know about this?"

"Sort of. Gwen told me the other day when I spoke with her. She and Gracie were dog sitting while Andy was at work."

Anne gave her son a very perplexed look. "You have a job and a dog?" She gave Martin a rather hostile stare. "I knew we shouldn't have left him here alone."

"Calm down, honey," said Martin soothingly. "He's old enough to have a job. Besides, it's only part-time at the county airport."

Emily could tell her mother was getting more stressed by the second. Even she didn't know her father knew about Andy's job.

"Look, let's all go into the family room and I'll tell you all about everything." Andy led the way down the hall and into the family room. He noticed his private pilot's book laying on the sofa and quickly picked it up and sat in a chair close by stuffing the book between him and the side of the chair. There was no reason to make things more strained than they were already. He cautiously waited for his parents to get seated on the sofa and Emily slid into the rocking chair.

"Okay, I found the dog in the backyard on Sunday morning. He was scared and hungry and I fed him. Gracie and I took him with us that afternoon when we flew our drones. That's when we found the dog's owner, Fanin Murphy in the village cemetery. As far as the police could tell the man had gone to visit his wife's grave on her birthday, had a heart attack and died. He'd been dead for at least a day."

"Wait a minute," said Martin with concern. "You and Gracie found this dog's owner dead in the cemetery."

"That's right. Of course at the time we didn't know the dog belonged to Mr. Murphy because he didn't have a collar or anything. He'd lost it. It was Dr. Duncan, the coroner, who recognized the dog as belonging to Mr. Murphy. Anyway I took the dog to Doc Schafer, you know the vet down on Main Street. He found the dogs identity chip and he recognized the dog as Mr. Murphy's too. So I've been taking care of the dog."

"This Mr. Murphy, does he have any children or relatives?" asked Martin.

"Oh yeah. He has a son and a daughter and a granddaughter teaches at the grade school here."

"Well, why didn't you give them the dog?" asked Anne.

"They didn't want him. Besides, the son lives in California and the daughter in Hawaii and none of them really like animals. I asked the son on Thursday if they wanted the dog when he came here for his dad's funeral and he said I should keep him."

"I see," said Anne. "Now what about this job at the airport?"

"Gracie asked me to take her to the aero club open house at the county airport on Tuesday. Major Reese was there and he gave us a ride in his airplane. Gracie is thinking about getting her private pilot's license. She thinks it will be helpful with her engineering degree. Anyway I thought I'd like to get a job and it looked like an

interesting place to work. So I asked and they said yes. That's all."

Emily had been quietly sitting in the rocker listening to the conversation and playing with Rascal's tennis ball when she accidently dropped it. Rascal quickly jumped from Andy's lap and raced for the ball. When he did Andy's book fell onto the floor. Before he could pick it up Emily noticed the title and realized there was perhaps one more piece of information her brother needed to share.

"Interesting book you have there," she remarked. "You plan on learning to fly too?"

Andy looked at her and frowned. "Maybe."

Both his parents gave him a quizzical glance. He let out a long frustrated sigh. "Okay, yes, I plan on learning to fly. I've signed up for ground school class and it begins on Monday after school at the airport. There, satisfied?"

"Yes," answered Emily smugly.

"Is that why you wanted a job?" asked his mother.

"Yes, so I can pay for the classes and flying lessons."

Rascal was happily playing with his ball near Emily's chair and everyone appeared to be relaxing at last. Emily glanced at her watch and noticed it was nearly 9 o'clock.

"Oh Dad, did you remember to call Pat when we landed in Dayton?"

Martin wearily shook his head. "No, I completely forgot." He got his phone from his pocket and placed the call.

"Well, if no one minds I think I'll go to bed," said Emily. "It's been a long day and I'm exhausted. See you in the morning." She made her way upstairs to her bedroom and didn't even bother to stop in the kitchen for her suitcase or backpack. Slowly she put on her pajamas and crawled into bed. Five minutes later she was sound asleep.

Emily woke up Sunday morning to a gray cloudy sky. "I don't believe this," she grumbled. "It couldn't have followed us clear across the ocean. I thought we left all those gloomy skies and rain in Ireland." Gradually she slid out of bed and made her way to the bathroom. More than anything she just wanted a nice hot shower and some breakfast. She noticed that both her brother's and parents' rooms were empty. *Wonderful,* she thought happily, *they let me sleep in. I'm going to take a nice quiet long hot shower.* Then she remembered, it was Sunday. That long hot shower would have to wait. She would need to hurry especially if she wanted breakfast.

Downstairs Anne was fixing French toast and sausages while Martin had his nose buried in the Sunday newspaper. Andy had taken Rascal outside for his morning walk around the yard. The temperature had dropped into the low 50s overnight and as Andy glanced at the sky he knew it wouldn't be long before the rain would begin. He hoped it would hold off until after church.

As soon as Andy and Rascal were back inside Anne was putting breakfast on the table. Andy took his seat and filled his plate. Martin glanced at the dog laying peacefully on the carpet between the kitchen and dining room. "So, son, what do we do with the dog while we're gone? Do you just leave him to roam around the house or do you have a crate or something for him?"

Andy stopped midair with the piece of French toast he was about to put in his mouth and put the fork and toast back on his plate. "Um, I don't know exactly what to do with him. He's usually with me or with Gracie and Gwen. I've never left him alone."

Martin nodded his head thoughtfully. "Well, he does seem to be house trained so I imagine we could just leave him here. But just to be cautious we should probably close all the doors to the bedrooms and bathrooms. We shouldn't be gone but a few hours."

"Okay. He'll probably just lay there and sleep."

"Good morning," said Emily gloomily. She sat down and put one piece of French toast on her plate.

"And what has you so cheerful this morning?" Her mother asked as she gave her a glass of orange juice.

"The weather," she answered. "I thought we left all those gray skies and rain behind us when we left Ireland."

"This is April," her father said. "The saying is, April showers bring May flowers. Be thankful it isn't snow."

"Ha, ha," responded Emily moodily. She finished her breakfast and took her dishes to the sink.

"Cheer up," said her brother. "The next few days are going to be sunny and the temperatures are supposed to get up into the sixties."

"Wonderful," Emily replied. "We won't be able to get out and enjoy it, we'll be stuck in the classroom all day."

"You can always go outside after school," he told her.

"All right, enough," said their father. "Let's clean off the table and get your coats. We don't want to be late."

After the church service the Parkers stopped in the church Fellowship Hall to visit with friends before going home. It was here that Andy recognized Eric Murphy sitting at a table with their friend Matthew MacBrian. Mac of course saw the Parkers and motioned for them to join him.

"Hello folks, good to see you made it back from Ireland. Hope you had a good trip."

"Yes, we had a very good trip," said Martin standing beside Mac, "and we're glad to be back. Whose your friend?"

"Oh excuse my manners," said Mac running his hand down the back of his snowy haired head. "Let me introduce you. Martin, Anne, Andy and Emily, this is Eric Murphy and his sister Wanda. They're in town for their father's funeral, Fanin Murphy."

"It's nice to meet you," said Martin. "We're sorry for your loss. Please accept our condolences."

"Thank you," said Wanda kindly.

"Yes, thank you," said Eric. "We are also very grateful to your son, Andy there. He's the one who discovered our father's body last week."

Andy stood there quite uncomfortably and felt the blood rush embarrassingly into his cheeks. He had no idea how to respond and remained silent.

Eric noticed Andy was having trouble with the situation and changed the subject. "I hope my plane isn't causing any problems at the airport."

Andy swallowed uncomfortably and shook his head. "No, sir. There's no problem. It's just fine in the hangar."

"Oh, that's good. It looks like I'm going to be here at least the rest of this week taking care of my dad's affairs."

"That's fine" said Andy nervously. "Take as much time as you need. I'll let the manager know if you like."

"Well, thank you very much. I appreciate it."

"Why don't you folks have a seat?" said Mac. "There's plenty of room. Get yourselves some coffee, juice and some food."

"We would like to Mac but we need to be getting home. We left the dog there on his own and we're not sure how he is doing. Andy's never left him alone before," said Martin.

"Sure, I understand. He is a cute little guy and I imagine he's probably doing just fine. I'll see you later and you can tell me all about your trip and what exciting things you found at that archaeology dig."

"Will do," Martin assured him. "It was a grand dig for sure." He winked at Mac then escorted the family out of the church.

When they reached home and headed up the steps to the back porch they heard an excited Rascal jumping at the door anxious to get outside.

Martin unlocked the door and Rascal came bounding out nearly jumping into Andy's arms. Andy was so startled he almost fell down.

"There's no doubt in my mind whose dog this is," said Martin with a grin. "You're his buddy for sure."

Andy urged the dog into the backyard and Rascal gleefully ran around watering his favorite trees and shrubs. Emily leaned against the porch railing watching his escapades. He sure was energetic. Eventually he tired himself out and laid down in the grass panting. Emily walked into the yard and knelt down to pet him. It was then that she noticed the unusual pin fastened to his collar.

"That's a rather remarkable pin you have on the dog's collar. Where'd you get it?" she asked.

Andy looked at the pin she was pointing to. "Oh, Gracie found it when she found the dogs collar. So I just took it off that one and put it on this one."

"Was there anything else on the collar?"

"Just the normal stuff, his dog license, his name tag, a Home Again tag and that pin. Why?"

Emily ran her hand smoothly down the dogs curly haired back. "There was an elderly gentleman I met in Blarney. He had a pin on his coat just like this. He was Fanin Murphy's brother-in-law. Mr. Murphy's wife was Mr. O'Keeffe's sister. Anyway, I promised him I would take a picture of the grave and send it to him."

"Either Gracie or I can show you the grave later this week," said Andy as the first raindrops began to fall. "Right now though we need to get inside unless you want to get soaked." He picked up Rascal and they all ran into the house.

Chapter Twenty

After school on Monday Andy stopped by Major Reese's classroom to see what he had wanted to discuss with him about the competition that week. The major was straightening his desk and putting homework papers in his briefcase when Andy entered.

"Hello sir," Andy greeted him as he stood in front of his desk. "You said you wanted to talk to me about this week's competition after school."

Major Reese who had been looking down at his briefcase when Andy stopped at his desk slowly raised his head and looked at him. "Have a seat, won't you?" he asked with a small smile and indicated the chair next to his desk. Andy carefully sat down unsure of what the major wanted to discuss. "I really don't have anything to discuss with you about the competition. I was just using that as an excuse to talk with you."

Andy leaned back in the chair a little and stared at him. "What did you want to talk with me about."

"Your future," said Reese informally. "I know I've only had an opportunity to know you through the drone club but I've talked with some of your teachers. They are all very impressed with you. You're an excellent student and they were very impressed with your results on the aptitude test they gave the juniors and seniors this year. I believe your knowledge is beyond the high school level. I'd say it's closer to college. When it comes to math, science and even foreign language you exceed what is being taught here. I know you are taking Spanish because you had to take a foreign language and that's the only one they offer here. But Mr. Perez said you speak the language like a native. He would know because he's from a duel language family and has been speaking Spanish all his life. I know you and your family have lived many different places so I'm going to presume you learned various languages in various countries you were in.

Andy sat there trying to understand just exactly what Major Reese was getting at. "Yes, I did learn different languages over the years," he admitted. "It was just the natural thing to do. I mean you had to be able to talk to the people working at the excavations and not everyone speaks English."

Reese nodded his head. "That makes perfect sense. So what other languages do you speak?"

"Well, I can speak Hebrew, Arabic and Javanese. I speak a little French and German, not much but a little bit. Why?"

"Do you find it easy to learn different languages?"

Andy gave him a very puzzled look. "I've never really thought about it. It's just something I do." Andy's puzzled look became a frown. "I don't understand why you're asking me all these questions about foreign languages and what it has to do with my future. You aren't trying to talk me into joining the military are you?"

Reese just shook his head and quietly laughed. "Oh my God, no. I think enough people have already approached that idea with you. So relax. That's not where I'm going. Although what I am thinking about does involve working with the military as a civilian."

Andy relaxed a little bit and viewed Reese with curiosity. "So what exactly are you thinking about?"

"The Air Force needs people who can speak, read and translate various foreign languages. They could use someone with your talents. And the good thing is you could work for them while you go to college as an intern. Then when you get your degree you'd be able to work for them full time. The pay is good and the people are generally nice and easy to get along with. It's just something for you to think about."

"I see," said Andy. "Well, it is something for me to seriously think about. Thank you." He stood up to leave.

Reese stood up also. "You're welcome. I know how difficult it can be trying to decide what to do with your life. I've been down that road myself. Give it some thought. You may decide to take a different path and that's fine. The important thing is to find something you like to do and do it. No matter what path you decide to take if I can help you please let me know. I also know it's not always easy to talk with parents so if you need someone to talk with I'm available."

"Thank you, sir. I appreciate that. I will give this some serious thought and let you know what I decide. Graduation is just around the corner and I need to come up with a plan."

"Okay," said Reese. "Well, you best be getting to work. Oh, one more thing, the military aren't the only ones who need drone pilots. I'm looking forward to the competition later this week. I know you are going to do great. So long." He followed Andy to the classroom door.

"I think we'll all do fine. Good-bye," said Andy as he headed down the hall and out the door.

Gracie was pushing Gwen's wheelchair through the Kirksborough Cemetery and Emily was by their side. The weather was nice and they decided to come right after school since the cemetery was closer to the school than to their homes.

"Thank you both for taking the time to come out here with me," said Emily as they made their into the cemetery. "I know it's a bit of a walk and I'm sure it would take me forever to fine Mr. Murphy's grave."

"We're glad to do it," said Gracie. "I was surprised to learn of Mr. Murphy's connection to that man you met in Ireland. That was a really strange coincidence don't you think?"

"Absolutely, but you know me, weird things are always happening to me."

Gracie rolled Gwen's chair down a path, past one of the benches and came to a stop at the grave site. Mr. Murphy's death date had been added to the double headstone and fresh sod covered the recently dug grave. "Well, here we are," she stated pointing to the headstone. She moved her sister a little closer so she could see better.

Emily stood at the foot of the grave and tried to imagine what it must have been like for Andy and Gracie when they discovered

Mr. Murphy's body laying there. It gave her goosebumps. She pulled her phone from her pocket and snapped several pictures of the tombstone so she could send them to Mr. O'Keeffe. When she finished she put her phone away and walked back to her friends.

Well, are there any other graves you want to visit while we're here?" she asked.

"No, this one is enough for me," stated Gwen pleasantly. "I'm ready to go home and get started on all that homework they gave us."

"Yeah, me too," said Emily. "Although I'm really not looking forward to all that homework."

"Oh well, the school year's almost over," said Gracie happily. "Just think, comes fall and you'll both be high school freshmen and oh the classes you'll be taking. Algebra, English literature, science where you get to dissect worms and frogs …" She started to laugh.

"Oh, you are so impossible sometimes!" said Gwen with a grin. "Come on, let's go home."

Explore More

Druids:
https://www.irishcentral.com/roots/history-irish-druids
https://www.ancient-origins.net/history/female-druids-forgotten-priestesses-celts-005910
https://www.historic-uk.com/HistoryUK/HistoryofWales/Druids/
https://www.livescience.com/65822-burial-mound-island-of-druids.html

Irish Archaeology:
https://www.thejournal.ie

Author

Nancy Potts is a former staff writer, columnist, and editorial editor for the *Fairborn Daily Herald*. She was also a staff writer for the *Beavercreek Daily News* and a freelance writer for the *Dayton Daily News*. As a journalist, she covered everything from human-interest stories, school board and city council meetings, to murder trials.

After leaving the newspaper business, she went to work for the National Aviation Hall of Fame (NAHF) as their communications coordinator. At the NAHF she wrote for their quarterly magazine and designed several pages for children in the publication. She also researched and wrote video scripts on the inductees for enshrinement. Additionally Nancy wrote many of the enshrinee biographies for their educational display and website.

As an Air Force wife, Nancy has had numerous opportunities to volunteer both in the United States and overseas. She has taught art to kindergarteners in England and tutored grade-schoolers in the States. Nancy has also shared her love of scouting with girls from the east coast to the Arizona desert to Fairborn, Ohio. She has served as a leader, neighborhood chairperson and as public relations chairperson.

Nancy graduated with a degree in Mass Communications from Wright State University. She has been a member of the Society of Children's Book Writers and Illustrators for over 20 years and enjoys writing books for children and teens.

She lives in Enon, Ohio, with her husband Bob and their two adorable dogs, Bonnie and Leo.

Artist

Daniel R. Kinney is a talented self-taught artist. He has loved art since he was young and it has always been a side passion for him. After retiring from American Electric Power, he has had more time to focus on his love of painting. Dan lives with his wife, Diana, in Columbus, Ohio. He has been a friend of the author and her husband since high school.